ONE NIGHT EVER AFTER

TERE MICHAELS
ELLE BROWNLEE
ELIZAH J. DAVIS

Dreamspinner Press

Published by
Dreamspinner Press
5032 Capital Circle SW
Ste 2, PMB# 279
Tallahassee, FL 32305-7886 USA
http://www.dreamspinnerpress.com/

Cover Art by Aaron Anderson
aaronbydesign55@gmail.com

Cover content is being used for illustrative purposes only
and any person depicted on the cover is a model.

ISBN: 978-1-62798-286-3

Printed in the United States of America
First Edition
October 2013

eBook edition available
eBook ISBN: 978-1-62798-287-0

TABLE OF CONTENTS

JUST A DRIVE

TERE MICHAELS

To E & E: This is a book born out of great friendship, laughter, and determination. I could not ask for better unicorns in my life.

CHAPTER 1

WYATT WALSH uncapped the bottle of water, imagining he was actually decapitating the diva-in-training currently stomping around the set. Better for his career and reputation to tighten his fingers around plastic and not her neck.

"Chantel, dearest? I understand how uncomfortable this is for you—I do. But...." Wyatt made a helpless gesture as she stomp-stomp-stomped past him on another circuit. "What can I do? This is what the label asked me for."

That was a lie, of course. He'd pitched the Alice in Wonderland theme for Chantel Baller (Seriously? Did they not notice that was a porn name?) for her debut album and if nothing else, Soundsource Records listened to their creative director.

Sometimes.

"I hate it! It's ridiculous! I look like a freaking freak!" she whined, stopping to stand in front of him with her arms crossed over her chest. "I want to look cool!"

See, they never listened to him when he told them not to pluck seventeen-year-olds out of Kentucky.

Was it too much to ask for the "next best thing" to not be a spoiled brat?

A knock saved Wyatt from explaining to Chantel that neither her waifish looks nor her thready, auto-tuned voice were going to go anywhere, so why not dress it up as quirky—and he turned to thank his savior.

The day went from crap to fabulous in four seconds flat.

His current favorite adorable young man appeared as if lifted from a dirty dream in Wyatt's regular repertoire. Benji Trammell stood in the doorway and fidgeted, clearly uncomfortable as the entire loft of folks involved with the shoot turned to stare.

"Uh… sorry. I needed to talk to Kala?" His gorgeous baby browns darted around the room, desperately seeking the producer in the crowd of overdressed, overworked, underwhelmed peons.

"She's somewhere," Wyatt chirped, his mood and demeanor changing as he left Chantel in the dust. "Are you sure you didn't come all the way down here for me?"

He'd been staring at the kid—an engineer of some sort, the particulars didn't matter—for six weeks now, as they were thrown together while Soundsource blew their party budget for various nonsense reasons. Most of said reasons stemmed from upcoming divorce proceedings between the president of the label and her "singer" husband.

It was going to be the bitchfest of the year.

As Creative Director, Wyatt had enjoyed free-flowing top-shelf booze, amazing buffets, and hot and cold running catering waiters. But the treat of the night had been the brief but delectable appearance of Mr. Trammel and his ass-worshipping jeans.

Praise high fashion.

It hadn't progressed past flirty small talk and making bedroom eyes at each other, but Wyatt was determined tonight would be it.

He was getting a piece of that.

Wyatt found a PA out of the corner of his eye and hissed a "find Kala" before coming to invade average height, dark, and handsome's personal space. "Can I get you anything while you wait?"

Me. A cocktail and me. Me.

"No. But thanks. I'm just…. It's a thing with the album and I was upstairs at a meeting so…." He gestured toward Chantel, who had begun ranting at the guy who brought their lunches, whom Wyatt suspected didn't speak enough English to care.

Benji was the thing that fantasies were made of, at least for One-Night Wyatt. Young enough to be doe-eyed and confused, old enough to be legal. Slender build under an ironic hipster T-shirt and five-hundred-dollar distressed jeans. A thick head of espresso hair, chocolate eyes and, yeah—Wyatt yearned to lick coffee ice cream off his delicious-looking jaw. The shy thing he was working just made it even more appealing—the closer Wyatt got, the more Benji blushed, and it was adorable.

Erotically adorable, if that was a thing.

Benji smiled and Wyatt's pants got tight.

"How's, you know, the shoot going?"

"Oh, fabulous. Chantel loves my ideas," Wyatt said brightly, shaking his head at the same time.

An even bigger grin made Wyatt's mouth water a little.

"She's a dream to work with," Benji whispered, mimicking Wyatt's head shake, a fake pout on his lips.

"No wonder Kala's in the bathroom drinking vodka and texting her therapist." It was just a guess.

They shared a moment of smiles and Wyatt couldn't help himself—he leaned against the doorjamb and batted his eyelashes at Benji. "So are you going to the party at Bryant Park Grill tonight? Maybe we could get a drink together—I feel like we could both share our Chantel misadventures and purge our souls. You know. To save our sanity."

Benji stared down at his basketball sneakers; the height difference meant Wyatt got a nice view of the back of his neck and that caused the lean to deepen. Like a moth to a porch light. Or a seasoned perv to a gorgeous young man.

"That sounds... nice." Benji looked back up. "You know—to keep us sane."

And naked.

"Fantastic." Wyatt whipped his phone out, scrolling to contacts with practiced ease. "Give me your number and I'll let you know when this delightful and very special afternoon with Alice in Bitchland is finished."

Benji recited the digits slowly and Wyatt repeated them back. Then he took a step away from the door to point the phone at Benji.

Who blinked in surprise.

"Come on, sunshine—I need a picture to go with those numbers." He snapped it before Benji could school his face out of "adorably confused." "Perfect. I'll call you later?"

His face a vision of "wait, what?", Benji nodded. A second later, the muted sounds of the set were broken by a shout of "Kala!" and a slew of swear words.

"Kala's off the toilet," Wyatt said cheerfully. "You talk to her, I will divert Chantel's attention with a ball of yarn, and this day might end at some point."

Benji nodded as Wyatt turned to join the fracas. There was a definite sashay to his step as he approached Kala, who was trying to shove Chantel off her arm but was largely unsuccessful due to all the tulle.

One more look over his shoulder left Wyatt delighted to see that Benji's expression was one of dumbstruck joy at the retreating view.

Feed the ego. Feed it well.

This was going to be a fabulous night.

HE MANAGED to convince Chantel that the shoot actually captured the essence of her music—pretending not to notice that this occurred after Kala gave her an "aspirin"—and finished the shoot before he did, indeed, die of job-related stress. After doling out cab fare (and beer money) to the stylists, Wyatt found himself on the corner of Fifth Avenue and 14th Street, phone in hand.

The cool flush of the air-conditioned loft gave way to the muggy August air of Manhattan. At nine thirty, the rush of tourists and home seekers had reduced to a trickle. He toyed with the scroll for a second then dialed Benji's number—first taking a moment to enjoy the upward tilt of his eyes and the pale olive of his skin. Someone's parents had played the exotic-combination-of-genes card and it had worked out beautifully.

"Um, hey," Benji said, clearing his throat a second later. "Hey. How'd it go?"

"Chantel's still alive, Kala didn't need an emergency admit to Bellevue, and we got enough stuff for the cover. So all in all, the perfect day." Wyatt laughed. He started walking toward Sixth Avenue. "How about you?"

"Oh—well, it was good. Not as crazy as yours." Benji cleared his throat again. "You still, uh—up for that drink?"

"God yes. The prospect has actually made this day bearable." Wyatt dodged some chatting girls who didn't seem to understand the concept of sharing the sidewalk. "I'm downtown still. Are you at the studio?"

"Yeah—you want to just meet at the party?

Wyatt let visions of a studio quickie fade, as it was probably prudent to show up at the work event—mingle, have a free drink, and then disappear into the night with his end-of-the-workday treat.

"That's a great idea," he said. "I'll be there in twenty, God willing."

"Awesome." Benji's voice perked up. He hung up almost as soon as the words were out of his mouth.

"Lack of conversation skills duly noted—thank God you have that ass," Wyatt muttered as a cab swerved to the corner to accept his business.

HIS phone rang about three blocks into his cab ride; if it was anything but crickets chirping, he would have sent it to voice mail. Crickets, though, meant Raven, and Raven was the only human being on earth Wyatt would interrupt a booty call for.

"Baby girl," he said, feeling his body unhitch and relax.

"I hate being in bed so much," his best friend whined dramatically.

"Said no one ever."

"Bed rest is hard."

"Bed rest is actually the opposite of hard. I told you pregnancy would make you dumb."

"Well, then we can finally have a conversation you can follow."

"That nurturing thing hasn't kicked in yet—you're still mean."

Raven sighed with theatrical flair. "Growing humans is hard, okay? And I'm growing double the normal amount."

"Condoms, Rae. Condoms. We had this talk." Wyatt riffled around in his pocket for money as the cab dodged vehicles into midtown.

"You could be a little more sympathetic to me, your dearest and only friend. Your godfather privileges will be revoked."

He would never say this to Raven—his reason for being alive today, his reason for not being a total abusive dickbag—but if she unnamed him godfather of her impending twins, he would not be sad.

Children terrified him. Responsibility for other human beings in general? Cold sweat and horror. But he couldn't say that to Raven, who'd turned her back on everyone from "back home" except Wyatt.

Who'd let herself thaw and grow and evolve to the point where she had a husband and a home and two humans entering the world in fifteen weeks.

See? He paid attention during their weekly chitchats.

"No, please, no," he said weakly and Raven laughed.

"Douche."

"You know you need to quit cursing like a syphilitic sailor before your kids are born."

"I figure I have until they're eight months old or so before I have to give it up."

"Harder than cigarettes, right?"

"Shit, yeah."

Now it was Wyatt's turn to laugh. The driver was pulling over, Bryant Park illuminated up ahead.

"Okay, I gotta go. I have a date."

"You mean dinner and a fuck."

"Actually free appetizers and a fuck, but that's too many words." He stuck a twenty through the plastic opening for the cabbie. "Receipt, please."

"Fine, fine. Call me in the morning and entertain me," she commanded. "Rob has an early meet-and-greet breakfast in Spencer with some potential recruits."

"I'm sorry, I don't speak Midwestern." Wyatt pocketed his change and the receipt. He managed to stay on the phone, gather his bag, and slide out the door without face-planting—no mean feat.

"Asshole. I'll talk to you in the morning." Raven blew kisses into the phone. "Myrtle and Myron send their love as well!"

"No."

"Okay, I'll keep looking."

They exchanged "I love yous," then Wyatt hung up with a sigh. He was in the middle of the sidewalk as New York City rushed around him in all its energetic beauty, about to have free cocktails and a fuck with a beautiful boy and….

He squared his shoulders and got his feet moving.

WYATT accepted a bacon-wrapped scallop from a passing waiter, the other hand wrapped around his third vodka tonic of the night. Bryant Park Grill was hosting Soundsource's annual "New Artists Night," with a full spread, an open bar, and enough interoffice drama to satisfy Wyatt's appetite. For the moment.

At least until his handsome young engineer booty call showed up….

A few frantic texts alerted him to Benji having an "emergency meeting" and his impending lateness with a host of apologies. Wyatt planned to parlay this guilt into at least two blowjobs.

"Fifty says Bianca falls out of her dress before the night is over," Betsy said as she tripped by, already unsteady on free booze and ill-conceived five-inch heels.

"If she does, it's on purpose. There's enough double-stick tape on her tits to repair a dike."

"I'd like to repair her dike." His petite boss leaned against him, barely coming up to his shoulder. He didn't pay her dirty rambling any mind as he chewed on his tiny snack. She was totally straight when there weren't a dozen or so Slippery Nipples coursing through her bloodstream.

Wyatt scanned the room. Everyone was in their own department groups—stylists, PR, marketing, A&R—while the eager wannabes flitted around, trying to impress. At some point there would be performances, and Wyatt would immediately take his leave. The straining vocals of newbie artists all trying to be Mariah Carey made little pieces of his soul die with each warbling note. No, he would head for the door—

With Benji in tow.

"Speaking of a fabulous ass…." Wyatt sighed happily.

"I thought we were talking tits." Betsy ignored him, wandering away to find the young ingénue Bianca and her amazing rack.

Across the room, Benji had arrived; he fidgeted in the doorway, looking around as he bit his bottom lip. Wyatt suppressed the urge to fan himself. He sucked down the rest of his vodka tonic with a dirty slurp, then deposited it on the tray of another circulating waiter.

Time to get down to business.

Benji straightened up, smiling brightly as Wyatt came to a halt in front of him.

"Hey gorgeous, I was thinking you weren't going to show up."

"Sorry. I got tied up with this stupid meeting," Benji said.

Wyatt's eyes twinkled. "Mmm… tied up. Now I have a lovely mental picture."

Benji's mouth did something—a cross between a smirk and a shy smile—and Wyatt tried to read the look in his eyes (just big and brown and lovely). It was an awkward moment of breath-holding confusion as Wyatt tried to keep his fantasy on point.

Sexy innocent thing meets king of seduction Wyatt. And then, as quickly as possible, a parting of ways after the orgasms were had. It was his recipe for a perfect one night stand.

Then Benji ducked his head and all but kicked the floor bashfully.

And Wyatt found his bearings.

"Let's get you a drink, gorgeous," Wyatt murmured, linking his arm with Benji's.

IT WAS the eyes, Wyatt decided; they were gold and green, almond-shaped with a corner tilt, and lashes that went on for miles. There was something hypnotic about their exoticness, setting this otherwise average-looking guy a notch above the rest.

He also had a perfect ass, but Wyatt saw the eyes first. He thought that made him seem slightly less shallow.

They were at the bar, in the far corner behind a large potted plant and featuring a distinct lack of light.

It was perfect.

Wyatt had his body pressed against Benji's side, using every opportunity to reach across him, to shift his hips, to touch every part of the young man's body he could without grabbing his ass.

It was getting harder and harder.

That's what he said.

The top-shelf shots flowed, courtesy of a sardonic bartender who decided it would make the night go faster if she helped Wyatt get Benji absolutely plastered.

There was a fifty in her pocket to seal the deal.

"More tequila?" Wyatt asked sweetly, pressing his lips to the strong curve of Benji's jaw. He liked the shiver it produced and slid his hand down to the small of Benji's back to keep him in place.

"No... no. I really shouldn't...." Benji turned his head just enough to brush their lips together, in not quite a kiss. "Tequila makes me crazy."

"Tequila makes me want to fuck someone beautiful," Wyatt whispered.

Those big doe eyes were bleary, but Wyatt saw the spark as his words registered in Benji's brain. He would have pushed harder but lust coursed through him and he leaned in for a kiss.

"I SERIOUSLY need to fuck you." It was the first thing Wyatt managed to say in almost twenty minutes, as his tongue had been otherwise occupied in the mouth of the most adorable young man.

"Uh...."

Benji knocked his head against the wall currently holding them up as the party whirled on behind them. It was quarter to twelve, there wasn't a sober person on the island of Manhattan, and Wyatt's flat-front trousers were about to become a casualty of their little make-out session.

"Seriously. My place is downtown...."

"I'm—closer. West 50th," Benji choked out, licking his sweet swollen lips, much to Wyatt's delight.

"That's the sexiest thing you've said all night," Wyatt purred, grinding his hips against the kid's stomach as he ran his palm along the warm line of Benji's spine.

So, so close. Wyatt's smile bloomed. "I'm going to go grab my bags from coat check. Meet me out front, okay? 42nd Street side."

Benji just nodded as Wyatt peeled himself off the younger man. He didn't care what people thought of his "habits" but there was no need to flaunt a pickup within the incestuous world of Soundsource Records.

He dropped a kiss on the back of Benji's neck, enjoying the shiver under the damp hair curling just above his collar. The view was stunning—how much better would it look when he was naked?

The kid squirmed in Wyatt's embrace at that moment, panting as his hips strained to get more friction. Oh yes, squirming. Wyatt leaned down to take a nice big inhale of the pheromones being thrown off.

"Do you have to say good-bye to anyone?"

Benji shook his head, quick and sure. He swallowed hard as Wyatt nosed behind his ear.

"Okay. I'm going to do a quick circuit, then meet you outside. Five minutes."

Another nod and then a muffled groan as Wyatt stepped back to give them both air and a less humpable distance.

"Five minutes," Benji murmured, adjusting the tight-fitting clothes currently plastered to his slender body.

Lord have mercy.

Wyatt watched as Benji practically ran for the front door of the Bryant Park Grill, dodging drunken coworkers and the catering waiters who had said screw it and were currently dancing to the raucous music.

Wyatt sauntered through the crowd, looking for Betsy or Sable, the label's owner, but they were nowhere to be found.

"I tried," he murmured, grabbing one last glass of champagne off a tray as he headed for the door.

One-Night Wyatt had fulfilled his professional duties and now he was going to go bang a pretty boy. It was a good night.

AS REQUESTED, Benji was waiting outside in the humid night air, flipping through his phone. He frowned as he began to furiously type something.

"Oh no, I don't like that look," Wyatt said as he strode across the sidewalk, dodging the tourists and Friday night revelers stumbling through midtown.

Benji looked up, his face easing into something resembling a smile. Wyatt couldn't seem to evoke a full grin, but he resolved to try—even if he had to fuck him twice.

"Sorry."

"Work?" He eased up next to the kid, pulling him against Wyatt's hip.

"N-no. Family." Benji waved his hand then pocketed his phone. "It's nothing."

"Awesome." Drama and details of a personal nature were not what this was about. The kid probably had some unstable home life—all the better to get in and out. Literally. "Let's grab a cab. The quicker we get to your place, the quicker I can get you out of those pants."

Benji blushed and ducked his head.

Mercy.

The entire cab ride took ten minutes, and Wyatt's hand spent the time high on Benji's thigh. Everything smelled like "boys in heat" and Wyatt wanted to bottle it.

A discreet check of his watch said half past twelve—which meant a few hours of fun and he'd be able to make the eleven a.m. spin class.

"This is it," Benji said suddenly, and Wyatt leaned over to see where they were. A dumpy walk-up? A crappy older building with questionable locks?

None of the above.

He paid the cab driver, trying not to let his jaw drop too much. This was where the kid lived?

Wyatt wasn't expecting the young engineer to be a resident of Longacre House: twenty-six floors of chic high-rise and a doorman to boot.

"Mr. Trammell," the elderly man said, opening the door. "Sir."

"Hi, Edgar." Benji seemed a little unsteady so Wyatt kept a hand at his back, enjoying the damp warmth and tremors—evidence of how turned on he was.

They walked through the modern lobby, with Benji fumbling through his pockets for the elevator key and Wyatt trying to behave himself the entire time.

"Nice building," he said casually, trying to reconcile his fantasy of the messy bedroom in a fifth floor walk-up with the reality of a place that easily ran at least three thousand a month for a studio.

"Uh, yeah. Thanks." Benji's face was flushed as he turned back to Wyatt; he bit his lip as they waited for the elevator. Wyatt, for his part, tried to remember his rule against sticking his tongue down someone's throat in front of the doorman.

No wait, that wasn't a rule he had.

"Roommate?" he asked, trying to break the tension.

"What? No. No. Just me."

The elevator chimed; Wyatt guided Benji inside after the doors opened—and just kept going, until they were leaning against the back wall.

"What floor?"

"Twenty-two." Benji was panting as Wyatt reached back and pressed the little circle before returning to align his entire body against Benji's.

The height difference, the size difference—Wyatt almost moaned at how perfectly this kid felt, fitted between the wall and Wyatt's body like he was a granted wish. He smelled rich and worked over and that just made Wyatt hungrier to mess him up even more. Everywhere their bodies touched Wyatt felt overwarm; he let himself sink over Benji, hiding him from the glaring light of the elevator.

"Oh my God." Benji laughed, resting his forehead against Wyatt's shoulder. "Seriously—you're killing me here."

"Sweetheart, I'm not even warmed up yet," he whispered, ducking his head to drop a kiss on Benji's temple. "I've been wanting to fuck you for weeks."

Those big beautiful eyes came into view again when Benji tipped his head back. Wyatt took in the sexy features, the dazed expression— that full-lipped mouth that was going to look amazing around his dick— and he smiled.

"You're the best decision I've made in a long time," he purred.

They were forced to break apart long enough to leave the elevator; Benji stumbling out, Wyatt close behind, crowding him just to watch the way the muscles in his back jumped when he got too close.

THE apartment was indeed a studio—a large living area with floor-to-ceiling windows on one wall and filled with leather couches and enough musical instruments and recording equipment to rival any studio at Soundsource Records. The art on the walls was big, splashy and red, sensual swirls of torsos and limbs in dancer's poses. It didn't fit the room or the man but Wyatt pushed aside those thoughts for the moment.

He was here for the night, for the man, and for the fucking. Then he was gone.

"I—can I get you something?" A disheveled Benji was standing in the divide between the living space and the sleeping alcove at the other end of the apartment, taken up almost entirely by a queen-sized bed.

"Water's good, honey. And you can point out where you keep your supplies." Wyatt stripped out of his lightweight jacket, looking around for a place to lay it down.

Benji nodded, gesturing into the alcove behind him. He walked past, took Wyatt's jacket with him without a word, then disappeared back down the hall toward the front door.

Wyatt sat down on the corner of an oversized armchair, sharing the space with a stack of music books and a tangle of cords and wires. He made quick work of his boots, tucking them next to the chair so he could find them quickly when they were done. When Benji didn't return right away, he moved into the bedroom to make himself comfortable.

It took a second to find the light; a switch on the wall finally made itself known and Wyatt let himself cast a judgmental eye over this room too.

The messy part he got right; there were jeans and T-shirts and gym clothes lying on the floor in the corner, next to a full hamper. Hardcover books stacked on each nightstand, teetering precariously. The bed itself was carelessly made, with pale-blue sheets and a chocolate-brown comforter in a lumpy mess. At least there weren't any posters on the walls of sports stars or muscle cars. Instead, a gorgeous landscape done in pale greens and blues filled the wall next to the sole window.

"Sorry, I wasn't expecting to bring anyone home...."

Benji's voice cut through his observations, and Wyatt turned around with a big smile on his face.

"Don't worry about it. I... like it. Your place is really nice. Homey."

Benji handed him the glass of water, a plastic tumbler with a Princeton logo on the side, ice cubes plinking against the side. "Thanks. I, uh... let me get what we need."

The breathless anticipation had gone out, and Wyatt frowned as soon as his back was turned. He watched Benji walk around the room, kicking clothes out of the way and moving some of the books to the floor. All of a sudden he seemed nervous instead of excited, and Wyatt wasn't really interested in that being the case.

So Wyatt put the water glass on the floor near the bed, then stood up, stripping out of his vest and belt with quick ease. He kept his eyes on Benji's back, watching the way he bent over and moved, retrieving things from the bottom drawer of his nightstand.

"You're gorgeous, you know that?" Wyatt said softly, unbuttoning his shirt. "The first time I saw you, at Mitch's birthday party, I nearly walked into a wall."

Benji's back stiffened slightly; he straightened up, turning as he did to face Wyatt from the other side of the bed.

"I can't imagine why you noticed me," he said, dropping two condoms and a bottle of lube in the center of the comforter.

"Didn't you hear me, sweetheart? I thought you were gorgeous." His shirt slid off his arms and he laid it on top of his other clothes, stacked neatly on the bench tucked against the footboard. "And when I got close… whoa, took a look at those eyes of yours. Well—I was a smitten kitten," Wyatt teased. He rested his hands on his hips, giving Benji a flirty smile.

Benji's lips quirked. He didn't say anything, though; after a sweeping blink of those long lashes, Benji pulled his T-shirt over his head, tossing it onto the looming laundry pile behind him.

And Wyatt hadn't been wrong about that tight body—there was not an ounce of body fat on the kid, just wiry muscles and taut tan skin, a smattering of dark hair on his arms, and a treasure trail disappearing into his slacks.

"Damn." Wyatt whistled appreciatively.

"Not so bad yourself." Benji crawled onto the bed and Wyatt bit his bottom lip. "You work out?"

"Stop with the flattery." He reached for his fly, unhooking it as he leaned down. "Come here and kiss me."

The crawling was ridiculous. Seriously. By the time he made his way over to the other side of the mattress, Wyatt was kicking his linen pants across the room. Fuck it; he didn't care at this point.

"Can I kiss you here?" Benji asked, soft and sweet as he nuzzled the front of Wyatt's Y-fronts, right where a damp spot was forming.

"Oh, sweetheart, you go right ahead...." Wyatt slipped his hands into those glossy brown locks and pulled him closer.

THE headboard slammed against the wall, and Wyatt's feverish brain had a moment of concern they were going straight through and down toward 44th Street in a fucking death spiral. Or rather, a spiral of fucking.

"Come on, come on," Benji whispered, hands gripping the backside of his knees as he sweated and strained under Wyatt's body.

Not a screamer, a slight disappointment, but then again, Wyatt wasn't done yet.

He slowed down until it hurt, until his muscles screamed at him and the sweat pouring off both of them threatened to become a puddle. He braced himself on the headboard and rolled his hips, eliciting a whine from Benji that almost made up for his aching balls.

"Fuck, you're pretty," Wyatt murmured, arms straining as Benji tried to buck his hips up. But Wyatt had twenty pounds on him and the top position—he wasn't going anywhere. "And that dick makes me reconsider several of my life choices...."

Benji huffed out a laugh and Wyatt sped up his thrusts.

ROUND three found Wyatt staring up at the ceiling in order to keep from popping his cork too soon—because he was absolutely correct when he'd presumed that Benji's pretty mouth would look perfect around his cock.

Perfect.

Almost good enough to warrant a callback, Wyatt thought hazily as Benji slurped and swallowed his length like a champion. He tightened a hand in Benji's sweaty hair, a bit of warning as if his jackhammering hips were not indication enough that all the backward counting in the world wasn't going to stop this.

Wyatt's hips jerked up and he came stupid hard into the condom as Benji's mouth worked its magic.

THE shower was hot, the water pressure a national treasure, and everything in the small stall came from high-end men's stores. Wyatt was impressed. This kid had a big dick, a tight ass, and good taste. Not to mention a job that apparently gave him some bank.

The whole package. Someone with a brain should be dating him.

Maybe Wyatt knew a guy with a brain.

He shut the faucet, then toweled off with a shower sheet that smelled like lavender. The small café au lait bathroom was surprising clean and tidy, indicating a professional made regular visits. How much was Soundsource paying their engineers, and did that mean Wyatt deserved a raise?

Wrapping the towel around his waist, Wyatt stepped out and opened the door, letting the cloud of steam dissipate. He'd lost track of time somewhere between the second round of fucking and a quick nap (before getting woken up by the second blowjob—the kid was a vacuum with no gag reflex). It was still dark, so maybe another catnap wouldn't hurt.

Wyatt walked into the bedroom and found the bed remade—clean sheets, another comforter, this one in a robin's-egg blue. It looked so damn inviting, as did Benji, naked and curled up in the center, snoring face first into the pillow.

A strange sensation of "hey, he's fucking adorable" washed over Wyatt, but he chalked it up to a lack of sleep and possible dehydration. He dropped the towel over the hamper, then slipped into the bed. The air conditioner hummed quietly in the background, harmonizing with Benji's snores.

It only took him about five minutes and one "what the hell am I doing?" moment before Wyatt fell back to sleep.

HIS eyes flew open, the disorientation of "not his own bed" flaring before he rolled over and encountered the sprawled form of Benji. At some point he must've gotten up and showered because he smelled delicious—and the urge to wake him up almost got the better of Wyatt. But the bedside clock said six thirty, which was way past his usual "thanks for the fuck" good-bye, and he needed to get home.

With perfected grace, Wyatt slid out from under the covers, tucking them back over Benji's back. He gave him a smile and a salute before he went to find his clothes.

In a few quiet minutes he was in the living room, locating his boots and taking his phone out by force of habit.

Six missed calls since one in the morning.

Wyatt sat down hard in the chair. Six? They were all from the same number, and that's when panic set in.

Raven.

He hit her number and waited anxiously for her to pick up.

CHAPTER 2

"RAVEN? Rae? Calm down...." Fear clutched at Wyatt's chest at the heartbreaking sobs coming through the phone. Every few seconds a bit of wet static filled him with panic—like the connection would cut out and he would never hear her voice again. "What's wrong?"

The babies, he thought. Problem pregnancy, bed rest, her blood pressure—he'd been hearing this for months, none of it quite connecting to the level of seriousness before this moment. Something had gone wrong—but in that case, Rob would have called....

"Rob," she choked out, as if on cue. "Car... accident." His best friend and foster sister nearly gagged on the word, choking and crying even harder.

"Oh shit, oh God, okay, okay." Wyatt pulled himself out of his frozen state, looking around frantically for his bag. "Is he... Rae? Come on, honey." He would have to get to her, wherever she was—East Bumfuck, Pennsylvania, where corn-fed "'roid-heads" were recruited by Rob Beeler to play football for his alma mater.

He had no idea how to get to where she lived.

"He's... he's... the car... a tractor trailer... surgery...." The words spilled out into a story of Rob on yet another recruiting trip getting smashed by a trucker who needed a nap. He was alive—that much Wyatt understood—but Raven was stuck in bed, unable to move, and her husband was sixty miles away in another hospital.

"I'm going to get out there, okay? Just—okay, you're at Unicello Medical Center, right?" He'd sent her a care package earlier that month.

She hiccupped a sob. "Yes."

"I'll be there as soon as I can, and I will help you take care of Rob. I promise." Wyatt's heart took residence in his throat because he'd promise just about anything to Raven—but this was the biggest thing so far.

"Wyatt." It was just his name, but they spent a moment in heavy silence, just breathing. "Hurry, please," she said finally and Wyatt nodded.

"I'm out the door in five minutes. I love you and everything will be all right."

He didn't want to hang up, but he had to figure out how the fuck to get out in the middle of nowhere with no car, no license, and no friends with either of the two. A car service? All the way out there? It was almost Ohio, for Christ's sake. He was still futzing with his boots, thinking frantically and verbalizing his litany of roadblocks, when he heard the floorboard creak.

And looked up to see his about-to-be-ditched one-night stand in the doorway of the living room.

Benji's eyes were wide, his mouth a straight line. He was also naked but that only barely registered.

"I'm...." Wyatt sighed as stood up. "I'm sorry. Sorry I'm a dick who was about to split without waking you. But I've got a fucking family emergency right now and I...."

"I heard—where do you need to go?"

Wyatt tried to pull his thoughts together. "Spencer, Pennsylvania. Small town—it's practically Ohio and just—I need to find a car service who's willing to drive all the way out there right now—"

"I can drive you," Benji interrupted. "We have to take the train to New Jersey—my car is with my parents." His voice was neutral. Even. But his eyes were everywhere but Wyatt's face. "But—I'll take you."

Overwhelmed, he stared dumbly for a moment. "You don't have to...." Then Wyatt caught himself. Uncomfortable be damned. He had to get to Raven as soon as possible. "Thanks. Just... thanks. So much. I'll pay for gas and the train and whatever."

Benji shrugged. "Let me get dressed. Do you need to stop at your apartment?"

He hadn't even thought of that.

"Yeah. Thanks."

"Let's say ten minutes we'll head out. Stop by yours and then head for my parents."

So logical and calm. Wyatt felt his heart rate drop slightly.

"Thanks," he repeated.

"It's fine."

And with that, Benji disappeared into the bedroom.

Wyatt would feel like an asshole tomorrow.

IT WASN'T until Benji emerged—in another version of last night's expensive jeans and faded band T-shirt—with an overnight bag that Wyatt realized this wasn't a jaunt to Cape May. They were going to be driving for hours and, chances were, staying overnight.

His palms sweated a little.

"You don't have to…," he tried again, hearing Raven's cries in the back of his mind. It must've shown on his face because Benji didn't even pause. He strode around the living room, picking up his phone and charger, a laptop case, his sneakers.

"Train leaves in about an hour. That should give us enough time. I'm going to need addresses at some point for the GPS."

The stuttering kid from last night was all but gone, and this responsible adult with carefully tousled hair and an air of control left Wyatt feeling off-kilter.

"Sure." Wyatt started to say more but Benji was already turning away and walking into the kitchen.

THE cab ride to Wyatt's apartment was utterly silent. No canoodling this time. There wasn't much traffic as they cruised downtown, and the Village hadn't yet filled with tourists and Sunday morning brunch seekers. Benji looked out the window.

Wyatt looked at his phone, jiggling his leg nervously.

What would happen if Rob died? Who would take care of Raven and her twins? He'd move them to New York—the apartment was small but they'd manage. His lack of giving a shit about children was well-known but this was Raven—they were going on thirty years of taking care of each other and nothing was going to change that.

She was so excited about these babies. Rob was excited. She kept saying "Rob's so excited" whenever they talked, like it was the greatest news she'd ever heard. Him not living to see his kids born—well, Wyatt's stomach twisted painfully. All sorts of shitty parents seemed to live forever (like his, like Raven's), tormenting their kids into middle age. Or dumping them without a second backward look. What sort of world would take a person away who actually wanted to be a dad?

"Wyatt?" Benji's voice pulled him out of his sad spiral. He blinked and looked around—they were on his corner in front of his building.

"Sorry." He went for his wallet but Benji was already pushing him out the door.

"I took care of it."

Wyatt stood on the curb and watched Benji struggle to get his bags out of the cab. He seriously had no idea who the guy was and yet he was about to get into a car with him and drive six hours into the middle of nowhere.

He was crazy.

But then Benji looked up at him, all serious and concerned, and Wyatt felt a weird sensation.

Trust.

WYATT thought about apologizing for the mess, but fuck it—he was frazzled and sick to his stomach. The small apartment building had no doorman and smelled like lemon furniture polish, but that it was cheap and had no drug dealers were excellent trade-offs. They walked to the fourth floor in silence.

"Give me like ten minutes, okay?" Wyatt gestured toward the leather sofa and then hurried into his bedroom.

He had a bag half-packed at all times, thanks to all his work-related travel. That saved time. He grabbed jeans and light shirts, a jacket. Loafers. With each thing dropped into his leather duffle, he felt a stab of fear. Small town, rural, closed community—he knew that world, and he didn't like the potential for asshole behavior. Been there, survived that.

Raven swore it was a nice place, but then Raven had the luxury of passing for straight and "normal."

Her hair wasn't purple anymore, the nose ring was almost fashionable, and no one could tell her number on the Kinsey scale by looking at her or her life.

His best friend passed. Wyatt had never had that luxury, not once in his whole life.

For a second, panic swamped him, and it had nothing to do with Raven and Rob. There was a reason he'd left small-town living behind as soon as he had a diploma in his hand.

A knock startled him and he turned to find Benji peeking inside.

"Sorry but, uh—the train. If we want to catch the next one, we have to get to Penn Station," he said, apologetic. As if he should be sorry for getting Wyatt where he needed to be.

Wyatt nodded, not quite ready to trust his voice. He zipped everything up, took his laptop case off the desk, and hoisted it over his shoulder.

The next hour was a blur after that—another cab, Penn Station, the ticket counter. Again, he didn't pay for anything, and dimly he thought he should start keeping a tab. Benji had very little to say, just leading the way through the train station, directing Wyatt from place to place.

If he wasn't ready to cry with worry and fear, Wyatt would have been really annoyed at the lack of control he was having over the situation.

"Where do your parents live?" Wyatt asked finally, as they sat on the hard plastic bench to wait.

"Hawthorne—it's just outside the city. Half hour, tops. We can walk to the house from there."

"They're okay with you borrowing their car? I don't want you to get into trouble." As soon as it was out of his mouth, Wyatt felt himself cringe a little. Lord in heaven, he should have found out exactly how old this kid was.

Benji looked at him strangely, eyes dark and unblinking. There was something in the shift of his mouth as if he were holding in words, which told Wyatt he'd said exactly the wrong thing.

"It's my car," he said finally, then gestured toward the platform. "Our train's coming."

Wyatt followed him, wishing the train had a bar car.

THE train let them out in spectacular New Jersey suburban glory—neat rows of houses with proper lawns and little flags proclaiming their love of America, flowers, and the New York Yankees.

Wyatt tried not to break into hives.

A still silent Benji led him out of the train station and out through the parking lot. As they waited to cross the street, a family on bikes—mom, dad, three kids with helmets—whizzed by. Wyatt's throat closed up.

Okay, God, you and I have no business with each other anymore but Raven and Rob need help. You should do something about that.

After five minutes of walking, they arrived at a tiny brown cottage tucked into a lot at the end of the street. It was dwarfed by the giant Colonials on the street, all of which looked more recently updated and expertly placed on well-manicured lawns. This one, however, seemed to be caught in a '60s time warp.

Benji's shoulders—already tense—had risen to somewhere around his ears at this point. There was a Prius in front of a beat-up free-standing garage, and Wyatt had a Thelma and Louise moment of suggesting they throw their stuff in the back and flee.

"I need to get the keys. You can stay out here." Benji's sharp-edged voice startled him.

Wyatt didn't respond; he stood on the scraggly lawn of weeds with his bags, sweating through his khakis and polo.

Was the kid in the closet? Did he not want to explain the giant queen on his folks' lawn?

He didn't even care at this point. So long as he got to Raven, nothing else mattered.

BENJI came out a second later, trailed by a tiny Japanese woman with a cranky slant to her mouth and a silver fox in a T-shirt that read "Clean Water is Not a Luxury."

"Just—could you move the car? I need to get going. It's an emergency," Benji was saying, walking to the garage.

"You show up for five minutes to get your keys and that's it?" The woman—Wyatt guessed that was Mom—was on his heels, making grabs at the back of his shirt. "This isn't a hotel."

"I know, I know." Benji fumbled with the lock. The woman pushed into his personal space. "I've been busy."

"Busy?" She scoffed at the word. "You're not busy. You're hiding."

"Tina," the guy whom Wyatt assumed was Benji's father said, standing back and shooting Wyatt occasional looks as he folded his arms over his chest. "Let's not do this right now."

Actually the silver fox didn't look pleased either, now that Wyatt saw him close up.

Tina stomped her foot as she stepped back, then turned on her heel to head back toward the front door. "Don't take his side," she snapped.

"I'll stay longer when I return the car, okay?" Benji's voice went from sharp to resigned in nine words. He stopped, shoulders slumping all the way down. "I'm sorry. But my friend has an emergency and I need to help him."

Silver Fox handed over the keys from the pocket of his dad jeans.

"We're going to hold you to that promise," he said sternly, then threw his attention over to where Wyatt was standing.

Oh Christ. He couldn't do this, not today.

But Benji's father didn't go for a confrontation or questioning. He just nodded and raised his hand in a wave.

"Hope everything turns out okay," he said.

Wyatt tried to smile but his face didn't seem to want to move. "Thank you."

There was a whispered conversation between Benji and his father as he pulled open the garage door, but Wyatt missed most of it as the moving of cars began.

Dad moved the Prius and a few minutes later, Benji exited the garage driving a Bentley.

A fucking Bentley.

He pulled down the driveway and stopped where Wyatt was waiting, slack-jawed. The trunk popped and Wyatt heard a door slam.

Benji's mom had disappeared with a very loud bang.

"NICE car," Wyatt said finally as they sped down Route 80 West. Sunday traffic was light and, with the GPS humming between them, they were on their way to Raven.

"Thanks."

"I mean... I'm sorry, what the hell do you do again? I thought you were a freelance engineer?"

"I am." Benji's face was covered with sunglasses and cool reserve. The latter was growing with each passing mile and the sunglasses—well, Wyatt knew his shit, and they retailed at about $500 a pop.

"Are you also a drug dealer?"

Benji cracked for just a moment. He almost laughed. Almost. The moment passed and he schooled himself.

"No."

Then the conversation—if you could call it that—was over. Benji said, "Music, track twelve," and the car filled with sounds of the big summer song from two years ago. "Love You Like Sunshine" had been everywhere—radio stations, commercials, movie trailers. Wyatt couldn't escape it. It was nothing but a frothy mess—with a hypnotic hook and perky chorus you couldn't stop singing.

Wyatt wanted to stab himself.

"You like this song? Seriously?" he blurted out, unable to stop himself.

Benji's reserve slipped again. Another almost smile.

"It's a piece of shit. Deep as a water stain. Best-selling single of the year, and we sold the shit out of the rights. If they wanted it, we let them have it."

We.

Wyatt swallowed.

"We?"

"Wrote and produced it my senior year of college." Benji switched lanes with practiced ease. "My roommate's sister did the original vocals before Katy got it. Made a shitload of money. Also got an A on my senior project."

"Oh."

Wyatt slunk down in the seat—the seat of the very expensive car Benji had bought with money made off a shitty song.

"Capitalism is great," he said finally.

Benji snorted. "Tell that to my parents."

The track ended—mercifully—and Otis Redding's crooning voice blasted from the speakers. Benji ticked the volume up a bit, and they were silent through the rest of New Jersey

CHAPTER 3

WYATT woke up with a start; he didn't remember falling asleep, and the disorientation caused him to hit his head on the window.

"Ow. Goddammit."

"You okay?"

He registered that the car had stopped and that Benji wasn't in the driver's seat anymore. Wyatt squinted through the windshield. They were at a rest stop.

"Yeah." Wyatt sighed as he stretched and turned. Benji stood next to the car, sucking on a straw stuck in the biggest cup of soda Wyatt had ever seen. "Are we crossing the desert or something?" He gestured toward the behemoth.

Benji slurped another mouthful—loudly—and Wyatt's eyebrow raised of its own volition.

"I got you some water. You need to use the, uh… facilities?"

"You're like the world's weirdest field trip chaperone," Wyatt grumbled, but he opened the door of the Bentley a second later. Clutching his phone, he put his arms over his head to try to unhook his spine. "Give me a few minutes? I want to call Raven."

"Course." Benji ducked back into the car and shut the door.

"RAE?"

"Oh thank God." Raven sounded a bit calmer, at least. Wyatt checked the faded map in the entryway of the rest stop, trying to determine how much longer it would take for them to reach her.

"We're about three hours out," Wyatt said, trying to find a key on the map, to make sure it was somewhere in the current century.

"Thank you, thank you so much. I didn't know who else to call." Her voice trailed off and Wyatt sighed. They didn't have any family to speak of, and Rob's fine upstanding folks lived in the 1950's—they'd ceased contact when he married a black girl with a nose ring.

There was no one.

"Any word on Rob?" he asked gently, pushing open the door to get into the main area of the building. People bustled around him seeking caffeine and snacks; Wyatt spotted the men's room and started over, dodging kids and crowds.

"He's out of surgery. They had to put steel rods in his leg." She sniffled. "The doctors said they might be able to move him here but not for a few days."

"Do you want me to go there or come to you?"

He heard her hesitation, felt it. Raven the strong, Raven the brave, Raven the badass.

"Come here? Please?"

"Oh, honey—that was my first choice. You sound like you need a hug."

He didn't mean to make her cry again but boom, there it was, open sobbing through the line.

"I'm so scared."

"Why? Rob's going to be okay. You're going to bring two great kids into the world. We got this, Rae—totally got it under control." The noise rose around him until he couldn't take it; there was a tiny alcove holding a pay scale and a soda machine, so he tucked himself into a corner to find a little quiet.

"We've been through worse," she answered, sniffling.

"So much worse. This is bad luck and a big fat lawsuit against the trucking company. You're going to end up with a 24-carat gold toilet when the lawyers are done with that asshole driver."

Raven hiccupped a laugh. "I don't care about that. I just want Rob to be okay. I want him where I can hug him and hold his hand."

"When I get there, we'll call the doctor again and try to figure out the transfer thing, okay? Maybe you can even share a room! I've seen that in movies, so I'm sure it happens in real life."

Five minutes later he was able to convince her to nap so he could take a piss and get back on the road. Thankfully she was too emotional and stressed out to ask how exactly Wyatt was getting to her.

Because he didn't have friends he could call with something like this—except Raven. Sable—Soundsource's owner—and Betsy—his boss—were fabulous ladies with sass and class and Wyatt loved working with them. But they weren't pals. They wouldn't be willing to drive him to practically the mid-fucking-west at a moment's notice.

And they'd known him for years.

Wyatt washed his hands, avoiding a look in the mirror. He looked fucking terrible and felt like roadkill. And then there was the matter of Benji Trammell—not a dumb kid but a really rich kid with a strange compulsion to help guys who played the fuck 'em and leave 'em game.

Or maybe he was one in a long line of guys Benji kidnapped and dropped into a well.

HE FOUND Benji curled up in the car, AC running, radio playing faintly. As quietly as he could, Wyatt opened the door and slid into the seat, but Benji shook awake a second later.

"Sorry."

Benji rubbed his face with both hands. "No, it's fine. We should get going." He yawned widely, then ran his fingers through his hair. "Did you reach your friend?"

"Raven, that's her name. You should probably know the person you're helping me… help." Wyatt put the bag of food he'd snagged on the floor between his feet, then put on his seat belt. "She's my sister. For lack of a better word."

"Cool." Benji shifted the car into drive. "I have an older brother."

They left the parking lot, headed for the highway.

"Is he in the music business too?" Wyatt dug around the bag; those fries were begging to be eaten. The lack of food since the canapés last night was making him lightheaded.

"God no. He's a doctor. He works mostly in the Sudan now—he used to be with Doctors Without Borders." Benji's tone was somewhere between "Isn't that cool?" and "Fuck him." Wyatt actually knew it well.

"Wow, that's impressive."

"So very impressive." Benji changed lanes and sped up.

Wyatt didn't mention the speed limit, contenting himself with the greasy greatness.

"Your folks are, ah… I take it not in the music business either?" He hoped that was polite.

Benji snorted. "No. I'm not sure they've ever switched the radio from NPR to something that plays music. They uh, they work for an organization that builds wells in third world countries."

"Wow, that is also impressive," Wyatt said through a mouthful of fries. He brushed a fall of salt off his pants.

"Yeah. The whole family is ridiculously altruistic and well-meaning. And then I messed up the tree by doing frivolous stuff for money…." Benji gestured to the dashboard of his expensive car, which looked like something out of the Classy NASA collection.

"Did you buy this car to piss off your parents?" Wyatt asked, admiration growing.

"I don't know what you mean. But if I did, it would be adding insult to injury to ask them to store it at their house when I can afford a spot in the city," he answered, deadpan as could be.

Wyatt handed him a fry.

They pulled off the highway a few hours later, having spent time discussing the endless gossip at Soundsource (that was mostly Wyatt) and various fashion trends that were influencing some of his CD cover decisions (also Wyatt). Really, Wyatt talked for a few hours and Benji made "uh-huh" noises.

That must be why his throat was tight.

Or maybe it was the way this part of the country looked like upstate New York, where towns were isolated and minds changed slowly, if at all. Since leaving West Conrad, he had steadfastly avoided the spaces in between big cities, content with tall buildings and chaos and noise and strangers who kept to themselves.

The quiet open made him crazy.

"Should be, like, another thirty minutes," Benji said suddenly.

Wyatt nodded, gaze still locked on the countryside flying by.

"Is there a hotel or something I can check into?"

That gave Wyatt pause. "I don't know, actually. I haven't ever been out here. Last time I saw Raven, she and Rob came to New York."

"Oh."

He scrubbed his hands over his face, trying to shake his brain back into working. "I don't want you spending more money than you already have. Just stay with me at the house for the night." Wyatt gave him a side glance. "If you trust me."

Benji chuckled. "I'm sincerely hoping this isn't an elaborate ploy to kill and eat me."

"Technically, I already ate you," Wyatt said dryly. "And vice versa. So we're safe."

The face Benji made was painfully cute. He scrunched up his face like he smelled death. Or the lingering scent of cow manure leaking through the closed windows.

"So we've determined," Benji said, "there will be no eating of flesh and/or killing."

"That means I have to believe you're just a nice guy doing a stranger a favor… which is almost as weird as you being a brilliant serial killer."

The tone was light but the sentiment was accurate—who in this day and age did something like this?

"Wow, cynical."

The disembodied GPS voice indicated an upcoming right. Far in the distance, a large white complex loomed. The medical center where Raven was.

"Yeah, I'm cynical."

THE medical campus resembled a small city, and they drove around for five minutes to find the visitors' lot. Wyatt's palms were sweating and he fiddled with his phone as Benji parked the Bentley on the top of the structure. He shut off the car; Wyatt was already halfway out the door.

"Do you want—should I stay here?" Benji asked.

Wyatt leaned down to look back into the car. Benji pulled the sunglasses off, and he felt himself relax a bit at the sight of those big eyes. "No. I mean—you can if you want. But why don't you come in? Use the facilities," he teased weakly.

"Good idea." Benji gathered the trash while Wyatt got his computer bag out of the backseat.

They walked side by side down the stairs; Wyatt felt his legs getting heavier and heavier.

"What the hell do I do when I get there?" he blurted out. They were almost to the huge sliding glass doors of the entrance; this place looked like a hotel. "I don't have a single clue. I have to talk to doctors and ask them what?"

"Hey." Benji grabbed his arm, slowing their walk. They stopped on the sidewalk. "Relax. Talk to your friend first. See what she needs. Then you can see if the hospital has a social worker—they might be able to help you figure out what to do next."

Wyatt swallowed. "Okay. Okay. That's good."

"If we need to drive over to the other hospital, we will."

The "we," the grip Benji had on his arm—Wyatt took a deep breath. "You might be the nicest person I've ever met," he murmured.

"Better than a cannibalistic serial killer?"

"I might know how to handle that better."

They shared a smile, then Benji seemed to realize he was holding onto Wyatt. He dropped his hand and stepped back.

"Let's go see your friend."

THE lady at the front desk had a cute pink lab coat, a peony on her lapel, and a very helpful computer. She typed in Raven's name and, after giving Wyatt two laminated squares of neon-green paper, directed him to the fifth floor.

Visiting hours were almost over, but they had thirty-five minutes to see her.

"I didn't think about visiting hours." Wyatt sighed, leaning back against the elevator wall. "Plus it's a Sunday—I'm not going to be able to do much until tomorrow."

Benji fiddled with his sunglasses. "So you start first thing in the morning."

Wyatt rubbed at his face. "I wonder what the cab service is like out here?"

"Why…?" Benji stopped talking midquestion.

"Why? Because you are a fucking saint, but I don't expect you to stick around for as long as I need a ride." It came out cranky and Wyatt shook his head as the words left his mouth. "I appreciate this more than you can imagine, but I cannot impose with such an open-ended obligation."

"How about you let me worry about it? I don't have anything until Thursday." Benji shrugged, studying the floor. "You have my car and chauffeur service until Wednesday evening. How's that?"

The elevator door chimed and opened. Wyatt hadn't even realized they'd stopped.

"Thank you," he said finally as Benji held the door open. "I'll figure out a way to repay you."

He walked past Benji and onto Raven's floor, completely overwhelmed.

RAVEN'S room was at the end of the hall. A bed filled each corner; three were occupied. Raven was fortunate enough to have scored the one near the window.

Her face was drawn into a sad frown, her hands rubbing circles over her massive middle. An uneaten dinner sat on the tray in front of her.

"Hey, sweetheart," Wyatt called softly, trying not to disturb the other ladies—but everyone turned and looked at him in the doorway.

"Wyatt!" Raven's head jerked up and a tearful smile emerged. "Oh God."

"No, no, don't cry." He hurried over, dropping his bag on the floor before wrapping his arms around his friend.

Raven cried anyway.

Wyatt might have squeezed out a few tears as well; Raven felt good in his arms, like he finally had confirmation she was okay.

He felt her tears seeping through his shirt.

"Hey, come on, beautiful. We're going to figure this out." He rubbed her back, awkward and starting to worry he wasn't doing this right.

"I got to talk to him on the phone." Raven sat up, clutching at his arms. "He's really out of it but... he knew who I was." A fresh wave of tears fell.

"Were you scared he wouldn't? Rae, you need to stop watching movies about people with amnesia on Lifetime."

She laughed wetly and Wyatt felt himself breathe a little easier.

"He told me to calm down, to just worry about cooking the babies."

"Oh God, that sounds so gross, don't say that." Wyatt rested their foreheads together. "Not that I can replace Rob and his wholesome rugged Boy Scoutness, but I'm here to help, okay?"

Raven nodded, then sat up straight. "How the hell did you get out here so fast?"

"Oh." Wyatt turned around, where Benji was visible through the doorway only by the tips of his sneakers and a few curls from the top of his head. "Benji?" He smiled back at Raven. "Coworker. Sort of. He was there when I called you, and he was nice enough to offer his driving services."

Raven looked confused. "You called me at six... ohhhhh...."

"Shut up please," he murmured between gritted teeth as Benji's footsteps indicated he was joining them.

"Hi," he said to Raven, shy and sweet. He looked like a kid again, and Wyatt saw Raven's eyebrows go up.

"Hi." Raven extended her hand.

They shook and Wyatt distracted himself by smiling at the ladies in the other beds. They looked... confused.

"So what do you need right now? This second." Wyatt clapped his hands together. "Please say food because whatever that is"—he pointed to the plate next to him on the tray—"it's inedible."

"Food would be good, I guess. I couldn't eat all day." Raven settled back against the cushions. She resumed rubbing little circles on her stomach.

"I'll go down to the cafeteria," Benji volunteered. "Then you two can talk, figure out what needs to be done tomorrow."

"Thank you, that's so nice of you," Raven said politely.

He took his leave with a little wave and as soon as his back disappeared around the corner, Raven reached over and swatted Wyatt hard.

"Your booty call drove you here?"

"It was an emergency," Wyatt whispered. The ladies in the room were gawking at this point; he got up to close the curtain around Raven's bed. "What did you want me to do? He's staying until Wednesday to drive me around."

Raven's jaw dropped.

"How amazing were you in bed to warrant this sort of assistance?"

"I won't even dignify that an answer. Because you already know it."

Wyatt sat back down on the bed. "He appears to be a nice person. For the moment, at least. I have no idea how this happened. But it's good luck for us because he was willing to bring me here and willing to stick around so I can get stuff done."

Raven nodded. "That's really sweet of him."

"Seriously sweet. And weird. I haven't figured out his angle yet." Wyatt sighed dramatically. "Can he stay at your house?"

"Of course!" Raven pointed to the bedside table. "The keys are in there." The fretting started again; he could see the way her hands fluttered. "What are we going to do when he leaves? Cabs are going to get expensive."

"We'll worry about that later." He dug around pens and a paperback until he found the Go Cougars! key chain. "We need to get Rob transferred here. After that...." Wyatt didn't know but he smiled brightly. "Well, one thing at a time."

BENJI returned with a mixture of food, healthy and not. Wyatt took the chips and made Raven eat fruit (he let her have a pudding when she was done). Perched on the edge of a chair, Benji ate two ham sandwiches, quiet as a church mouse while Raven and Wyatt discussed what needed to be done.

She had two more weeks before the scheduled C-section. There were plans that had to be made regarding Rob's care. A ramp for the ranch. A hospital bed for the living room. Wyatt kept a calm façade during the entire conversation; at one point he realized that Benji was taking notes on his phone and he wished, desperately, for a stiff drink.

This was going to take more than a few days or even a few weeks. He had to call Betsy, to tell her—what?

He was quitting?

His stomach hurt. This was his career—he'd worked his ass off for years to reach this position and now— Well. Raven needed him.

The curtain rattled. A nurse stuck her head in, smiling politely. "Mrs. Beeler? Visiting hours are over," she said gently.

"Thanks, Viv." Raven pointed to Wyatt. "This is my friend, the one I told you about."

"Ah, your New York friend." Viv adopted a motherly manner, patting his arm. "Nice of you to make the trip."

"Anything for Rae." Wyatt went to grab his bag but Benji already had it over his shoulder.

"And that's Benji. His *friend*." It was the way Raven said "friend," Wyatt assumed, that made Viv's pale eyebrows disappear into her platinum bangs.

Benji offered a quick smile, then gave Raven a wave. "Take care. Nice to meet you." He disappeared through the white curtain before anyone could say another word.

"Well, he's a cutie!" Viv said, overly bright. She fussed with Raven's covers, and Wyatt was seized with a burst of annoyance.

"Bye, sweetheart. I'll be here in the morning." He kissed her cheek, ignoring the nurse.

"Love you."

"Love you too."

HE FOUND Benji at the car, sitting on the hood and drinking a bottle of water. Another one sweated next to him.

"Raven's really nice."

Wyatt nodded. He leaned against the side of the car; the sunset had begun, all peaches and reds across the wide-open space. "She's the best."

"You've known her a long time."

"Kindergarten." He took the water bottle, then unscrewed the cap.

"Ahhh, so she knows all your secrets." Benji hopped off the Bentley, jiggling his keys in his free hand.

"Only the ones I've told her."

Raven and Rob's house was a compact blue ranch a few streets away from the center of town. Wyatt spied a small supermarket, two banks, a nail place, a diner, a bar, barbershop, and drug store—Main Street, USA staples.

It felt like home and Wyatt hated it.

CHAPTER 4

WYATT unlocked the front door as Benji stood behind on the stoop, holding their bags.

"There's a cat. I should have mentioned that. Are you allergic?"

Benji shook his head as Wyatt scooted through the door.

"Mimsy? Mims? Where are you, devil cat?" Wyatt called out as he made his way through the open floor plan, turning on lights. The ancient giant white puffball was sitting in the kitchen, parked in the middle of the green tile floor with a pissed-off expression on her face.

The fluff ball was going on twenty-one, and Wyatt was convinced at this point that only pure hatred of humanity and her desire to torture them kept her alive.

"Yeah, I know. Daddy got into an accident and Mommy is trying to birth your replacements." Wyatt dropped his bag on the counter between a bowl of green apples and a bright pink blender.

Raven's kitchen looked like a set from *Suburban Monthly*.

"I put everything in the living room," Benji said, hovering on the other side of the island. "What do you need me to do?"

Make dinner? Feed the evil demon cat? Fix my life so I don't have to quit my job?

"Uh—check the fridge for food?"

Wyatt opened and closed cabinets until he found the pile of cat food cans. Mimsy hadn't moved; she just stared at him with those piercing blue eyes.

"Fridge empty but I found a menu," Benji said, sounding triumphant. "Says they deliver."

The sound of wet cat food hitting the plate made Wyatt gag. "Is there an ethnicity to this blessed delivering food factory?"

"Uh… American sandwiches and, well, let's call it bar food."

"Awesome. Some sort of fried meat with cheese with a side of fries. Please." Wyatt put the plate on the floor, right under Mimsy's nose. She blinked twice, then ducked her head to eat.

"That's an interesting cat."

"She's Satan birthed in feline form. I have a twenty-year-old scar from one of her numerous attacks."

Wyatt washed his hands, then wandered through the kitchen. It was clean but Benji was right—the inside of the fridge had an echo, though bless Rob for having a six-pack of Heineken in there. They would have to venture out to the grocery tomorrow.

First, though—he had to talk to Betsy.

"I'm making a call," Wyatt said, resignation in his voice. Benji nodded, phone to his ear as he waited to place their order.

The house wasn't big—kitchen, adjoining living room, two bedrooms, and a bathroom, all on one floor. It was suspiciously devoid of sass or pictures of girls in bikinis posed on cars—which had been the style du jour of Rob's dorm room back in the day. Wyatt found himself in the nursery, a mélange of greens and browns, owls and pussy willows painted on the walls, two of everything tucked into opposite corners. He settled down in the oak glider.

"Why are you calling me on a Sunday night?" Betsy said, skipping all that friendly conversation stuff. "What's wrong?"

"Family emergency."

"You have a family?"

"Betsy, I am too tired to banter. My foster sister's husband got into an accident, she's on bed rest with twins stuffed into her little body—so long story short, I'm in the backwoods of Pennsylvania and I need some… emergency leave?"

"Holy shit."

"Nice summation." Wyatt leaned back into the chair, his body heavy with worry.

"How long do you need?" Betsy started to sound panicky.

"A month?" He winced at the sound she made. Like she'd been stuck with a pin.

"Jesus."

"I can work from here. I have my laptop. It's just—" He blew out a breath. "Betsy, I never ask for anything. You probably owe me a million dollars in overtime and lost vacation days. Please."

Betsy's sigh was long-suffering. "I can swing two weeks, three at the most. Sable is on a tear about budgets because of the divorce. To replace you, I'm going to need at least two freelancers...."

"Have Sasha handle the Brannigan cover art and give Brick the scut work for Chantel's promo. Then you just need one freelancer—I'm going to go ahead and recommend Alicia from last summer because she doesn't do coke—and with me working on things from here, voilà!" He talked as fast as he could, speeding ahead of Betsy's protestations. "I may have just saved you money."

His boss breathed heavily for about two minutes—two minutes closer to the nervous breakdown Wyatt was crafting out of sheer terror.

"Three weeks, you work from wherever you are at least six hours a day, and we talk frequently—as in daily," she finally said, begrudging as all get-out. "I'll try to make this work with Sable."

"Call her after lunch on Tuesday. She always drinks too many martinis going over the books with Lyle." See? So helpful.

"Ugh. This is such bullshit, Wyatt. Seriously." Betsy's pout was audible.

"Believe me—I didn't choose the gangster life. It chose me."

BY THE time Wyatt hung up with Betsy—he may have promised her things he could not deliver regarding men and shoes and plastic surgery—he was starving and deeply convinced his only chance at happiness was that six-pack of beer in the fridge.

When he emerged from the nursery, he found Benji setting the table.

"How'd it go?"

"Betsy—my boss? Yeah, I may owe her internal organs for three weeks off." Wyatt flung himself into one of the straight-backed chairs.

Benji stopped mid-napkin-fold. "Three weeks? That seems optimistic."

"It's all I could get her to agree to."

Nodding, Benji finished his Holly Homemaker routine, then checked the clock. "The food should be here in, like, ten minutes. Can you take care of it? I need to call the studio."

Wyatt nodded, his brain processing everything, thoughts tumbling in circles like hamsters on a wheel. "Sure. Considering you've paid for everything so far and drove me out here to the middle of hell—I can swing dinner."

Benji smiled then disappeared down the same hallway as Wyatt emerged from. Apparently the nursery was private convo central.

Wyatt dragged his ass out of the chair, determined to do something productive before the food arrived. He moved the bags into the bedroom—and suffered his first roadblock.

Sleeping arrangements.

Given they'd already fucked, it seemed a little dramatic to stick the guy on the couch. And Wyatt was far too tall and far too diva to fold his frame onto that floral lump anchoring the main space.

He dropped his bags on the left side and Benji's on the right and thought *fuck it, whatever,* which was fast becoming his mantra for the night.

Back in the kitchen, Wyatt opened a beer as he unpacked his computer bag. Laptop, phone, chargers. He plugged everything in between swigs of beer and felt a little bit more grounded with the set-up.

He could do this.

He could help Raven and Rob, keep his job, and survive the middle of nowhere with ease. No problem.

The doorbell was sweet to his ears; Wyatt grabbed his wallet and made his way to the front door, eyes peeled for an imminent Mimsy attack.

But there was no blessed food on the other side, just a cautiously smiling middle-aged couple, each carrying a bag of groceries.

"Oh hey, hi. I'm Joann and this is my husband Frank. From next door?" She nodded as if Wyatt knew what that meant.

"Hello." Wyatt realized he was holding the beer and tucked his hand behind his back. "You're maybe looking for the Beelers?"

The man shifted, cans clinked, and Wyatt realized the bag he was holding wasn't light.

"Rob and Raven—of course. Are you a friend of Rob's? We just wanted to drop off the weekly groceries...." Joann's smile started to flicker.

"Actually I'm a friend of Raven's. You need me to grab that?" Wyatt motioned for the bag Frank was losing his grip on.

"Sure." His deep voice matched his broad shoulders and beefy arms. He looked like an escapee from *The Sopranos*.

With the hand not holding the beer, Wyatt rescued the groceries. "Rob—well, he had a little accident," he said, unsure of how close they were to Rob and Raven. "So I came to help out."

"Oh no, no! That's awful." Joann looked genuinely upset.

"He'll be fine. He's at the hospital in Kenville with a broken leg and I'm minding Raven so...." Wyatt gestured for Joann's bag. "This is so nice of you. I'll let Raven know in the morning and I'm sure they'll appreciate it."

Frank seemed to get the dismissal before Joann did; he was side-eyeing Wyatt, his scowl growing. Maybe he thought it was a hoax so Wyatt could steal their television.

"Jo—give 'em the bag," he said.

She was flustered for a moment. "Oh, sure. Okay. Here you go. Um... our number is on the speed dial if you need anything."

"Awesome. That's so great, thank you." Wyatt took a step back, managing groceries in one hand and the beer in the other. "I will definitely call if we need anything. You guys have a great night."

With one last glare, Frank put his arm around Joann and led her down the walkway.

Wyatt let the door slam with relief.

"The food here?" Benji appeared, tucking his phone in his pocket.

"No, but the potluck train started. We have groceries."

"Wow. People just show up with stuff?"

"You have no idea. I just pray things with condensed soup have gone out of style." Wyatt headed for the kitchen.

"This doesn't happen in the suburbs of New Jersey, by the way." Benji trailed behind him—then reached around to divest him of his beer.

"You're taking your life into your hands, mister."

The doorbell rang again and Wyatt moaned.

"Allow me. Maybe it's people with cake." Benji darted for the front door.

Wyatt stepped over something blocking his way—Mimsy sprawled on the line between the entryway carpet and the kitchen floor.

"Maybe we'll trade Mimsy for cake," he muttered as conversation filtered in from the front door. Benji was chatting someone up—it was probably the most animated tone he'd heard from the kid... ever.

Inside the bags from Joann and Frank, Wyatt found boxes of spaghetti, jars of store brand pasta sauce, generic raisin bran, two boxes of Oreos, and a full bag of tiny cans of cat food. Spoiled Mimsy. At least they had something for breakfast—if Benji didn't mind beer-flavored cereal.

"Dinner. No casseroles," Benji announced. He headed to the island to drop the bags.

"We have Oreos. We won't starve."

THEY ate without much conversation, and halfway through Wyatt registered that they'd only known each other for twenty-four hours.

He swallowed a mouthful of chicken.

"I don't know much about you," he blurted out, catching Benji as he took a sip of his beer. Like it had just dawned on him

Benji wiped his mouth slowly. "Uh—you know enough? I promised not to kill you. I told you my deep dark pop princess secret. Everything else is... boring." He ducked his head and seemed to squirm for a second under Wyatt's gaze. "Actually—can I ask you a question?"

"Considering how many miles you put on your car on my behalf—shoot." Even as he said the words, Wyatt felt his fake smile settling in, his shoulders tightening.

"This morning, if you hadn't—you were just going to leave?"

It sounded curious, not accusing, and Wyatt relaxed. He hadn't had to deal with this sort of thing since college, when occasional dates led to boys thinking stupid things about love and relationships—and Wyatt had to give them a sweet, sad song about not being that kind of guy. Because he did not stick around to give guys the time and space to be assholes.

"I know—dick move. But I had this thing and I didn't want to wake you." Wyatt reached over and patted Benji's hand. "Nothing personal, honey. I had the best time. Seriously. I'll write you a recommendation letter."

"Oh." Benji started to play around with his french fries, stacking them fortress-like around what was left of his burger. "So if I saw you at the office, say—tomorrow? And asked you to dinner, you would have said...."

Wyatt sighed as he leaned back in his chair. "That I had a thing and...."

"Nothing personal," Benji finished, bemused.

"Exactly."

"Fair enough."

"Come on—you're like, twenty-five and rich and wicked hot. You do not want to be having second dates." He went back to his dinner. "Seriously. Take it from an old man with a comfortable life—relationships are complications you don't need."

When Benji didn't answer, Wyatt looked up from his dinner. Benji was watching him like a bomb that needed defusing. Then he shrugged.

"Like I said, fair enough."

TWO hours later, Wyatt was internally bitching about shitty water pressure in the pale-peach recesses of the Beelers' bathroom—he and Raven were having a serious conversation about paint colors when she got home—when the floral-patterned shower curtain was yanked aside.

In all his beautiful naked glory stood Benji, half-hard and expectant. "This isn't a second date," he said before climbing in. "Just so you know."

Wyatt didn't even think to protest when Benji slid to his knees.

Chapter 5

AFTER feeding Mimsy and checking his e-mail, Wyatt waited for Benji to wake up from his dead-to-the-world slumber. They'd swapped blowjobs the night before but fucking seemed way too much work, so they'd rolled over in opposite directions—space for an entire extra person between them—and fallen asleep.

But Wyatt didn't sleep well in strange places and so at six he was awake and revving to go. They had a while before visiting hours started, so he went through his inbox to show Betsy how serious he was about making this work.

By the time he heard shuffling from down the hall, everything had been delegated or handled.

Wyatt snapped the laptop shut with a touch of gloating.

"We have no milk," he announced as Benji appeared, naked yet again.

"Hm?"

"No milk. Are you a nudist?"

Benji leaned against the counter, ruffling his bedhead with one hand. "Sorta."

"Fabulous. I will make sure we keep the curtains closed." Wyatt leaned his elbows on his knees. "No milk."

"You mentioned."

"Which means our options for breakfast are cat food, pasta, Oreos, and beer."

"Wow, it's like college all over again."

Wyatt snickered.

"I saw a diner when we were driving in. You up for eggs fried in grease and overbuttered toast?"

Wyatt's stomach gurgled in response.

IN HIS khaki shorts, white tee, and boat shoes, Benji emerged with yet another version of himself for Wyatt to examine. Nerdy engineer, college bum, rich kid with a Bentley. He didn't even know what to call this new look as Benji slid his expensive aviators on.

Wyatt wished he'd brought shorts of his own; the air could only be described as baked and he was starting to feel crispy.

Benji turned the air conditioning on in the car.

"Did you get any work done this morning?"

"Yeah. I have to make sure Betsy doesn't get nervous and give my job away."

Directing the car through the nearly deserted Main Street area, Benji shook his head. "Why would you assume she'll give your job away? Haven't you been there for a while?"

"Since Soundsource was born. Hell, I was actually an intern at Fiddler's 6 before the buyout. It's the only place I've ever worked—if you don't count Kmart when I was in high school."

Benji laughed.

"What?" Wyatt rolled his eyes. "This is what you find funny?"

"You in a Kmart? Yes. Hilarious."

"It helped me to hone my style instincts. For example, I can tell you what any piece of clothing or an accessory costs."

"This is a valuable skill?" Benji didn't seem convinced.

"Oh, absolutely. It tells you a lot about a person, what they spend money on."

"For example...."

Wyatt settled back and eyed Benji critically.

"For example—your shorts are last season Topman and I'm betting you got them on sale because they look new. So—clearance rack? The T-shirt looks cheap but it's Calvin Klein and it's been tailored. Those shoes are a knockoff but you can barely tell. Good eye."

"Thank you."

"You're welcome. Oh, and those aviators are at least five hundred bucks and you drive a ridiculously expensive car, not to mention all that equipment back at your apartment. You like toys, Mr. Trammel, particularly ones that identify you as a grown-up who can pay his own way. But that feels a little too showy, maybe? Whatever the reason, you try to soften reality with this whole shy-kid thing, which is a total hoax."

"Interesting." Benji worried his lower lip with his teeth. "But that shy kid is who you wanted to fuck."

Wyatt cleared his throat. "Point."

"And you did."

"I did."

Benji pulled them into the parking lot of the diner, already starting to fill with early risers. He parked, then turned to look at Wyatt.

"I used to be that kid. He's very nonthreatening." His face seemed to soften as he talked.

Wyatt wished he'd pull off the sunglasses.

"You thought I wanted passive…," he said, realizing he'd been played a little.

Benji shrugged. "You saw me at Mitch's party—I saw you as well. Saturday wasn't a stroke of luck. I could have just called Kala."

"You came to see me?"

Benji shut off the car and unlocked the doors. "I did."

And then he got out of the car.

WYATT trailed him nervously into the diner. Maybe he should suggest a hotel. Or for Benji to head back into the city. Because this was starting to feel strange, and with Raven's troubles, he did not need this shit.

And then it got worse.

He stepped into the diner, taking in the hard maroon booths and long Formica counter, the rotating dessert cabinet to his left, the makeshift bar behind the registers to the right. It was like getting kicked in the ass and flying back through time to the shithole you've done everything in your power to escape.

"I got us a table," Benji was murmuring all of a sudden and Wyatt snapped back. People were starting to stare at him, turning from their plates of flapjacks and eggs.

"Right this way," said a middle-aged woman in a floral shirt and rayon pants. She wielded two giant menus like they were the Ten Commandments.

Benji led the way and Wyatt tried to keep up, but out of the corner of his eye he spotted a few whispers between companions and his blood boiled.

When they passed the guy with the confederate flag T-shirt, he almost bolted.

"You boys want coffee?" the woman asked as they settled into a far back booth. She handed them their menus with a flourish.

"Please," Benji said politely. "With milk for me."

"Same." Wyatt stared at the menu and saw nothing. Could Benji feel all the eyes trained on them?

She toddled away and the clatter of the restaurant seemed to rush back. Wyatt blinked a few times, then ducked his head.

"Do you want to leave?" Benji asked suddenly. Anxiously.

Wyatt dropped the menu to stare across the table.

"No," he snapped, then took a deep breath. "Sorry. No. Let's eat breakfast and head to the hospital."

With a nod, Benji went back to the menu and Wyatt focused on the all-important task of choosing between waffles and pancakes.

"Wyatt Walsh?" a soft voice asked, and Wyatt almost hurt himself looking up. The voice belonged to a teenaged girl, with black hair that came from a bottle and clashed horribly with her sunny yellow church dress.

"Uh—yeah." Wyatt dropped the menu, his body tensing before he realized it was happening.

"I'm Belinda—I work for Raven as a mother's helper sometimes." She laughed nervously, then shook her head. "I mean, I will, when the babies are here, but for now I just, like, help around the house and stuff."

Wyatt nodded. "Hi, Belinda." He shook her hand, thin and damp, then gestured toward Benji.

"Benji Trammell," he said and watched as they did the friendly nod thing.

"I heard what happened to Rob...."

Wyatt nodded, taking a deep breath as he resettled himself. "Have you talked to Raven?"

"Yeah, this morning. Oh my gosh, I'm so upset about Rob. He's the nicest."

The floral-shirted lady arrived with coffee cups; she and Belinda dodged each other for a moment before she disappeared again.

"I'm sure he'll be fine," Wyatt said, staged smile, canned words.

There was an uncomfortable smile as Belinda looked from Wyatt to Benji and back again.

"So, did Raven need for you to do something at the house?" Benji prompted. Belinda's grateful smile was huge.

"Yes! She wanted me to take care of groceries for you guys and um, just tidying up. Plus...." She pulled out a phone in a bright pink case with bunny ears. "Here's my cell. School doesn't start for another two weeks, and my shift at the drug store is usually late, so any time during the day...."

Benji kicked Wyatt under the table, which clued him to take out his own phone. They exchanged numbers, Wyatt adding her name under "Yellow Sundress" so he would remember.

"Thanks for, uh—well, that's going to be helpful," Wyatt said, putting his phone away. Floral blouse showed up again, a pad of paper in hand with pen poised. "So we're going to order and then I'll call you tomorrow, maybe? After I find out what Raven needs at the hospital."

Belinda nodded enthusiastically. "Okay, super. Text me a shopping list, okay? I know my parents dropped off a few things last night, but they never remember the stuff you actually need. Like milk." She rolled her eyes in dramatic teenage fashion, like she couldn't imagine their shortcomings were allowed to exist in the world.

"Last... oh, Frank and Joann." Wyatt smiled harder. Fabulous. "Lovely people."

"Who forgot the milk," Benji offered, deadpan and adorable, and Belinda tittered like he was on the stage with a microphone.

Seriously?

"Oh gosh, top of the list, okay. But I want to get everything right, so...."

"A list," Wyatt broke in. "Promise."

Floral-blouse lady sighed loudly.

"Sorry, sorry. Sorry, Angela!" Belinda stepped aside.

Wyatt ordered pancakes and bacon because it was the least amount of words he had to get out of his mouth. Between the staring and the Belinda whirlwind and Benji's "yet another personality"—he was veering closer and closer to done. And they still hadn't made the trip to the hospital.

"Same," said Benji, collecting both menus and handing them over. Floral blouse disappeared but Belinda remained.

Benji gave him a glare but smiled up at the girl. "Would you like to join us?"

"Oh no, no. Thank you! But I really have to get going. I just stopped by to see my friend." She blushed a little and Wyatt wondered which of the pimple-faced busboys was hers. "I'll text you guys later."

"Okay, thanks again." Wyatt used the last wattage of his fake smile—and as soon as Belinda's back turned, his face dropped.

He slumped against the back of the banquette, hearing the pleather creak in protest.

"She's nice."

Wyatt's eyebrows ducked into his hairline. "Yeah." Benji didn't seem too pleased with him but who the hell knew; Wyatt waited for the food by matching the stony silence with his own as he glanced around the room.

Business had picked up; the tables were filled and the noise level rose. Wyatt watched as surreptitiously as he could, waiting for the look or the words or the confrontation he feared from places like this.

A body came into view and Wyatt looked up to see an attractive dark-skinned teenager wielding a water pitcher in one hand and a coffeepot in the other.

"Refills?" he asked. His name tag said Eli.

"Sure." Benji pushed his cup forward but Wyatt just looked down. He hadn't even taken a sip of his.

"Just refresh it, thanks," he said wearily.

"So you guys are friends of the Beelers?" Eli asked and Wyatt swallowed an exasperated sound. They were never coming here again.

"I am."

Benji just drank his coffee.

"I'm playing football at Field's next year, so—he's the best. Tell 'em I said get better soon."

"We will," Benji chimed in.

Eli gave them a smile, then disappeared into the crowd.

"What are you doing?" Wyatt finally snapped, his voice low as he leaned closer over the table. "I don't need to make conversation with every person in this place."

"I'm being polite. Because you're rude." The matter-of-factness made Wyatt see actual red spots.

"I'm...."

"Rude. When I leave in a few days, you're going to be stuck here without transportation or assistance. And while you don't care about what people think, this is your friend's home."

Wyatt felt his blood pressure spike.

"Fuck you."

"I'm trying to help."

"Well, I'm done with your help so feel free to fuck on back to New York. Let me know how much money I owe you and I'll write you a check," Wyatt snapped.

"Pancakes and bacon!" Floral blouse announced, dropping the food on the table. By the time she'd stacked up the butter and the syrup and extra napkins, Wyatt thought he was going to shoot off through the roof like a rocket.

How dare this... asshole? Wyatt did things for a reason. Because of his experiences. And here comes this little shit... he knew the nice-guy routine was too good to be true. Just another dickhead who wanted to control Wyatt's behavior.

Benji started in on his pancakes, painting on butter and drizzling syrup without even looking up. Wyatt gripped his fork as floral blouse asked if they needed anything else.

"No, thank you," Wyatt said as nicely as he could manage.

She left.

Benji took another container of syrup from the center of the table.

"Tell me how much I owe you and...."

"You don't owe me anything." Benji tucked the napkin across his lap, finally glancing up at Wyatt, placid face mask in place. "I offered to help you and so whatever I spent—it's fine. We're even. I'll drop you off at the hospital and then...." His voice trailed off, the confidence suddenly wavering.

"Thank you." Wyatt loosened his grip on the fork so he could feel his fingers again.

They ate in silence. Wyatt paid the bill—overtipping a ridiculous amount—as the food sat in his stomach like a rock.

Eli waved at them as they walked out the door and Wyatt returned it with a nod, not watching where he was going. The impact as he slammed into someone was jarring.

"Shit, sorry," he muttered, turning around fully.

The guy was just… a guy. Polo shirt and jeans, heavy gold watch, badly styled blond hair. Nondescript. But the sneer? The sneer felt as familiar as his own name.

He got no answer, so Wyatt just stepped around the guy, feeling Benji fall into step behind him.

"Fags," came the whisper behind him.

Wyatt stopped in midstep, jerking around to say something—because no, no fucking way—but Benji shoved him through the doors.

WYATT didn't stop until they were back at Benji's car; he was shaking, breakfast threatening to make a repeat experience. The pounding in his head was like a bass drum installed directly into his ear.

"Just get in," Benji was saying. The door opened and Wyatt felt himself being maneuvered into the front seat. With a slam Benji moved to the other side of the car.

Wyatt closed his eyes and tilted his head back against the rest. He heard Benji get in, heard the motor start.

Air conditioning.

Radio.

The GPS whispering directions to Raven.

Raven.

Shame crept over Wyatt. He couldn't handle this—couldn't help his friend in the middle of these shitty circumstances. He felt powerless; sixteen and scared and his family gone and no one seeming to give a shit about everything going on with him….

"Hey—I know you're not okay, but we're going to be at the hospital in a minute and I need to know if I'm dropping you off or not or what." Benji's quiet calm voice broke through his head.

"Can you do a lap?"

"Not a problem."

The GPS complained but Benji kept going. Wyatt opened his eyes, finally, blinking against spots in front of his eyes.

"So, I know you're mad at me but if you want to talk, I'm sort of a captive audience."

Wyatt blew out a breath.

"I'm not—I'm not mad, okay? I just hate being here and you're... here. And you pissed me off."

"Sorry." Benji sounded contrite—in the same way he did after the little song and dance with his parents when they went to pick up the car.

"No, I'm sorry." Wyatt whacked his head against the headrest. "Okay, here's the thing. I grew up in a town like this. Like, you could assume cloning was a factor, that's how close it was," he said softly, his throat aching with unspoken anger. "Raven's my foster sister because my father kicked me out when I was sixteen."

"Oh. Wow." Benji slowed the car down, then pulled onto the side of the road next to a copse of trees. "I'm sorry."

"It wasn't because I'm gay—so, you know, not a very special Logo movie." Wyatt ran his fingers over the door handle. "He knew since I was a kid. My mom knew. They didn't care enough to damn me to hell."

"Then why?"

"They were moving to Louisiana. And they didn't want to take along an extra mouth. So I got my stuff and fifty bucks, and that was it." He heard the dullness of his voice—it was such a stupid story sometimes he wanted to make it into something else, to embellish. "Raven's foster parents took me in so I could finish high school."

Benji exhaled. When he reached over the console to touch Wyatt's knee, it seemed so nice and so ridiculous at the same time.

"But you know what? That's not the worst part. The worst part was the people in town—wholesome small town values and Jesus and neighbors helping neighbors and what the fuck else they decided applies to them—those people? They blamed me for getting kicked out. They thought I'd done something terrible to make my family move out of town."

"What? That's crazy. You were a kid."

"A mouthy gay kid whose parents up and moved twenty states away. Oh, the rumors—they were amazing. I'd molested my kid brother.

I was cooking meth in the shed and my parents were in witness protection because they turned me in. I was some sort of creepy pervert they couldn't control." Wyatt laughed, bitter and exhausted by the retelling. "I'd already gotten shit in school for being gay but this was— this was full-out war. I primed the gossip mills for two fucking years, until I graduated and got the fuck out of there."

Silence filled the car; Benji continued to stroke Wyatt's knee.

"That's bullshit," Benji murmured finally. "I'm glad you got out."

"They were supposed to be nice people, okay? They prided themselves on that Biblical bullshit about treating other people the way they wanted to be treated—which apparently means being spit on and getting your ass kicked by douchebags who traveled in packs."

His voice cracked.

"I hate being here. Hate it. Hate remembering that life because I have worked my ass off to forget."

Benji leaned over, pulling him into a loose hug. Wyatt's stomach clenched even as his body reacted; he let himself be drawn in closer, let himself be comforted.

Dangerous territory.

EVENTUALLY Wyatt pulled himself together and Benji drove him back to the hospital. This time he didn't park, he just pulled up to the front entrance, car idling.

"Listen, I get you don't want my help," Benji murmured, hands tight on the steering wheel. "But I feel really uncomfortable leaving you here without a ride home."

"I was a massive asshole to you at the diner but could we just... peace treaty this out for a while longer?" Wyatt asked. He had no right to, and Benji had zero reasons to say yes, but....

"Of course." Benji half smiled as Wyatt opened the door.

"Thanks."

Wyatt got out of the car as quickly as he could.

RAVEN was beaming when Wyatt showed up, a hastily purchased jelly donut and five obscenely pink Gerbera daisies in his hand.

"Well, that's what I like to see—a giant smile. Good news?"

She accepted his cheek kiss as he sat on the bed. "Very positive sonogram this morning—the babies are awesome."

"Not surprised—amazing parents and all."

Her smile dimmed a little as she took the flowers and the little bag of sugary goodness.

"I have to call Rob's doctor in a little bit...."

"My timing is perfect, then."

He held her hand tightly and Raven—because Raven knew him—leaned forward to get into his very personal space.

She didn't say anything; she just let him lean against her.

And oh, how guilty that made him feel.

ROB'S doctor was named Halsey; despite sounding gruff, he was very helpful with information. Raven got reassurance and Wyatt got a list of dates.

The date they could move Rob to Raven's hospital. Two days from today.

The date they could consider moving Rob back home. Eight days from today.

Add to that the thirteen days until Raven's C-section and three weeks seemed a tip of the iceberg. Betsy wasn't going to like this at all.

BENJI never turned up in the room.

Raven asked about him, but Wyatt deflected with "work" and moved the conversation to Belinda, Frank, and Joann and how many places delivered so he never had to leave her house.

"It's not like home," Raven said for the umpteenth time. "It really isn't."

"Some guy called me a fag at the diner this morning," he retorted.

"And that never happened in the city?" Raven shifted, trying to get comfortable.

"That doesn't make it right."

"Of course it doesn't! It also doesn't make it just a small-town problem."

A nice nurse brought chicken soup and crackers so they called a stalemate. While Raven napped, he texted furiously to Betsy to keep everything on track. When she started mentioning giving "Brick more of the load," Wyatt tap-danced away his bonus and gave Betsy dirt on who the head of IT was banging. That mollified her and Brick got squat.

Wyatt was going to need an app on his phone to keep track of the peace treaties he was currently negotiating.

VISITING hours ended and Wyatt found himself dragging his feet to leave the hospital. He got to the lobby, pulled toward the doors by the throng of folks leaving.

Through the doors and there it was. That gleaming Bentley with the cute boy behind the wheel.

"I MADE dinner," Benji said, as soon as Wyatt buckled in.

"Oh, okay."

They didn't talk; Wyatt was still in a mood, moving rapidly between "no one touch me" and "man, I'm an asshole" in his thoughts.

"It's my mom's family recipe." Benji's voice cut through the quiet. He sounded nervous.

"Huh, that's really nice of you." Wyatt made a stab at a smile. "Why don't we stop and I'll get a bottle of wine. As a contribution."

"Sure."

THE liquor store was on the highway, more a liquor warehouse than a simple place to pick up wine or whiskey. Past the cases of beer the size of a hatchback, Wyatt found a worker stocking shelves with bottles of champagne.

"Japanese food," he said a little desperately. "What have you got that'll go?"

The guy looked like he just got hit with a pop quiz.

In the end, they used Wyatt's phone and discovered it depended on what was being served. Wyatt thought it would be a close race to see who cried first.

"Chardonnay," the man said eventually. His name was Billy and this was his second job (he also worked at the oil refinery) and Wyatt didn't mind the chatter as they selected a slightly more expensive bottle with "pear undertones."

"I usually just drink the sake and beer the waitress brings with my sushi." Wyatt sighed as he whipped out his credit card.

"From the city, huh? Philadelphia?" Billy rang him up.

"New York."

"You're a long ways from home, son."

Wyatt gathered his bag and credit card and slipped Billy a ten. "You have no idea."

AT THE house, Wyatt let Benji carry the wine in. He had a list on his phone of things that needed to be done.

Run the sprinkler for an hour.

Put the garbage out.

Check to make sure raccoons didn't get into the garage.

He didn't bother with the last one because seriously—what the hell was he going to do if they were there? He would feed them Mimsy and buy Raven a kitten later.

Inside, the house was lit up, the table set. From the doorway, he could see Benji opening the wine in the kitchen.

Wyatt sighed, one hand to his forehead.

The level of off-kilter he was feeling was starting to resemble a roller coaster. He just wanted to get through tonight without having a panic-induced asshole attack.

WYATT washed his hands, spying Mimsy at her bowl, eating daintily.

"You fed Satan's spawn."

"Well, she was glaring." Benji stood next to him at the sink, facing the other way. "Listen, I'm sorry for today."

"You aren't the one to be apologizing."

"Listen, full disclosure. I wanted you to be interested in me at the party," Benji said softly, looking at the wall. Wyatt watched his profile, the tense tilt of his body. "And I got a little pissed when you were just going to leave in the morning. Okay? I didn't realize that you were...."

"Someone who doesn't do second dates," Wyatt finished.

"Right." Benji turned toward him and Wyatt was once again struck by his expressive eyes. "So, I apologize for expecting something you weren't prepared to give."

"You need to stop being such a nice guy." Wyatt blamed the day, the moment, the... whatever... for leaning over and kissing Benji's cheek.

"It was beat into me as a child," he said dryly. "Let's eat."

"Right." Wyatt watched him straighten up and walk to the dining room.

Wyatt sat down, focusing in on his wine. "Oh wait, let me check the drawers for chopsticks," he said as Benji approached with a covered casserole dish.

The confusion on his face was pronounced.

"You eat spaghetti with chopsticks?"

"Oh God." Wyatt felt genuine horror at his faux pas as Benji put the dish on the table. And opened the top to reveal a pile of thick spaghetti, covered with red sauce and fat meatballs.

Wyatt's mouth watered even as he wanted to crawl under the table.

Benji started to laugh.

"Seriously, Wyatt?" Benji dropped down into his seat. "Chopsticks?"

"Jesus Christ, don't look at me. I just... you said mother and I assumed...." He moaned, burying his face in his hands.

"My mother is definitely Japanese but she can't use chopsticks to save her life. Also, her family's been in this country for five generations." He laughed again, rich and warm. "Her nanny was from Sicily. This was my mother's favorite dish as a kid."

Wyatt refused to look up, even as he heard the clinking of silverware and the rich aroma of dinner came closer to his covered face.

"Everyone assumes I'm good at math," Benji continued, mirth still lacing his tone. "That's the big one besides food. Oh, and that being musical and part Asian, I must play the violin. For the record—I don't play the violin."

Eventually Wyatt peeled his hands away and looked up—to find Benji twirling spaghetti around his fork.

"I'm starving so you better hurry up. I'll eat the whole damn plate of it."

Wyatt finished his wine and poured another glass before he picked up his fork.

"So if you don't play violin, what do you play?"

Benji's gaze went from his plate to Wyatt, a curious glint to his eyes. "Piano, mostly. It's where I write."

"Poppy summer songs about love that smells like suntan lotion?" It was a gentle tease.

"Yeah, and… other stuff." That faint blush was back.

"Why haven't you released any more music?"

"Mmmm—nervous, I guess. Me and a piano isn't as glamorous as Katy in a mink bikini dancing on the top of a giant beach ball. I'd like it to be mine this time. Meaningful to me and not just a good hook I knew would sell."

Wyatt stuffed a forkful of pasta in his mouth—he would have answered but he was too busy moaning.

"Good, right? That's some excellent Japanese red sauce right there," deadpanned Benji.

WYATT insisted on doing the dishes. He cleaned the kitchen as penance and served Benji Oreos and milk in the living room for the same reason. The full fridge reminded him he also owed Belinda a thank-you for her shopping trip—at this point he might as well download an app called "Say Thank You, You Ungrateful Bastard."

When he finally settled down on the couch where Benji was sleepily watching SportsCenter, the question he was eager to ask fell off his tongue.

"Why are you really doing all this?"

Benji started, rolling over onto his stomach to meet Wyatt's eyes. "I told you...."

"You liked me and then you realized I'm a douche. I followed that up by being an ungrateful ass to you two mornings in a row. Your response was to make me dinner." Wyatt shook his head. "What do you want?"

Shaking his head, Benji laid back down on the couch. "Nothing."

"You should want something."

"Wyatt—sometimes you just do nice things, okay? That's it." The annoyance in his tone told Wyatt that this was a pile of lies.

"Well, you shouldn't. Not just for anyone—especially not one who's going to take advantage of you," Wyatt huffed. "That's it. I'm not going to mention it again."

"Fine."

THAT night, Benji slept on the couch.

CHAPTER 6

WYATT crept out of the bedroom at five to collect his laptop and phone. Benji was sprawled facedown on the couch, snoring into a throw pillow.

Guilt-laden, Wyatt slunk back into the bedroom with Mimsy at his heels.

With the cat watching him from her perch on the dresser, Wyatt booted up to check his e-mail. Every one was bullshit—things he could handle without being in the office, and then a string of messages from Betsy in which she lamented how things were already going to shit without him.

The last e-mail—from last night—was an entirely different tone.

Wyatt,

You have six week's leave, with pay. If you need more, let me know. Sable sends her love.

Brick is an asshole, by the way, and he wants your job. Did you know that?

Betsy.

Wyatt rubbed his eyes, unsure if he was dreaming.

He didn't even check the time when he dialed Betsy's cell.

"Are you kidding me?" she sputtered, her voice thick with sleep.

"Why do I have double the leave with pay? You said three weeks—what's going on?"

"Only you would be suspicious of something good."

Wyatt started pacing the room. "Did Sable okay this?"

"A request was made of Sable, Sable called me, I told Brick to fuck himself. It was a busy day."

"Wait—who asked Sable to grant me leave."

Betsy snorted. "Sweetheart, how did you get to East Bumfuck?"

"I…." Wyatt stopped walking. "Benji."

"Mr. Trammell has great sway with Sable," she said crisply. "And he put in a good word. And you should say 'thank you' and let me get back to sleep."

Wyatt hung up the phone in shock.

HE WAS going to wait until at least seven to wake Benji but that went out the window about five seconds later.

Wyatt dropped Mimsy on Benji's legs.

There was a brief cartwheeling of arms and legs and then Benji was sitting up precariously on the edge of the couch.

"What the hell?"

"Mimsy wanted to say good morning," Wyatt snapped. "Who are you?"

"What?" Benji struggled with the throw blanket and stood. He looked bewildered.

"One pop hit gets you a shitload of money, I got that. What exactly gets you sway with Sable Vincent?"

"Oh."

"Oh?"

Benji took a deep breath and stepped back. "I own five percent of Soundsource."

Wyatt resisted the urge to smack his head against the wall.

"SABLE needed some cash last year, I needed an investment—her niece and I went to college together." Benji was babbling and Wyatt sat on the edge of the couch with a throbbing headache.

"So I technically fucked one of the owners of the company I work for," he cut in. Mimsy sat on the coffee table, staring him down. He knew he was going to lose this contest.

"Yes. Technically."

"Please tell me there isn't anything else you haven't told me."

"I'm pretty sure that's it."

"If you put my career in jeopardy...."

Benji was already shaking his head. "It's not like that. Not at all."

"Fine," Wyatt snapped. He stormed into the kitchen to feed the stupid cat.

TEN minutes later, the doorbell summoned him to find Frank of Frank and Joann standing on the front steps.

Scowling.

"What?" Wyatt bit his tongue. "Sorry. Hi." He faked a smile. "What can I do for you?"

"Belinda said she'd be stopping by with some groceries later."

"Uh-huh." Wyatt bit the inside of his mouth. Be nice, be nice.

"I know she's almost an adult but I wanted to have a chat with you before she starts coming around," the man said gruffly. He put his hands on his hips in full lecture mode. "Two men in a house, both of them strangers—I want to know what your intentions are."

Wyatt blinked. "Wait—do you think Benji and I are going to... hit on her?"

"I don't know you," Frank said, deadly serious.

"Uh, okay. Quick rundown. Two gay guys, one mean cat, no drugs, a little liquor, and that's about it."

Frank's frown lessened slightly. "You're gay?"

"You didn't figure that out?"

The man looked surprised. "It's not like you're wearing a sign!"

Wyatt put his hand up. "Sorry. Okay, let's start again. What do you need to know so your daughter can bring us groceries?"

Which is how Frank ended up at the kitchen island, drinking coffee with Wyatt.

"I'm just sayin'—he hasn't made a good movie since *Casino*."

Wyatt was already shaking his head. "Come on—*Silver Linings Playbook* was excellent."

"De Niro should stick to what he's good at. Mobsters." Frank took a sip from his cup.

"He's a genius!"

"At playing mob guys! Why mess with success?"

"This entire conversation explains your pants from the 1980s," Wyatt said tartly, suddenly realizing he was being bitchy again as soon as the words flew out of his mouth.

Frank's face scrunched up, then he shrugged. "See, now you sound a little gay."

Wyatt's mouth opened, then closed.

"But you're not wrong about the pants."

"HE'S a nice man," Benji said after Wyatt returned to the kitchen from seeing Frank out.

"You say that about everyone."

Wyatt heard the "Not saying it about you" muttered under Benji's breath as he leaned back over his raisin bran.

THEY reached Raven's room by ten. Wyatt had literally taken four steps inside when his phone rang. The nurse at Raven's bedside gave him a dirty look.

"Sorry, be right back."

The screaming fight with Brick that ensued was epic, full of harsh language, three threats of bodily harm, and a "Don't make me call Sable" threat that finally stopped the madness. After, Wyatt emerged from his spot in the bushes behind the meditation bench.

He missed New York so much.

Wyatt texted Betsy, updating her on the Brick smackdown, trying to ignore the fact that he was slightly aroused by the entire incident.

It must be the fresh country air.

Back in Raven's room, he found Benji and his best friend chattering away like... best friends. He paused in the doorway to watch their bright matching smiles and clasped hands. His eyes narrowed.

"Wyatt!" Raven spotted him first and he very clearly saw the red spots on Benji's cheeks as Raven squeezed his fingers in hers. "Everyone okay?"

"Yes, I got to be mean to a stupid person. It was awesome." Wyatt sauntered into the room and kissed Raven's cheek. He tried to ignore the brush of his body against Benji's.

"And they pay you for that; how nice."

Benji got up to relinquish his spot to Wyatt. "I'm going to head back to the house—I have some work of my own to do." He winked at Raven. "See you later?"

Raven smirked back. "Absolutely."

"I'll pick you up at seven," Benji said to Wyatt, still not meeting his eyes.

"Sounds fabulous."

Wyatt watched him leave then turned back to Raven's full-on delighted face.

"I love him, he's amazing," she declared.

"No."

"Seriously, so awesome."

"Raven Louise, shut up, right now. It's not happening."

She pulled a wicked pout, shaking her head so her hair fell in her face. "That's sad."

"Cute when you were seven, really pretty embarrassing right now." Wyatt patted her head. "We have work to do, ma'am."

WHEN he was sixteen and everything fell apart, Raven wrapped him in her optimistic embrace and told him it would be fine. They were yin and yang—Wyatt the pessimist and Raven believing in happy endings. The only thing they had in common was how difficult it was to trust people.

The sparkle in her eyes over Benji made him nervous.

"ROBERT, I'm going to kick your ass when you show up," Wyatt said, as soon as Raven handed him the phone.

"A tractor trailer took care of that," his friend responded dryly. He sounded like shit but Raven insisted he was "much better."

"We're going to sue them until they cry and give you a lot of money."

"I will get right on that, as soon as I'm not peeing into a jug."

"Safewording on your urination issues."

Rob laughed and Wyatt gave Raven a wink.

THE next day an ambulance would bring Rob to Raven's hospital. He would be on a different floor but through the miracle of wheelchairs, they'd be able to see each other.

Raven burst into tears.

"Hormones," she said, weeping into Wyatt's shoulder.

"Of course, honey, of course."

AT SEVEN, Benji showed up at Raven's door with two bags.

"Presents," he said, smiling shyly. Books—best sellers, romance novels—and so many magazines—one of everything as far as Wyatt could tell—and a bowl of fruit salad that made Raven moan with delight.

"Peaches?"

"And blueberries, as requested."

Wyatt watched them, filled with quiet pleasure after the long day. His ass hurt, he missed the sun, and one more sip of cafeteria coffee was going to end in tears and bloodshed. But Raven looked smiley and content as she cooed over pictures in a baby magazine, and that was all that mattered.

"BELINDA brought groceries, Mims is fed, and I left some pizza in the oven," Benji recited as they made the now familiar trek from hospital to house. "And I have to drive back to New York tonight."

Wyatt was shaken out of his half daze. "Oh."

Benji's fingers were tight on the steering wheel. "It's a meeting I've been trying to get for a while and it just sort of came up, so—I'm sorry. I can't stay the extra day."

"It's fine. You've done plenty." Wyatt tried to ignore the pang of disappointment; he chalked it up to the fact that he was now sans a ride or companion.

"I talked to Joann. She's going to be your ride." Benji smiled thinly. "I hope that's okay."

"Literally? I need you to stop apologizing for being a decent human being. It's exhausting." Wyatt threaded his hand through his messy hair. "It'll be fine. Seriously."

Benji drove them back to the house, quietly.

AFTER Benji left, it was Wyatt and Mimsy, lying on the couch.

The ceiling fan wick-wick-wicked over his head, the CD player sang some Ella Fitzgerald. Mimsy licked her paws, then the fabric of the couch, before falling asleep against Wyatt's ankle.

Wyatt decided to enjoy the peace and quiet of being alone.

It lasted half an hour.

He missed his apartment. He missed being alone there. He missed New York, loud and impersonal and rude outside his window. He missed yelling at Brick in person.

He missed his ordered life.

When they were at FIT, Wyatt and Raven had dreamed of their coming days with fabulous fashion careers and money to spend on shiny pretty things. They would work together—of course—and share an apartment on the Upper East Side, with spectacular views and big closets. They would woo and be wooed, go dancing every weekend.

Grand plans.

Then Raven said, "I'm going to visit Lucy's boyfriend's college with her—it's Pennsylvania! We've never been!" and Wyatt had said, "Dear God, no."

So he stayed at the dorm and watched movies, and Raven went to a kegger and fell in love.

He forgave her, eventually. Forgave her for leaving New York after graduation, for trading in her promising fashion career to design displays for a chain of bookstores. Forgave her for marrying Rob.

Because Rob was a good person and he made Raven happy.

He forgave her everything, even leaving him alone in the big city, with a degree and all his plans now at half power.

Wyatt had a good life in New York. This trip down memory lane—the angry panic he felt being reminded of his younger years—had just unsettled him. That was the reason he was staring at the ceiling, already over the quiet privacy.

At two in the morning he opened his phone and typed a quick message.

Get home safe.

CHAPTER 7

HOME. Technically last night. So—good morning.

Good morning—and good to hear it.

Traffic jam in Jersey. Stuck for almost two hours. Wrote two songs about bumpers.

Everything wrong in the world in one text. What time is your meeting?

Eleven.

Good luck.

Thanks Wyatt.

Rob's at the hospital with Raven. He says thank you.

Tell Rob I didn't really do anything.

Just say you're welcome and move on.

You're welcome.

See? Wasn't that easy?

No.

How'd the meeting go?

Really well.

Congrats.

How's your day?

Breakfast with Frank. He ordered Silver Linings Playbook *on Netflix. Not sure how that happened. Driving with Joann to the hospital. She likes old-school country so I got to hear Loretta Lynn this morning. Raven's been convinced that color in her bathroom is an insult to people with eyes. And Rob taught me to play Uno, which I then mastered after playing it for four hours straight.*

Wow.

JUST A DRIVE | 77

Also, Belinda is dating Eli, and I know this because when I came home they were making out in a parked car in the driveway.

At least now I'm caught up with the gossip from Small Town America.

Dinner at my parents tonight. Dad sends his regards.

I feel like you've texted the wrong person.

Had to tell them why I bugged out so fast. You were the scapegoat. So thanks for that.

You're welcome.

I feel like that was sarcasm.

I need a font that conveys the surety of that thought. So wait— didn't your mom send her regards?

She's not speaking to me.

Because of the car thing?

No, because I'm ungrateful and hard to handle.

Has your mom met you? You're the nicest person ever.

Thanks.

I'm serious.

Thanks.

Seriously here.

Thanks.

Now I need a font to express my annoyance. Don't let her get to you.

Too late. Night.

It's ten o'clock!

Sorry about last night. I was just stressed out.

You don't have to apologize for having feelings.

That's what you think.

I saw the babies on the sonogram. It was creepy awesome.

They should use that in their marketing campaign.

Listen, I have the weekend off. Did you need anything from the city?

You're coming out here again?

If you want.

Sorry I took so long to get back to you. Yeah. You should come out. If you want.

Just say thank you, Wyatt.

Thank you.

CHAPTER 8

"DOES New York miss me?" Wyatt sighed dramatically, standing in the doorway as Benji came up the walkway.

"Yes. It asked me to send its regards." Benji's smile was divine but the name stamped on the bag in his right hand—that sent Wyatt's heart soaring.

"You didn't."

"I did. It needs to be warmed up, though. I also got some wine."

"I'm willing to pay with oral sex," Wyatt said happily as he relieved Benji of his packages. Groceries from Trader Joe's. Chinese from the Crystal Palace. A bag of fresh clothing from Wyatt's apartment.

"Is that my reward or yours?"

Wyatt hustled him into the house. When they exchanged a quick kiss in the doorway, they both blushed.

WHILE Benji washed off the road, Wyatt warmed up the food. Two heaping plates of the very best the Crystal Palace had to offer. Old school lo mein, egg rolls, and pork fried rice, in all its greasy glory.

The smell made him miss home just a little bit less.

The bottle of red uncorked, Wyatt brought everything into the living room and set it on the low coffee table. A giddy rush had him lighting candles, sending a swirl of cinnamon and sugar and spices wafting through the room.

He shut the lights, lost the shoes, and settled down on the floor, back against the sofa.

Benji walked in about ten minutes later, damp and delicious in sweat pants and a tight black T-shirt.

Dinner got slightly less appealing.

But then Benji moaned in appreciation when he spied the food. "I'm starving."

"Did you stop for anything on the way?" Wyatt patted the pillow next to him on the floor.

"I wanted to get here."

Benji folded down next to Wyatt, cross-legged. He accepted a glass of wine from Wyatt, avoiding his gaze.

"Thanks," Wyatt murmured. He bumped their shoulders gently.

"I was in the city. It wasn't a big deal to…."

"No. For coming back." Wyatt sank down a little more, so they were leaning into each other, touching from shoulder to hip. "I appreciate it."

With a shrug, Benji sipped his wine; after a moment, he finally turned to face Wyatt. He looked pleased.

He looked gorgeous.

"We better eat," he said, a smile quirking at the corners of his mouth.

"What's your hurry?" Wyatt purred out the words, punctuating it with a flick of his tongue against his lower lip.

"I was promised oral sex."

THEY actually ate two plates each and finished the wine as the candles burned down. The quiet darkness, the way they curved into each other—it was the most relaxing evening Wyatt could remember having. He didn't look at the clock with a sense of growing dread and panic. Benji was warm and pliant against his side, the conversation casual with periods of silence that weren't the least bit awkward. When Benji's head tipped onto his shoulder and his breathing went shallow, Wyatt felt awash with contentment.

Mimsy wandered by, giving them a haughty glance. It seemed remarkably close to "I told you so."

"Stupid cat," Wyatt muttered.

He let Benji sleep, fighting his own heavy eyelids as the clock ticked quietly. A few of the candles were almost out and it seemed as good a time as any to head to bed.

"Benji? Come on, pretty boy—bedtime," he whispered, stroking his fingers through the waves on Benji's head to wake him up. "You'll be more comfortable there."

"Mmmm." That seemed to be a sound of agreement; Benji opened his eyes fully a second later, followed immediately by a yawn. "Bed sounds good."

"You go ahead. I'm going to blow the candles out."

"I love that song," Benji muttered as he rolled over and onto his feet. The unsteady colt thing lasted for a second and then he got his balance. Suddenly looking more awake, he gave Wyatt a sultry stare.

"Hurry up."

WYATT shut down the house with quick efficiency, fueled by the need to get into that bedroom, distracted from fire hazards and safety concerns and double-checking the front door by the thought of Benji naked. Maybe sprawled across the sheets. He moved just a little bit faster—and he wasn't disappointed when he stepped into the bedroom and found Benji in just briefs, lying across the foot of the bed.

Wyatt's jeans and shirt hit the wall with an impatient thump, thump. Benji watched him from the bed, lazily stroking himself through the damp material.

"You're gonna make me do all the work, aren't you?" Wyatt said as he stripped off his boxers.

"Maybe I'll get really lazy and have you tie me to the bed." Benji rolled onto his back, legs open, like a prize laid out.

Wyatt couldn't hide his smile as he pounced.

BENJI undulated beneath him; Wyatt blanketed him with his body, concentrating on the tight clasp around his fingers.

"You are so fucking sexy," Wyatt whispered. He pulled his fingers free in a teasing slide, until they both moaned at the sensation.

They kissed, tongues twining and searching, as Benji rocked his hips upward. Wyatt loved the way he was hungry for it; he sucked on Benji's bottom lip until the moment threatened to spill into rutting.

He didn't rut. He wanted to fuck.

When he broke away to get the condom, Benji was already struggling onto his stomach, hissing as he lay flat on the mattress.

The condom he put on first because he was running out of patience. Lube was next, his fingers tingling under the gel, his free hand stroking across Benji's shoulders.

Two fingers, in and out—the press inward, the clamp of Benji's ass—the sensation and stroking and the nonwords spilling out of Benji's mouth. Wyatt's body temperature soared to something incendiary, his tongue chasing a fevered burn over his lips.

Benji pushed back, meeting every stroke with needy shoves for more. Wyatt braced himself with a hand to the small of Benji's back, twisting his fingers to catch every nerve ending.

It was only a few minutes before Benji's body said "ready" and Wyatt's body said "right fucking now."

Wyatt sucked in a steadying breath; he took his cock in hand, slicking it wetly with more lube before brushing a kiss to Benji's back as he lined himself up.

Unable to deny himself another second, Wyatt sank into the exquisite tight heat of Benji's body.

Benji moaned as Wyatt bottomed out; there was no resistance but now, balls deep, Wyatt could feel the fierce shaking of his body.

The "yes, don't stop, please" was nearly lost in the sheets as Wyatt began to move. He pulled out halfway before shoving back in, eyes rolling back in his head as pure pleasure rocked through his blood. Another stroke—farther out, deeper in. Another and another until the punishing rhythm took over.

He watched the circle of Benji's body sucking in his cock and couldn't look away from the perfect give and take. It was hypnotic and it was pushing him over the edge far too quickly. Beneath him, Benji begged, his entire body dragging over the covers with each thrust. Wyatt could see each white-knuckled fist full of wrinkled sheet and focused on that as he picked up the pace.

"Don't touch yourself," he panted, hands braced on either side of Benji's. "That's for me."

Benji twisted and groaned, fighting each stroke with one of his own, a race to see who cracked first. Wyatt fucked him harder, pushed Benji flat on the bed so he could get more friction that way, so he could take it all, completely. It was overwhelming—the reality, the smell of sex and sweat filling the air, the angry wanting cries from Benji, the iron clasp of his body. Wyatt couldn't remember the last time he felt so completely out of control in the middle of sex. The strokes sped up until he was holding nothing back, to the point of pain.

His vision went a little gray as the orgasm rocked him with a sudden viciousness. He pushed down, hard, and pulled out, still pulsing in the condom. "Turn over," he said roughly.

Wyatt bent down, flicking his tongue over the swollen head of Benji's cock, teasing for a long cruel moment, and when he was sure Benji's eyes begged hard enough, he swallowed him down in one smooth stroke.

"Oh fuck," Benji cried, eyes fluttering shut and head flopping heavily back to the bed as Wyatt took him in.

Wyatt swallowed until Benji's cock hit the back of his throat, his fingers slipping back into Benji's body without announcement or prep, fucking him again.

Pulling off Benji's cock with the most obscene slurp ever heard outside of a porn movie, Wyatt kept his eyes riveted to Benji's face. His fingers continued their thrust and pace, unrelenting.

"Come on, come on," he murmured, twisting a third finger inside Benji's body.

Never losing the connection of fingers to ass, Wyatt shifted to his knees and shoved Benji's legs even farther apart with his free hand.

Wyatt never stopped, sucking and moving his fingers until Benji gasped and rocked and came. He swallowed Benji deep to catch the last few pulses of his orgasm.

CHAPTER 9

THE light from the half-opened curtain woke Wyatt. There was a luxurious moment of bliss; the air conditioning hummed, the blankets piled around them, Benji tucked under his arm—perfect.

Then the aching in his throat set in and remembrance of last night made him shiver. He curled around Benji's snoring form to grab a bit of his body heat and prolong the moment.

Because the freak-out was coming. He could feel it. All his walls were flattened out, until there was nothing but the frightening possibility of wanting to do this again. And again.

"What time is it?" A sleepy voice reached his ears as Benji turned in his arms, resting his forehead against Wyatt's shoulder.

"Eight thirty."

"We have stuff to do before we hit the road." Benji stretched and moved, sitting up as he missed Wyatt's body stiff and unmoving. "You want to shower first?"

"Go ahead," Wyatt murmured, stroking his hand down Benji's back.

Benji twisted and gave him a gorgeous smile. "You could always join me."

Wyatt shook his head. "Then we'll be late."

"True." Benji unraveled himself from the covers and stood up, stretching toward the ceiling.

"Stop tempting me."

Benji's smile made Wyatt's chest hurt. "You see through all my tricks, clearly."

Then he disappeared into the bathroom.

WYATT stripped the bed to give himself something to do. Everything smelled like sex, so he shut off the air conditioning and opened the windows.

Leaning against the wall, he looked out through the curtains. Down the street he heard a lawn mower start up. Kids were already screaming and shrieking in someone's backyard. It should have made him crazy frustrated, reminding him he wasn't home – currently stuck in a place he wanted to avoid. Except – it was kind of soothing. Signs the day was starting and everything, for at least the moment, was calm and peaceful. Hopeful.

Maybe this place wasn't the third circle of hell.

"Giving the neighbors a free show?"

Wyatt turned slowly to find Benji dressed in black basketball shorts and a sleeveless green shirt. He was just—glowing. A bright, good-hearted kid with a great future and everything going for him. And he was looking at Wyatt like he hung the moon.

Terrifying.

"Well, I won't be here forever. I want to give them something to remember."

Benji laughed, head tilted back and everything.

"All right, you Greek god, you—I'm going to make coffee."

IN THE shower, Wyatt tried to prepare his speech.

Listen, you are a great guy but I don't do relationships.

You deserve better.

We've had fun but these are extenuating circumstances....

I can't fall in love—it's too scary.

THE first thing Wyatt saw when he came out was Benji in the kitchen, cuddling Mimsy in one arm as he poured coffee into two cups.

Wyatt had the urge to run screaming from the house.

"Hey, before we head out, we should talk," Wyatt said, his voice unsteady.

Benji looked up in surprise. "Oh, sure. About what?" Mimsy struggled to get down, as if she knew what was about to happen.

"I just wanted to let you know, the past ten days have been great. You've been so terrific and helpful. And last night was—the best. I have had a really great time with you." Wyatt walked to the dining room, bracing himself on the back of a chair. "You are an amazing guy."

With each word, Benji's face fell.

Wyatt plowed on, fixing his eyes on the box of cereal on top of the refrigerator. "But I am not looking for a relationship. And we work together, which would make it even weirder, so—I'm hoping we can stay friends."

A horrific silence descended on the house.

Benji swallowed, then nodded slowly as if registering everything. Wyatt held very still, fingers digging into the fabric of the chair. He watched Benji take his coffee cup, watched him through the entryway and out the door.

Wyatt breathed out, then in, then hitched his back straight. There, it was done.

EVENTUALLY, Benji came back into the house. Wyatt was on the couch with his laptop working but he didn't look up. Not until the bags next to him suddenly moved.

"Listen, I meant what I said." Wyatt dared to look up. "I want us to be friends."

Benji nodded as he swung his bag over one shoulder. "Absolutely. We should probably get moving. We have that stuff to pick up for Raven."

Raven. Raven was going to kill him twice for this bullshit move.

His phone started ringing—"Walking on Sunshine," which was Raven's latest choice.

"Let me just get this—she's probably got a craving for movie theatre popcorn again."

Wyatt put his laptop aside to grab his phone; a second after he said, "Yeah Rae?" he heard Rob's voice.

"Get here now! Raven's in labor!"

"OUR entire… friendship… seems to revolve around food, sex, and frantic phone calls from Raven," Benji said, somewhere between the front door and the hospital. Wyatt tried to register the words while listening to Rob frantically giving him updates on the other end of the line.

Raven's labor couldn't be stopped.

The twins were mature enough to be born.

The doctors were prepping her.

And Wyatt was going to be in the operating room with her.

"I'm going to be in the operating room with her," Wyatt said as they parked in the lot. "With them. What the hell?"

Benji reached across the console to take his hand. "The doctors are there to take care of Raven and the babies. You're there to keep Raven calm and distracted. I know you can do that because you've been doing it for weeks."

Wyatt looked at their fingers intertwined, felt the warmth of Benji's words. "Maybe you should be in there to keep me calm and distracted."

Benji blushed. When he started to pull his hand away, Wyatt had to force himself to let him go.

TWO nurses commandeered him when he arrived outside Raven's room. There were scrubs to put on and a supervised washing of his hands that felt slightly *Silkwood*. He hadn't seen Raven or Rob yet, and Benji wasn't allowed back into this area with him.

Totally surreal.

"Here you go, right through here." Wyatt followed one of the women through a series of doors until he found himself in an operating room, filled with people taking care of business. In the center of the drama? Raven strapped to an operating table, her stomach exposed as a nurse swabbed her skin. To one side was Rob and his wheelchair, trying unsuccessfully to stay out of the way.

"All right, Beelers, I'm here, we can start." Wyatt darted over to place a kiss through his mask onto Raven's head. Rob's eyes—the only thing he could see—looked infinitely grateful.

"Benji's such a great guy. You're not going to meet someone like him twice. Don't be stupid, Wyatt," Raven murmured, still weak and finding her way out of the knockout drugs. She lay on the bed, one hand on Rob, the other on Wyatt's. The babies were snoozing in the bassinet nearby.

"That's random." Wyatt felt like he'd been run over twice, all the adrenalin burned off leaving him weak.

"I'm having a moment of clarity."

"Pretty sure it's the drugs." He kissed her cheek. "Don't worry about me."

Raven's eyes filled with tears. "I don't want you to be alone forever."

"How can I be? I have a nest of Beelers to keep me in my old age."

"Wyatt...."

"I'm not the marrying kind," he retorted, lighthearted in a way he didn't feel.

"Date him. Be his boyfriend for a little while. You'll regret it if you don't."

Wyatt looked over at Rob for support and found his faux brother-in-law had nodded off, chin on his chest. No help there.

"Rae—I love you. Deeply. This has been one of the most meaningful experiences of my shallow, glittery life. But there's just so much I can manage in one day."

She sniffed her annoyance. "Fine.

"We've agreed to be friends and that's—you should be so proud of me for doing that, okay? He's a great guy, a terrific amazing human being, and I'm working on being friends with him." The tightening of his throat—that was because of the strain of the day. That's all. "Now go to sleep. I'm going to go scope out some coffee."

Wyatt got up, kissed her on the forehead, and then headed out the door.

The hallway was empty, probably because it was after ten. Benji had probably gone back to the house; Wyatt sighed as he checked his muted phone, but there was nothing.

"Mr. Walsh?" Viv's voice filtered down the hall. "Congratulations are in order, I hear."

"Yeah, thanks." Wyatt slipped his hands in his pockets. "Quick question—did you see my friend around here? I sort of left him to his own devices while I birthed some babies," he joked.

Viv shook her head at him, amusement glinting in her eyes. "I didn't see him, but maybe Linda did. Hang on."

Wyatt waited in the hall, checking his phone again. He debated sending a text but he didn't want to wake Benji up....

"He left a note for you at the nurse's station." Viv returned and Wyatt looked up to see her carrying two furry brown teddy bears, a large envelope, and a smaller folded note. "And some presents for the babies. How sweet."

The cloying hint in her voice didn't irritate him anymore; he knew she thought he and Benji made a cute couple. His insides squirmed the tiniest bit.

"Thank you." She handed him the note and kept the rest.

"Let me put this in the Beelers' room. I need to check on her anyway."

"Terrific." Wyatt gave her another smile then leaned against the wall to read the note.

He expected "See you later at the house" or something along those lines so at first, the stark black printing didn't register. He was trying to read something that wasn't there and when it registered, Wyatt felt himself choking with grief. Because he knew what it meant.

It just said:

I lied. I can't be your friend. I'm sorry. You deserve someone who doesn't expect more than you can give. Take care of yourself, please.
—BT

CHAPTER 10

"DO YOU really have to go back?" Raven had Whitney at her breast, while Warren squirmed impatiently, waiting his turn, in Rob's arms. They were home—finally—settled into the little ranch house with a ramp, a day nurse, a night nurse, Belinda, Eli, and a spreadsheet of neighborhood folk on various duties. Including Joann and Frank.

Wyatt had even arranged for lawn care. He was a genius.

An idiot genius, as Raven had been informing him for the past three weeks.

"Yes." Wyatt stroked Whitney's fuzzy head, not even weirded out by the fact that Raven's breast was about an inch away. At this point, he was more intimately acquainted with both Raven and Rob than he had ever intended. Boobs were nothing—he'd seen her uterus, her *insides* for God's sake. "Work has been insanely open-minded about my absence, but I can't assume they'll keep my job open forever."

"I'm sure Benji could put in a good word," Rob said dryly from the wheelchair parked next to the couch.

"Don't make me give you a verbal smackdown in front of my godchildren."

"He's right."

"Thank you, Raven."

"I meant Rob was right. Actually, he was right to bring up Benji, because I'm running out of time to remind you you're a moron."

Wyatt sighed.

"Help, Whitney, help. Mommy and Daddy are being mean!" he whispered, dropping a kiss on his goddaughter's ear. "The car will be here shortly. Do you really want to spend our last moments chastising me for being incredibly wrong?"

Raven's face lit up like Christmas. "So you admit you're wrong?"

"Absolutely." He could feel the absence of Benji like the ache of a phantom limb. The past few weeks, even packed with helping Rob and Raven and the kids, had done nothing to lessen the missing.

He'd never missed anyone before.

"So what are you going to do about it?" Rob looked up from Warren's scrunched-up little face, expectant and serious.

"I'm going to go back and try—really hard—to prove to Benji I can be a good friend. How I'm accomplishing this—no clue. I'm hoping the endless miles of Pennsylvania countryside will give me an idea before I get to New York."

There. He said it. He was going to go back to the city and talk to Benji.

Raven rolled her eyes and seemed ready to speak again but Rob elbowed her in the side gently. They shared a look, a secret conversation that Wyatt couldn't interpret, so he focused on the babies. Warren looked increasingly angry and, well—Whitney was in baby heaven, held by someone who loved her without reservation, well-fed and adored.

He envied Whitney.

THEY saw him to the door, the entire family. Rob held the babies in his arms while Raven and Wyatt hugged and cried and made solemn promises to keep in touch better.

"You know the way now. You should come here more often." Raven sniffled, clutching Wyatt's arm tightly. "I love you. We're your family—don't forget that."

Wyatt's throat hurt from shed and unshed tears. "I love you too. Even your lunkheaded husband."

"If you saw me in a bar, you'd totally hit on me and you know it."

"Booty, not brains, Robert. Booty, not brains."

Wyatt gave him a kiss and a hug too. And maybe he cuddled the babies a little too long for someone who didn't like children—but they were family. They didn't count like regular people would.

By the time he loaded himself and his bags into the back of the sleek town car, Wyatt's heart hurt. He had a mad moment of considering going all *Green Acres* and taking his feather boas to the country, but this wasn't where he belonged.

And he had amends to make.

HOURS through flat green countryside, hours through highway and suburbs, over the bridge and downtown—hours of thinking and considering, and Wyatt arrived in New York City that night with no earthly clue what to say to Benji.

Sorry I'm a dick.

Sorry I'm self-absorbed.

Sorry I forget that other people have feelings.

Sorry I took from you without giving in return.

Sorry I don't know how to be a normal person when it comes to other people.

Fact was, Benji knew all that—it had been fairly obvious from day one. And he had still stuck around. Still did what needed to be done without taking anything for himself. What do you say to someone who's selfless and insecure?

I'm sorry, the note had said. It was a crumpled bit of paper in his pocket, worked over by anxious fingers for fourteen days.

Maybe his opening was—*I'm sorry too.*

THE driver got an extra hundred from his pocket, in addition to the tip on the company credit card. He tried to ignore the fact that this was also a courtesy extended by Benji and Soundsource.

On the third floor, Wyatt pushed open the door—and was hit by the fresh scents of lemon and lavender.

He snapped on the light.

And marveled.

The apartment was spotless. He'd left over a month ago, a whirlwind of anxiety kicking up the normal mess usually draped over his couches and tables. Now? It looked like a damn showcase. From the gleaming surfaces to the bouquet of lavender on the kitchen table, it was perfect.

His throat closed up.

In the bedroom, he found more neatness, and the scents told him it was Benji's cleaning lady who'd massaged this place into a sanctuary.

Wyatt dumped everything onto the desk, then wandered back into the kitchen. The full refrigerator was the final kick in the stomach.

He sat down at the table and cried.

WYATT woke up to his phone trilling faintly from his bedroom. It was pitch black, so by the time he stumbled in and retrieved it from his laptop bag, it was just a message.

Five in the morning and the message said, *Stop wasting time. Life's too short. Rob (and Whitney)*

Feeding time in Smalltown USA. And a reminder that Wyatt couldn't escape—especially when he threw himself into the sweetly scented sheets and wrapped himself in the comforter.

When he finally fell back to sleep, Wyatt dreamed of boys with beautiful brown eyes and hearts too big for their chests.

AT NINE in the morning, Wyatt was freshly showered, shaved, and dressed in his best red linen summer suit. His hair swooped perfectly—at least until the humidity showed up in full force, somewhere between his apartment and the office.

Everyone rained down hugs and kisses and happiness that he was back—except Brick, who saw his promotion disappear, and the receptionist, who was clearly having a bad morning. Betsy dragged him behind closed doors and spent the next two hours bringing him up to speed.

Most of it was gossip.

"Soooo—friends in high places," she said finally, sitting back in her chair. Her smirk was epic.

Wyatt shrugged. "A… friend. Who helped me out when he didn't have to."

"Uh-huh." Betsy tapped a pen on the desktop. "Sable is buying him out."

"What?" Wyatt sat up straight in the curved plastic of Betsy's visitor's chair. "Why?"

"To get leverage. He owns Paul's contract. If she buys Benji's share...."

"She controls Paul's career." Some relief trickled down his spine. Benji wasn't being hustled out. "Did you hear what... what Benji is going to do?"

"Take the money and run?" Betsy shrugged. "Sable said he's going to go out on his own, maybe record an album."

Something swelled in Wyatt's chest. "He's really talented."

Betsy threw her head back and laughed. "I'm sure he is."

BY SEVEN he'd come somewhat close to being caught up, mostly through delegation, deletion, and enough caffeine to blow up a hamster's heart.

"Go home," Betsy said at seven. "Or...."

Wyatt looked up from his screen. "Or?"

"Sable is having a cocktail thing at seven thirty. At her office." Her voice was sly and calculating; she was clearly manipulating him. Which was why she was his favorite.

"Uh-huh. And why should I show up there?" His heart beat a little faster.

"It's small and intimate. Good to show your face around again." She batted her fake eyelashes at him.

"To someone in particular?"

Betsy rolled her eyes. "Jackass. Ten minutes and I'm leaving without you."

SABLE'S office was a glass monstrosity in the penthouse of their building, an epic retelling of a love story between white leather and track lighting. If Wyatt believed in heaven, this was what he hoped it looked like. But with feathers.

"Wyatt!" Sable cried as soon as he and Betsy entered the party. People stopped schmoozing to give him a glance but Sable's enveloping hug blocked out the view. She smelled like vanilla ice cream and hugged like a force of nature.

"Hi, Sable."

"You are a sight for sore eyes." She stepped back to look him over critically. "You a hick now?"

"It was a month in the country. I've retained all of my New York sass."

"Praise." Sable pinched his cheek, then gave him a slap. "Your boyfriend was all direct and serious with me about you getting paid leave. It was sexy."

Wyatt felt his face go hot. "He's not my boyfriend."

Sable made a sound and turned away, her hand tight in his. "Shut up. He tried to tell me the same thing and I knew it was a lie. Let's have a drink."

Two waiters circulated with trays of champagne. Sable drank two glasses on the way to the bartender set up in the corner.

"Whiskey, neat. Two." Sable looked around the milling crowd as Wyatt stared at his shoes.

"He's over at the piano. Hiding." His boss sounded annoyed.

"He doesn't like crowds."

"He's hiding from you because I made him come." Sable let go of his hand to give him his drink. "You know about the deal?"

"Yeah." Wyatt threw down the drink fast enough to give his liver whiplash.

"He's going to get richer and have lots of time. You make sure he gets his ass into a studio."

"I'm not his—"

Sable thumped him on the arm. For a sixty-year-old, she had a serious right hook. "Then go be his friend and make sure he gets into the studio to record an album. Now."

Wyatt swallowed—then took her untouched whiskey.

"Fine. But if he throws a diva tantrum at me, I'm going to cry a lot in the office and wear a bathrobe."

Sable made shooing motions.

Drink in hand, Wyatt walked over to the far corner, where a white baby grand was framed by the floor-to-ceiling windows and the Manhattan skyline twinkled in the background. Hidden from the party was Benji, gently plunking at the keys.

He looked so good Wyatt had to suck down the whiskey before he did something unseemly like pounce on him.

Before he could let the whiskey unstick his tongue, Benji looked up. In his gunmetal-gray button-up and neatly styled hair, he was a grown-up. A serious, sad grown-up.

"Hi."

Wyatt sat down on the bench next to him, just resisting the urge the kiss him. "Hi."

"How's the family?" Benji stared at the keys, poking at them like they would give him an answer.

"They're good. Raven made me take a thousand pictures of those pesky babies," he said with fake exasperation. "So if you want to see them…."

A little smile played on Benji's face.

"She made you?"

"Twisted my arm and everything." Wyatt gave him a little shoulder bump. "Ow."

There was a long silence but it wasn't terrible. Wyatt didn't move, Benji didn't move; they sat shoulder to shoulder as the chatter rose and fell around them.

Wyatt felt words rattling around in his head. He didn't know which ones to pull out, which ones would speak to Benji the right way.

"I missed you," he said finally, holding his breath as the words slipped out of his mouth.

Benji tensed.

"You missed me… as a friend," he said, pressing the keys randomly until it started sounding like a tune.

Wyatt made a noncommittal noise in his throat. "I didn't really put a label on it. It was just general missing."

"You put a label on it, Wyatt—you want to be friends. I told you I couldn't." The tune took shape—and Wyatt realized it was that poppy summer single, slowed down to a melodic dirge. "I still feel that way."

Wyatt felt the warmth of Benji's body next to him, breathed in the familiar scent of him. "What if I insist…?"

"I don't want to be your friend." Benji's breath caught. He slowed the song down even more, until there were seconds of pause between each note.

Everything stopped—the sounds of the party faded, the notes under Benji's fingers muted, and Wyatt's heartbeat thundering in his ears was the only thing he could hear. He should get up; he had his out, he could blame everything on Benji. Because he tried. He really did this time.

But.

Wyatt couldn't seem to get up.

"I think you're the most dangerous person I've ever met," he whispered, laying his head against Benji's shoulder. He felt the tension, the sharp intake of breath.

"I'm harmless."

"Oh no, no. Sweet Benji—you are the scariest thing that's ever crossed my path. You make me want to break all my rules, and my rules—they're usually so important to me." He was helpless then— sliding his hand over Benji's on the piano keys.

"What rules did you break for me?" Benji's gaze was directed to where their fingers entwined, and Wyatt's heart filled his entire chest.

"A second night. A third one. Being there in the morning." He whispered each thing, coming closer and closer to put his lips right up close to Benji's ear. "Wanting more nights. And the waking up. Everything in between." Wyatt swallowed. "I think you make me want a boyfriend."

It was dizzying, letting it out into the open. Benji's breath was audible, his fingers tightened on Wyatt's and when he turned, it seemed only logical that they kiss.

Nothing frantic about it, just a twist of lips and a graze of tongue— but it was absolutely the best kiss of Wyatt's life.

When they separated, Wyatt smiled so wide it actually hurt.

"You want a boyfriend?"

"Possibly. But only if it's you."

This time the kiss was searing—Benji didn't hold anything back, tilting his head so he could slant their lips together, deepen the connection. Wyatt's free hand went to back of his neck to keep him in place and it was just....

At some point applause broke out but Wyatt didn't care.

"THANK you for taking care of me," Wyatt murmured into the back of Benji's neck, about four hours later. They were in his bed, flush and tired from emotion and sex and way too much champagne.

"Thank you for letting me." His boyfriend—boyfriend!—turned just enough to buzz a kiss on Wyatt's jaw.

"I'm going to start taking care of you. I've gotten better at cooking."

"Oh really?"

"I made microwave popcorn for Raven one night…."

The rumble of Benji's laugh was delightful.

"I'll handle the cooking, okay?"

"Fine. I'll handle the shopping."

"For food?"

"No. For clothing and shoes," Wyatt huffed. "You're in charge of music." He nuzzled against Benji's hair. "And bath products. I want to smell as good as you do."

"I might have to get out of bed and make a list."

Wyatt snaked a leg over Benji's, then tightened his arms, effectively locking him into place.

"Nope."

They lay there in comfortable silence for a while, locked into their own little world.

Wyatt felt little pokes of worry in the back of his head as the silence grew. Benji felt warm and heavy in his arms, his breathing growing deep. They would fall asleep—wake up in the morning, eat breakfast, head off to work. There would be texts and maybe a phone call. Plans for dinner? Another night together.

A well of panic began to fill.

What if he couldn't do this? What if he fucked up? What if he fucked another guy because he was stupid and shallow and scared?

"Ow," Benji mumbled, and Wyatt started out of his little spiral.

"What?"

"You're squeezing the hell out of me," he said sleepily, squirming against the cage Wyatt had created.

Wyatt released him, reluctantly. Whatever was fluttering through his head, his body had its own ideas. Like keeping Benji close.

Benji had the same idea.

He rolled over until they were nose to nose, sharing the same pillow.

"Hi," he said, his beautiful eyes lit up. "What's wrong?"

"Nothing." Wyatt closed his eyes. His lying skills sucked lately.

"Second thoughts." The tone was light but Wyatt knew everything that was underneath it and it hurt that it wasn't a question.

"I've never done this." This was easier in the dark. "I don't know how to do this."

"What? Have a boyfriend?"

"No. Be a boyfriend."

The quiet went on a little too long and Wyatt opened his eyes. The tight line of Benji's mouth was painful.

"We don't have to... you know. Use that word. We can just... take it one day at a time," Benji said, brave and quiet. "I don't mind."

"No—you deserve better. You deserve an answer. A—commitment."

"I didn't ask...."

"No, you didn't." Exasperation drove Wyatt to sit up, struggling with the sheet. "You don't ask for anything. Jesus Christ, Benji—please. Ask for something. Anything. Let me give it to you."

He let his words sit between them for a long moment. The dampening of his palms was directly related to how many times Benji blinked up at him.

"Come back down here, put your arms around me, and stop worrying so much," Benji finally answered, his voice quiet. "When you freak out, it makes me freak out, and honestly? I haven't slept much in two weeks. I want to close my eyes and not worry—"

He cut himself off, gaze dropping.

"Not worry that I'm going to leave."

Benji nodded.

Wyatt slipped back down, back to curl his body around Benji's. They were nose to nose again, twining their legs together under the blanket.

For a moment, they just breathed the same air.

"Go to sleep, pretty boy. I'll be here to burn your breakfast in the morning. I promise." Wyatt stroked Benji's back, little soothing circles he'd been using on the babies. He didn't mention that part, humming nonsense until his boyfriend fell asleep.

And Wyatt accepted that act of trust as confirmation that he could do this.

He could. He would.

EPILOGUE

BENJI shut off the last light in the studio, checking his phone with his free hand. When the doorbell rang, he didn't even look up from his scroll of messages.

But he smiled.

He grabbed his jacket and bag, then headed for the exit, the last light snapping off behind him.

On the other side of the door stood Wyatt, bright and smiling and clutching a picnic basket.

"He lives!" Wyatt said, lifting a hand to the heavens. "Hallelujah! I'm glad you remembered you weren't veal."

Benji shut the door behind him, leaning against it as Wyatt did his nightly routine.

Mock his long hours. Make a veal joke.

Then the best part.

"Hi," Benji said, matching his smile in wattage.

"Hi." Wyatt leaned down to smack a kiss right on that grin.

They shared a too-close lingering look, flirted with going cross-eyed, then Wyatt stood up straight.

"Come along, my little steamed dumpling. We are having a robust Italian feast in the park."

"I think that's racist," Benji mused, taking Wyatt's proffered arm.

"Robust Italian feast? That's what it said on the menu, I'm just repeating the deli's description."

Benji rolled his eyes as Wyatt gave him a hip check.

Benji's new studio space was a renovated townhouse on the Upper West Side, near Central Park. He'd shopped around the Village and Bowery but Wyatt was horrified by the "*Law & Order* crime scene cast-offs" and so there he was, surrounded by shrinks and aging socialites, working on his new album.

Wyatt, by his own description, was acting as head cheerleader and sex god.

They chatted about their respective days, enjoying the fall evening air. Benji knew Wyatt was holding back on his daily recitation of whatever fuckery had occurred at Soundsource, and the "So what did you record today?" and "Oh, that song with the snappy chorus—I like that one" comments were that much more special.

Just past 70th street, they ducked down the pathway. There was a particular bench they enjoyed, nicely shaded and tucked away enough to usually be empty.

"Still no squatting on our bench—I told you we were meant to stake our claim," Wyatt said happily.

Their bench, Benji had realized a few weeks ago, was a metaphor for them living together. Right now they were all over the place real-estate wise—their respective apartments, the new studio. Benji wanted to buy the entire townhouse and move there, and more than anything, he wanted Wyatt to share the space.

They weren't ready for that.

Wyatt wasn't ready.

Benji was determined to be patient.

"We have pasta salad, we have olives, we have cheese, we have bread, and you're going to need to promise to still like me naked when I'm fat...." Wyatt unloaded everything in the space between them, a tidy plaid cloth wrangling it all together neatly. "We have wine but we have to pretend it's grape juice lest the police arrest us," he whispered conspiratorially. "Now tell me more about your new song."

They worked their way through the food slowly. Benji talked about lyrics and the schedule and little things it felt nice to verbalize. Wyatt made "mmm" and "hmmm" sounds, asked questions, and all the while, their hands were entwined.

It was the best way to end the day, of that Benji was sure.

"Okay. I'm officially tired of talking about me." Benji did the cleanup as Wyatt kicked back and tried to catch a few last rays of light through the trees. "Your turn."

"I don't know what you mean. My day was positively bo-ring." Wyatt sighed dramatically—then turned his head to flash an adorable grin in Benji's direction. "Unless you want to hear how Brick and Sasha had a free-for-all in the kitchen over a missing eel roll...."

Benji laughed as he got up to throw away their garbage.

"Brick, Sasha, and an eel roll? I think I saw this movie. It ends in porn."

"Pish. This ended in tears and it was not Sasha." Wyatt patted his lap like a dirty Santa. "Come here, handsome boy, and I will tell you a story...."

Benji lay down on the bench, his head in Wyatt's lap. It gave him the perfect view of his boyfriend's animated face and gesturing hands as he launched into his tale.

"I love... when you tell stories," Benji interrupted. Wyatt stopped in mid-hand-wave and looked down at him, pleasure and surprise in his expression.

Benji blushed under the scrutiny.

"And I love... when you listen." Wyatt's smile was gorgeous and Benji felt everything in his middle shift and readjust.

"Sorry, continue."

"Mmm...." When Wyatt leaned down to kiss him, everything felt perfectly glorious.

TERE MICHAELS unofficially began her writing career at the age of four when she learned that people got paid to write stories. It seemed the most perfect and logical job in the world and after that, her path was never in question. (The romance writer part was written in the stars—she was born on Valentine's Day.)

It took thirty-six years of "research" and "life experience" and well… life… before her first book was published but there are no regrets (she doesn't believe in them). Along the way, she had some interesting jobs in television, animation, arts education, PR and a national magazine—but she never stopped believing she would eventually earn her living writing stories about love.

She is a member of RWA, Rainbow Romance Writers, and Liberty States Fiction Writers. Her home base is a small town in New Jersey, very near NYC, a city she dearly loves. She shares her life with her husband, her teenaged son—who will just not stop growing—and three exceedingly spoiled cats. Her spare time is spent watching way too much sports programming, going to the movies and for long walks/runs in the park, reading her book club's current selection, and volunteering.

Nothing makes her happier than knowing she made a reader laugh or smile or cry. It's the purpose of sharing her work with people. She loves hearing from fans and fellow writers, and is always available for speaking engagements, visits and workshops. Find her at http://www.teremichaels.com and on Twitter (@TereMichaels), and Facebook (https://www.facebook.com/tere.michaels).

JUST A
STRANGER

ELLE BROWNLEE

Elizah and Tere, your generosity of talent and friendship is a treasure. Alison, my words are always better for knowing you. Gratitude.

CHAPTER 1

THE club Andrew had wandered into was not his usual scene, but he wasn't looking for that. He was looking to get laid. He figured in a place with pulse-pounding music that drowned out conversation and lighting that made everyone seem mysterious and attractive, he would easily find someone else wanting the same.

Generally, he wasn't a clubber. He liked sports bars and mellow restaurants. But since his "generally" of the past few years had included almost zero adult social contact of any kind, he'd decided to skip to the main event and make the most of this one night he'd been able to wrangle as his own. He didn't need game updates or five courses or even conversation. He needed available and no strings and—oh, that guy right over there.

Andrew darted from the bar and pushed through the gyrating crowd toward a dark corner where the dance floor melted into a semicircle of plushly cushioned loungers. As he approached, his intended glanced at him and looked almost guilty at getting caught. It gave Andrew the sense that this guy had been checking him out in return, and that emboldened him, while his throat went dry and his stomach lurched with the strength of instant attraction. The guy smiled hesitantly. Andrew realized he had stalked over there as if on a mission, and while that was true, it was also enough to make him laugh at the absurdity and relax a little.

"Uh, hi!" Andrew yelled, and he almost rolled his eyes. Not exactly a suave lead-in. He felt himself blush and almost turned tail, but the guy squirmed around enough to make room on the lounger and patted it. He leaned into Andrew once he'd sat down.

"Hiya yourself! I'm Michael."

"Michael. Hey, hi. Hey."

They stared at each other, and Andrew forgot to even blink. Even in the strobing, ever-changing colored lights and dimness, Michael was gorgeous and perfectly typed to get Andrew's motor revving. He had a strong jaw that led to a cleft chin. He was olive complected with liquid dark eyes and equally dark, clean-cut hair.

Someone jostled into them and Andrew managed an apologetic smile. To distract himself from simply staring more, he downed his beer. He and Michael sat in the cacophony of techno beats and writhing bodies, an island of silent stillness. Andrew began to peel the label from his beer bottle.

It was almost pitifully comical that he'd homed in on the one person seemingly feeling as awkward and out of place here as he did. He was so bad at this, and so very out of practice. Maybe he should have gone to a sports bar or not bothered at all and just gone home.

"Wanna get out of here?"

"What?" Andrew whipped around to squint at Michael and their noses brushed. Tingles erupted from his nape and spread down along his skin in a delicious cascade that made him shiver.

Michael's eyes danced promisingly in response, and his squared, blunt thumb swept into Andrew's upturned palm. That only made Andrew shiver more. Michael grinned and leaned under Andrew's ear again.

"I asked if you wanna get out of here!"

"Yes! I do, yes—with you!"

Andrew almost groaned because, good lord, at one point in time he had known how to be a real person around other real people, but he figured his answer hadn't been completely inept when Michael's grin softened to a happy smile.

Michael pried the empty bottle from Andrew's hand and set it on a waiting side tray, then hefted him to stand. Andrew was a few inches taller and slim, while Michael was broad, with firm, wide shoulders that tapered to a trim waist. His movements were economical and smooth, which suggested physical labor or a good bit of effort put in at the gym. Either way, Andrew appreciated the results. He flattened his hand on the flex of Michael's abs, just visible under a thinly stretched tee. That action made it Michael's turn to shiver.

It was enough to ease a laugh from Andrew, and he led the way toward the main entrance. He liked when Michael snagged the center belt loop of his jeans at the back to keep them connected while they threaded through patrons and laden waiters and randomly strewn tabletops. He waggled his butt for show.

Once outside Andrew let out a long, relieved sigh.

"If you hate that kind of place so much, why bother going in?"

Andrew went for cheesy and bold. "I was looking for you." He flashed the crooked, charming grin that used to get him out of all kinds of scrapes when he was a teenager, then into better opportunities once in college. It still had its uses today.

Michael groaned. "Well, you found me, and here I am, so I think that earns me at least knowing your name."

"Oh." Andrew's smile turned wry. "Sorry? I didn't realize I hadn't—I'm Andrew." He carefully didn't give his last name and held out his hand. "Nice to meet you."

They shook and Michael lingered at the touch. He studied Andrew intently as if he'd noticed Andrew's reactions had gone from embarrassed and open to shuttered away again. But Michael didn't call him out on it, and Andrew was relieved.

"So, back at you." Andrew nodded at the club. "If you hate that kind of place so much, why were you camped out on their uncomfortable loungers?"

"Buddy of mine's birthday. I think he's still in there somewhere. Don't worry, he won't miss me." Michael shrugged almost apologetically and finally let go of Andrew's hand. "Where to?"

Andrew had to ball his hand into a fist, then release it a few times to get normal feeling back after their handshake. Even then it was as though his hand burned and the warmth was spreading up his arm.

"Actually, I have no idea. I'm not from Indy."

Michael eyed him speculatively, and Andrew found his disarming grin again.

"I'm on a business trip, some conference thing, and was on the verge of doing not-very-businesslike things to my boring colleagues. I thought rather than get into criminal activities, I'd let off some steam."

"Horticulture or pharmaceuticals?" Michael asked sharply.

"Excuse me?" Andrew blanched. He didn't actually want to say. He liked Michael a lot—too much already, truth be told—but he'd promised himself he'd do this, enjoy it, and give away as little as possible.

Michael pulled an annoyed face and waved his hand in the air, then he nudged into Andrew to start them moving again. "Now I'm sorry.

Jeez. There are only two big conventions in town this weekend, so deductive reasoning and all."

"Do you make it a habit to keep up with any going conventions, whether they interest you or not?"

Andrew watched as Michael chewed on his lip in such a way that made him want to lean in and follow suit.

"No, I kinda have to know—I'm a cop. Detective, even. It takes up like, three-quarters of my life? Sometimes it's hard not to be that way in the other quarter. It's a bad habit."

"Yeah. I can see how that'd happen." Andrew had cooled more than a fraction, and he knew Michael felt it too. He hadn't meant to, didn't want to, but there it was. His walls were ever present and returned full force far too easily. Michael wasn't the only one there with some deeply ingrained habits.

They wove into the parking lot, and Michael stopped them next to a generic four-door. The warm September night was humid, and the streetlights coated everything in a mellow, dusky haze. Andrew stared at the vague dome of the sky mostly reflecting Indianapolis's muzzy glow and discovered he missed being able to take in a night sky densely packed with stars. He'd become a small-town guy by circumstance, but he was discovering he fit there far better than he ever had in the city.

"Okay, look, I was going to tell you that I happened to know the perfect place for after-midnight coffee and pancakes and invite you there. I was also going to be awesome and charming and really funny about asking, then the whole time we were at my favorite diner, I was going to flirt with you mercilessly and play footsie under the booth. After that, I was going to mention the diner was walking distance from my apartment."

Michael scratched at the back of his neck in a disarmingly adorable tell of uncertainty, then straightened.

"But the truth is, I just want to skip to the 'my apartment' point in the proceedings. And I really like you? A lot. But I don't usually do this, like ever, so I can't even say I'm out of practice. And I've put you off by asking too much about you already—and I haven't even asked that much—so I can only imagine how breakfast tomorrow would go, and now I'm rambling which is another terrible habit of mine that, I'm told, becomes endearing after about a decade of knowing me and learning how to tune me out." His eyes widened. "I didn't mean to imply we had to, you know——"

Andrew took pity on Michael, and he also had to tamp down the stirrings of more-than-physical interest Michael's endearing ramble had disturbed in him. He cupped Michael's face in both hands and gave him a sound kiss, one that set off those sparks and fireworks he'd had hints of in the club. He trembled when he finally pulled away. Andrew told himself it was only horniness and having been dry and frustrated for so long, nothing more. Michael sucked in a breath, then pursued Andrew's withdrawal, grabbing him close into another kiss.

A loud, playful whistle finally separated them. Andrew came back to the world to find he had Michael pinned to the generic four-door. Michael's hands were in Andrew's shirt and pants while Andrew had Michael's wonderfully slinky hair tangled in his fingers.

"Wow, okay." Michael let the words out on elongated syllables and shallow breaths. "Guess I didn't ruin things after all?"

"Does your car have a siren?"

Michael looked at him blankly, and Andrew arched his eyebrows.

"I like pancake breakfasts. But I find I'm in a real hurry to get to what comes before that, so I'm hoping with you being a cop and knowing your way all around this city that you can, you know." Andrew twirled one finger in the air and made woo-woo noises.

"Oh, right. Yeah, I do! C'mon." Michael boosted out from between Andrew and the car, then held the door open.

Andrew wasn't even buckled in when Michael had the siren blaring and the car squealing out of the parking lot. It was an entirely irresponsible abuse of power—something Andrew could easily tell wasn't Michael's ordinary habit—but it did wonders for his ego and mounting desire to get straight to business when they got to Michael's apartment.

"For the record, Detective, I don't usually do this either. Try, never." Andrew cleared his throat and shifted in the seat. He knocked his elbow into Michael's arm and smiled in the hope he didn't sound desperate and dorky, but Michael only nodded with understanding and smiled back.

He watched Michael drive, competent and obviously thrumming with the same anticipation that had Andrew strung tight, and decided he'd only have regrets tonight if he walked away. Andrew wasn't lying.

He never did this. He didn't date, not seriously or casually. He hadn't even seen another guy naked outside of movies or the local YMCA locker room in years.

Michael cut the siren off a short distance before they turned into a nondescript parking area with an expanse of condos that looked like badly designed ski lodges. Michael curled his top lip ruefully. "Not my taste, but it's in my budget and takes care of itself. I don't exactly have a lifestyle that allows for gardening."

Andrew didn't complain, certainly not when Michael rushed him from the car up a narrow sidewalk and into the ground-floor unit. Michael didn't bother with lights, just fumbled the door closed and locked again before pushing Andrew up against it. Andrew moaned and opened his legs, then met Michael's seeking mouth in a dangerously appealing kiss.

They spun each other around and groped their way out of clothes and down the hall until Andrew backed into the bed and fell abruptly over onto it. He blinked rapidly when Michael snapped on a small side lamp. For a moment, he had those stirrings again, somewhere between his heart being glad that Michael seemed to be an actual nice guy, and his brain whispering they should get to know one another after this and how great that would be.

He bottled that thought up tight and banished it to some hidden recess that would hopefully never open again. Michael's life was here in Indianapolis, and it didn't even have room to mow some grass. Andrew's life was hours away and had no room to add anyone else, not even a nice-seeming guy who could turn out to be really great.

He levered onto his elbows and grabbed Michael down onto him, bit, then sucked Michael's full lower lip into his mouth. Michael melted against him with an encouraging groan. Andrew hummed intently and set to kissing Michael with thorough pleasure.

Andrew loved kissing. He loved making out and the sensations that could overwhelm his whole body when the kissing was good. Michael was very good. He fit against Andrew in the just-so way that allowed their hands space to explore and intermittent breaths without ever having to break contact. They teased each other in complementary moves and parries, with bites and swirls of tongue, then went back to open-mouthed kisses.

It had been so long since Andrew had felt anything like this, since he'd enjoyed the solid, sweaty press of an undeniably masculine body to his. He closed his eyes to indulge and heighten the sensations, restless and thrumming and nearly at the brink already. He grabbed at Michael, kneading then skating his fingertips around. He didn't want to miss out on anything within his reach.

Michael pulled back and eased away. Andrew protested then sat up to give chase. He didn't want to be so eager and desperate but he couldn't help himself. This felt so good; Michael felt amazing.

"Shhhh," Michael kept kissing Andrew, lingering presses to Andrew's jaw and neck then down his shoulders. He tugged at Andrew and positioned them as he moved. He lowered fluidly and smiled once he knelt on the floor between Andrew's legs. "I'm not going anywhere."

Michael kissed Andrew's thighs, his strong, competent hands pacing an unerring track toward the center, where Andrew's cock stood heavy and aching. Andrew widened his eyes—he wanted them open for this. When he tentatively brushed at Michael's hair, he got a deep, encouraging rumble in response, so he gave in to the draw and tangled his fingers into Michael's luxuriously soft locks.

"Oooh—" Andrew gasped a broken sob when Michael's adept mouth and hands finally met. He almost came when Michael tongued the head of his cock and thumbed across the taut strain of his balls. He barely held off and controlled his hips enough so he didn't thrust and choke Michael.

"Why don't we… yeah…." Michael spoke almost to himself. He wrapped both hands around Andrew's cock and twisted them in either direction with just the right amount of friction to be good, but not so much pressure as to hurt. Then he swallowed Andrew's cock until his lips touched the circle of his fingers.

Andrew couldn't control himself. His toes curled into the carpet and he rolled forward and avidly watched the gorgeously filthy stretch of his cock distending Michael's cheek. Michael stroked him faster, more firmly, and sucked harder. When Michael's tongue fluttered, Andrew was done for.

His hips lurched and his hands opened and flexed as if he'd been shocked. Heat coursed from his center to boil his blood and he went rigid until at last he pulled in a sudden, needy gasp. Michael worked him through his orgasm, grounding him, until Andrew fell back onto the bed in a dizzy rush.

"Hi." Michael's lips were wet and cool, and he shoved at Andrew to move them to the center of the bed.

Andrew blinked and looked around. He hadn't passed out as he'd thought, but he realized Michael had managed a trip to the bathroom to rinse, then get him pushed around without his being fully aware. It should have made him uncomfortable or nervous, because he was always aware, always on alert, but he chalked it up to being way too long since he'd come in hands that weren't his own.

"Well. That was—" Andrew blushed and wasn't sure what to say. He liked to think of himself as someone with stamina and reciprocity in bed, but Michael wouldn't know it from that.

"Nice. Incredibly nice." Michael shifted to straddle Andrew, now that they were actually lying on the bed properly, and he traced the grooves and lines of Andrew's abs. "Gotta be horticulture—no drug company drone would be cut like this," Michael teased and continued his lazy perusal. He tilted his hips as if to let Andrew feel the hot but lax weight of his cock, still definitely interested but satisfactorily spent, and revealed so much with just that. "It's been awhile for me too. Knowing we're in the same boat? Hey, not like I mind, not any part of that."

Andrew nodded and accepted it, even laughed. He ran his hands up Michael's arms. "Aside from knocking a guy out who's finally ending a—" He cough-mumbled playfully. "—years' drought, what else do you like?"

"Uh. Anything?" Michael grinned, and the open sincerity of it almost bent Andrew sideways.

It almost made him push Michael away, rear up, and run.

Before he could bolt, Michael leaned in and stole a quick kiss. "But I don't have a to-do list or demands. Thankfully, there's plenty that falls under the 'anything' heading. How about we just see where it goes?"

Andrew's arms and hands moved with a plan they hadn't told his brain about, and he greedily pulled Michael into another seemingly endless necking session. They kissed and grinned, touched and writhed, until finally Michael tucked his face into Andrew's neck and panted.

"Whew, you are good at that." He nipped behind Andrew's ear. "I love making out."

Andrew had to agree but only nodded. He couldn't bring himself to say "love" or even "me too" in answer to the word, even if it carried no specific meaning. He nudged Michael to lie back, then kissed and took his time exploring every inch, from the dark stubble showing on Michael's chin, to the dusky nipples, to abs more cut than his own. He took Michael in hand and went back to kissing, kept kissing while he used a maddening, leading mix of light strokes and sudden hard tugs. It didn't take long before Michael cursed and grabbed at Andrew, then pinned them together so he could grind against Andrew's thigh. Andrew dragged his teeth over the thin skin under Michael's ear, tantalizingly hot under his tongue from a rapidly beating pulse. Michael muffled a shout and came again.

Andrew stayed put so Michael could fit close to him. He didn't mind the mess, or when Michael sucked his fingers clean, or when they kissed to share the taste. Soon, they were hard again, and after they'd kissed past the point of Andrew's lips getting swollen and feeling bruised and nearly numb, they rutted together in steady, short thrusts to completion. Andrew gasped and stretched, opened up to lie on his back, and Michael flopped against the sprawl of his other arm.

They dozed. When Andrew found a clock on the table at the far side of the bed, he couldn't believe he'd been there for hours. But he didn't move except to respond when Michael made tiny, agonizing circles with a fingertip over his slit. He pulled Michael on top of him, then rolled Michael under, and then they were at it—locked in mutual absorption—once more.

The next time Andrew woke, it was morning. Five thirty and still dark outside, but definitely, for-real morning. He couldn't remember how many more rounds they'd gone, but he was weighted with that bone-deep lassitude of having come so many times that moving should be an impossibility. He moved anyway.

It almost killed him to leave, because he knew Michael expected him to stay, to treat him to those pancakes and coffee while they grinned and blushed and stared at each other bleary-eyed, and he couldn't deny wanting that too. But it would be even harder if he stayed. That wouldn't even be the long run; it'd be harder within minutes, and Andrew couldn't do anything to change that.

He eased from the bed, ignored how cold he felt and the foolish sense that he outright liked Michael. Absolutely did not allow thoughts of the friends they could become and how well they got along.

Absolutely did not replay the snips of things said and shared between hand jobs and necking that had made each other laugh or snicker dirtily.

Andrew wondered if Michael's being a cop meant there was some kind of radar or spidey-senses that would trip any minute now. But when he peeked at the bed, Michael was curled in the warm spot Andrew had left behind, half-smiling and exhaustedly gone.

He followed the trail of his discarded clothes and belongings back to the front door, then worried about an alarm system. When he didn't see or find any, he crept outside. Andrew went through a litany of self-derision and recrimination for finding himself in some condo development in a city he didn't know, getting dressed on the sheltered front porch of a guy he'd hooked up with.

A guy he really liked. A guy who was a cop and had noticed way too many things during their short time together. A guy who was a cop but didn't wake when Andrew made his escape, presumably because he'd really liked Andrew back.

Andrew sighed and pulled himself together. He scrubbed a hand through his hair which made it an all-around messy skew instead of the obvious walk of shame bedhead. He trotted through the parking lot toward the road. From there he picked a direction and in the near distance saw the glowing sign of a gas station. He'd use the bathroom, get some coffee, maybe a bear claw, and call a cab. He'd get to his hotel with time for a shower before check-out, and from there, drive home and back to reality.

He pictured Michael a last time, then filed it away. A guy he'd really liked who couldn't be his.

CHAPTER 2

MICHAEL hummed the pop song that refused to budge from his head and strolled back outside, fresh cup of coffee in hand. He threw a last wave at everyone in the coffee shop as the door closed behind him, then he pulled to the side and took in a long, appreciative whiff. Two sugars and a lot of cream and freshly made—perfect.

He turned to continue his counterclockwise circuit, and almost laughed when he thought about this being his new beat: the town square in his hometown of Starling, Indiana. He charmed the old ladies at the quilt shop, ducked into the Five and Sundry hardware shop for a chat session, and stopped in for free coffee at the Book'n'Brew—not exactly working anything except a lot of his charm and good public relations. It was certainly nothing like the homicide beat in Indianapolis, and he missed that: the rush, the challenge it presented, putting actual bad guys away.

But things were different, and Michael had no regrets. He knew in his heart he'd think back on having stayed in Indy to pursue his career and the endless docket of 187s instead of moving back home as the mistake. Especially as his reason for coming back was family, and that was the most important thing to him, hands down, no question. When Dad had the heart attack, the whole family had reacted the same way: *Here I am. What can I do to help?* No reservation.

Michael had ended up staying—had, for all intents, moved back into his old life. While his fiercely independent streak insisted he should mind, his heart and soul felt like he'd finally come back to where he really belonged.

He let out a breath and shook his head. Thinking of regrets and belonging always brought him back to the same place—Andrew. Cute, hilarious, whip smart and freaking sexy Andrew and their one night together. It didn't matter that it'd been months ago, and so much change and upheaval had happened in Michael's life to drag his attentions away—they inevitably found their way back to memories of Andrew.

Michael was almost fixated, despite having done his best to relegate the night to his "good time had, now let it go" file. He had adamantly decided it was because there would never be any resolution, not because he was pining.

Maybe he was still so caught up in Andrew because it had made him feel so out of step, like he couldn't trust his instincts and reactions after that night. He'd have sworn they were incredibly compatible, and not just in bed. That what was between them could easily evolve into something great, even if that had to be dirty e-mails when they were apart.

But Andrew had devastatingly proved that false, having left without even a kiss-off note, and zero anything since. Michael had woken that morning surprised he'd slept through Andrew leaving. He'd sat naked on his sofa, head in his hands, and tried to wrap himself around the idea that, despite their electric spark and seeming connection, it had been nothing more than a one-night stand. He'd had to admit a lot more than that as the months rolled on without any change. It made him almost hate how attached he got to people, so quickly and easily. If he'd spent a whole day with Andrew, it'd probably have broken his fool heart.

The happy shouts of children playing pulled his attention away from the beginning spiral of useless thoughts. He smiled and decided to go check things out. He needed something to shake up his routine, and while caffeine helped keep him sharp, he couldn't get too predictable.

Starling's courthouse was still in use and that, along with an action committee of persistent townsfolk, was what kept the old town square alive. Instead of letting storefronts go empty to fall into dismal ruin, they'd pressed the city to give incentives for businesses to stay or move in. Any time a lot cleared, it had been refurbished.

Michael was proud of it—in part because his mom was on the committee—because too many small towns were dying from the center out. His still had its roots but also branched out to adapt with the times, and that combination kept it vibrant and a going concern.

Several years ago, the façade on one of the brick buildings had crumbled, and it would cost more to repair the whole building than to simply tear it down. After it had been razed, the lot had been turned into a playground, small and trim and tidy, just enough space for one of those multilayered contraptions with a connecting bridge and a few benches sprinkled around.

There was more squealing, delighted laughter, and the rumble of feet. Michael could make out the figure of a man standing on the ground, playfully grabbing at the ankles of two little kids who ran back and forth across the bridge. A little girl and a littler boy, both towheaded, pink-cheeked, and adorable.

"Daddy!" the girl shouted. "Can't catch me!"

The little boy trundled alongside, still shaky with a toddler's learning legs, and echoed, "Meee!"

Michael watched the dad's patient repeat of the game and smiled fondly, because his dad had been great like that when they'd been growing up. He glanced over a final time before heading on to the hardware store and got a good look at the man. Bile scalded his throat as his stomach fell somewhere near his feet.

"Daddy" was Andrew. Andrew, his still-mourned-over could-have-been. The one-night encounter that had been enough to keep him awake nights or held in vividly frustrating wet dreams. A guy he'd really liked and had wanted to get to know so much better. Real and just as stupidly attractive as he remembered, right there in front of him. Impossibly so, attached to those happy kids, glowing with the genuine grin Michael had caught brief glimpses of during their night together.

Michael was an affable guy, generally good-natured and almost always in a good mood. But he could have a hot temper. When provoked, it went full throttle to searing heights. He was particularly vulnerable to losing it when things involved kids or lovers who were apparently living a huge, fat, selfish lie. That temper plowed through him now, cut out any hesitation or regard for the situation other than anger. He stalked over to the playground, right up to where Andrew stood, and made up for the few inches difference in their height with a sneering glower.

"Hey there, Andrew," he said through his teeth.

Andrew startled and reared back, eyes going almost comically wide at seeing Michael. All sorts of dark things ran through Michael's mind, from invectives to awful scenarios. He figured Andrew could read most of them on his face.

"At least it's finally explained why you up and ran that morning." Michael would have added a few choice curses, but he remembered his audience just in time. Still, his lip curled and he bit out sarcastically, "Surprise."

There was a short, tense silence. The little boy had taken shelter behind the girl's legs.

"Pumpkin?" Andrew patted her feet and smiled reassuring up at her. "Can you please get your coats back on, then take your brother to wait for me over there?" He pointed at the bench farthest from them but still in clear view. "I just need a minute to talk, then we can go home."

She crouched to look through the bridge railing. "Okay." She frowned at Michael. "Are you a real policeman? You're not being nice. So either you're always grumpy or Daddy's in trouble." It sounded like she spoke from experience. "Is Daddy in trouble?"

"Daddy is not in trouble." Andrew squeezed her ankles, then gave her a little push. "I bet he's worried we're littering." He winked and pointed at the pile of their belongings, discarded for playtime.

She studied them intently, but relented at Andrew's say-so. Her eyes were darker than Andrew's but just as startlingly blue.

After the kids had left, Andrew turned to look at Michael fully. Michael knew he should retreat. It wasn't fair to challenge Andrew in front of children, but he didn't feel fair. He felt betrayed and hurt.

"So what then? I'm the piece of ass that the closeted small-town guy nailed one anonymous night in the big city?" Michael set his jaw and laughed humorlessly. "In for a conference, you don't do this often, sure. Good act you put on. Boy, you had me fooled—with everything, clearly. Is there a wife included in this, just to round out the whole picture, or are you only lying to your kids after divorcing her when you realized you preferred dick?"

Andrew straightened and went glacial, enough to cool Michael's temper a fraction.

"Back at you, big city detective." His eyes raked up and down the Starling PD uniform Michael wore.

Michael slashed a dismissive hand through the air. "That doesn't even come close to comparing and you know it. Don't smoke screen or put this on me."

Where Michael was big gestures and all afire, Andrew had narrowed to a sharply motionless point.

"I don't know why you're here. I don't know anything about you. But you don't know anything about me." Andrew's words were staccato and precise. "It's not my habit to bother wasting time on assholes, and I never explain myself to strangers, but I'm insulted enough that you've earned hearing this, and not put to you nicely. More than anything, I don't want you ever treating those kids that way again, so I'm going to explain. After that, I'm walking away and I hope we never speak to you again."

Being called a stranger hit Michael harder than being called an asshole. The worst was having to admit it was true.

"Here's the short version." Andrew's expression was hard, and his wonderfully bright blue eyes were remote shards, focus kept just right of Michael as if he was reading a well-learned script he wished could be forgotten. "My sister and I grew up rough. I got away from it. She got two kids by two different men and had them way too young. Dad number two lives here, and she'd settled nearby so he could have access to the boy. Then man number one found her, and they fell back in together. He killed her in a drug-addled car wreck two years ago. There was no one else willing to accept full custody of both kids, so I came to take care of them. I don't drag anyone into their lives unnecessarily. Never have, never will."

Michael could tell Andrew hated every moment of telling him this, that even the terse, barely detailed recitation of events felt like giving everything away and revealing far too much. His detective instincts were on high alert as Andrew spoke, and his own anger faded. He could tell this was no bullshit. He could also painfully infer a whole lot of what was meant by "growing up rough" and everything that had happened to them after.

He pictured the boy—probably around three, which meant Andrew was really the only stable parent the kid had ever known. Who could say about the girl, but in the scant review of events and what had to be acres of turmoil and distrust rescued by Andrew's presence, no wonder they so naturally called him Dad.

His rage died as quickly as it had flared, but it was too late. Andrew was so calm it scared Michael, but he could discern under the touch-me-not façade a mixture of disappointment, disgust, and shame. The shame bothered him most, and he ached to take Andrew's face in his hands to reassure it away.

Michael imagined the playground cracking open under him, fissuring and splitting and swallowing him whole, then having an anvil land on him after he'd hit rock bottom. He didn't even deserve the sardonic puff-of-dust punch line at the end.

He stammered, partly in shock because who would ever think such a thing, partly in abject misery.

"Oh God, Andrew. I'm so sorry. I am such an asshole. I just— That night—and then you here—and seeing you with kids was just such a shock. Then my horrible temper…. I'm not usually like that, but— Obviously, it got the better of me and, obviously, I proved that trite adage about assumptions is absolutely correct in all respects." He reached out, but Andrew easily sidestepped the attempt.

"I meant what I said. Good-bye," Andrew clipped without meeting Michael's eye. He gathered the kids' bags and walked resolutely away.

Michael debated giving chase, but the girl's worried glance at him from under Andrew's arm stilled him. He didn't want to cause her any more stress. It hadn't been fair for him to challenge Andrew in front of the children in the first place. Instead, he stood rooted in the warm March sunshine, the playground gardens pretty with white and purple crocus heads announcing themselves while tree branches began to blush red with forming buds. Michael shivered, iced through to his core.

CHAPTER 3

ANDREW sat down and closed his eyes. He methodically went through the habitual steps that allowed him to decompress from being completely shut off. Eventually, he started to shake. Small tremors, nerves at last working out tension and fear and anger, held in check using ways to hide in plain sight he'd learned years ago. He wasn't always like this anymore, didn't always need to retreat from emotion until it was safe to react. Some days, it happened on purpose. Other days, it was like he was yanked back into yesterday and had no choice.

Unexpectedly seeing Michael and not wanting to freak the kids out had been a killer combination. He'd been on autopilot the entire day. Here it was, twelve hours and three beers after their confrontation in the playground, and he'd only started to unwind.

The memory of Michael had dwelled in a carefully separated compartment Andrew didn't often revisit, for good reason. It was too distracting, too impossible, too painful. He was good at not feeling, had become a master craftsman at repression, so that's what he'd done instead. Michael walking, talking, and apparently living in the same town as he did had erupted all those bottled emotions until they'd threatened to overwhelm him. If he hadn't had a lifetime's practice of hide-everything-or-suffer, he might have broken down on the spot.

As it was, he wished he hadn't told Michael so much. He wanted to be able to take it back, and replayed again and again what he should have done instead. Say hello in front of the kids, threaten bodily harm once the kids were out of earshot, then nothing else. It was none of Michael's business, and Andrew resented being made vulnerable.

But part of him had wanted to punish Michael, to shock and wound with the stark facts of his situation, because Michael's accusations and murky assumptions had hurt him.

It made matters worse that he'd actually sympathized with Michael's immediate reactionary extrapolation and anger. Apparently, his having slept with the guy made him uncharacteristically forgiving.

That and he'd been struck with the fleeting impulse to grab Michael, kiss him, then tease, "You idiot, come meet Chloe and Tanner."

Andrew sensed more than heard anything. He opened his eyes to find Chloe lingering in the long shadow that slanted across where the hallway joined the living room.

"Hey, Pumpkin," he said softly. "C'mere."

His shaking had almost subsided, and she never sought him out unless she needed something. She swished over to him in her long pink princess nightgown, and he helped her clamber up into his lap. He set the rocking chair going at a gentle creak. Her warmth, fresh-washed hair, and clean-nightie scent relaxed and reassured him, and she sighed and leaned into his shoulder.

"Why were you and the policeman mad?"

Andrew frowned. He had a policy to always tell the kids the truth, within reason, but this was tricky. "We weren't exactly angry."

Chloe grumbled indignantly, and it would have been funny in other circumstances. She knew the difference and saw far too much. She was too much like he'd been at her age—reserved, observant, aged too quickly into a mini adult with an all-too-fragile child's ego underneath. Andrew had suspected her apparent nonchalance toward today's encounter was false. But he was relieved she sought him out to talk about it, instead of dwelling on it.

"It surprised me that he was there. Seeing him scared me a little, and I think I scared him." Andrew settled Chloe more comfortably so he wouldn't eventually lose feeling in his feet. "The last time we saw each other, we had a disagreement, and I wasn't expecting to meet him again so soon. Like you not wanting to go back to school after that day you and Becca had a fight, because thinking about seeing her after being angry was scary."

Chloe and Becca's disagreement had been second-grade politics and something involving a cartoon about ponies that Andrew didn't quite understand the nuances of, but he figured the parallel tracked.

"Oh." Chloe absorbed the information. "Does that mean you're friends again?"

Andrew made a noncommittal sound.

"Becca and I had lunch together after saying sorry. I felt so bad I brought the sticker with her favorite pony on it for her, and then she put it on my folder." She shrugged. "Was it like that?"

He wished he and Michael could reach the same equanimity so easily. "Not quite. But don't worry about it, sweetie. It's nothing to do with you or Tanner, and he won't be mean around any of us again."

Chloe let out a long, thinking-on-it breath. "Do you like him?"

Andrew rested his cheek on Chloe's head and had a long think too. "Yes. I do."

It felt good to say it, to admit out loud, even if it was only to Chloe. The burden of a secret released, but shared in a way that wouldn't bring any repercussions to bear. He closed his eyes again and thought about Michael. It was true, even after today and all the previous months of so actively trying to forget. He could still easily and vividly remember them being together. How it had felt, their compatibility, and how lonely he'd been without it.

"Well," Chloe began, taking on the tone Andrew used when he was trying to reason with either of the children, "if he likes you, too, then you can be friends again. Right?"

"Right, sure," Andrew agreed carefully, because there would be no explaining to Chloe why that wasn't going to happen.

"Good. Are you okay now?"

Andrew couldn't keep from grinning. "Who says I wasn't okay?"

"You made dinner without any vegetables. Tanner wanted mac 'n' cheese and you said sure and that was it!" Chloe scoffed and waved her hands, as if that explained everything.

It was a startlingly accurate tell. Andrew was always conscientious and firm about them eating well, even when the meal was simple or they were rushed. Even if it looked like the grossest thing to them ever, he insisted they have at least one try-me bite. Tonight, he barely recalled making dinner. He'd done everything through a fog of red, focused on hiding the fallout of his reactions to Michael. He'd gone through the motions from when they'd gotten home through getting them cleaned up and into bed. He didn't even know for sure if he'd read to them.

Andrew resented that Michael had affected him that much, that he was already so far under Andrew's skin to have so much power. He wanted to shift the largest portion of that blame onto how stunned-then-furious he'd been over Michael's assumptions about him and Michael's behavior around the kids. So he only acknowledged the parts that were easiest to explain away. The feelings he'd worked to savagely repress had rushed back full bore when he'd seen Michael again, still too close to the surface.

"Yes, I'm okay. Tomorrow, we'll have brussels sprouts to make up for it, how's that?"

"Ugh," Chloe sighed, but she nodded.

He rocked them until Chloe drifted to sleep, and used the time to carefully repack and stow what Michael had brought out in him. Then he hefted Chloe to her bed, abandoned the fully warmed beer to be dealt with in the morning, and went to bed himself.

CHAPTER 4

"I AM such a jerkface," Michael lamented, voice muffled by the kitchen table. He had his jerkface pressed against the cradle of his arms.

As soon as he'd showered and changed after getting off duty, he'd headed straight there, to the predictable comfort of the homestead kitchen, where everything important happened. The journey to find this comfort wasn't far and could be made on foot; Michael lived in the largest of the barns on the farm property, the hayloft converted to an apartment with its nooks and crannies and vaulted ceiling.

It wasn't where he'd imagined himself being several years ago when he'd left home, ready to make it and prove himself in the big world. He'd thought his return to the old farmhouse would be visits only, not moving back in, and certainly not moving back after exchanging a big-city detective's badge for a small-town beat. But the longer he was here—and here to stay—the more he was grateful fate had forced his hand.

He liked it here. He belonged here.

It was Friday just after lunch. Almost everyone was around, helping to clean up or busy with the endless small tasks that kept a farm in constant busy motion. Aaron had begged off and left already, back to town and his office—he'd become a lawyer, of all things—and Ava was rarely here anymore, as she lived an hour away with her husband and three kids. Otherwise, the kitchen was stacked with Michael's siblings. He was torn between wanting to spill and be bolstered by their reactions of sympathy and blunt honesty, or slinking to bed to hide under the covers until tomorrow.

"What? The last thing you are is a jerk." Moriah, closest in age to Michael and his lifelong compatriot in all things, leaned over him with a quick hug and a cup of coffee.

Michael groaned miserably. "I saw a guy I met in Indy and had really liked, and trust me, I was a huge jerkface to him." He'd have called himself worse but his mom didn't like such language.

An interested stillness descended over the kitchen. Nothing came to a halt—Moriah continued peeling potatoes for dinner, Daniel kept sorting the catch-all screws and nails bucket, Sarah remained busy with her college work—but Stephen shut off the water from doing the dishes, and his mother Rita's bustling around got a lot less bustle-y.

"This wouldn't be that guy you went out with once, then never heard from again, would it?" Sarah asked, so very casually.

"Oooooh," Moriah drew out. "That guy."

"So that guy turned out to be a jerkface, is that it?" Diana had appeared from upstairs as if by magic, drawn by the unmistakable siren call of family gossip.

They all knew exactly who "that guy" was, because Michael was seemingly incapable of coolly putting Andrew behind him and moving on without dwelling on what-might-have-been. At one point, Daniel had suggested they pool their resources to track Andrew down to deliver either a punch in the face or a plea to take Michael and his torment off their hands.

Michael half-expected the phone to ring with Aaron and Ava on a party line, ears pricked up for the news. He sighed. "No, he is most assuredly not a jerkface."

"Mikey is the jerkface," Stephen noted helpfully.

"Ahhh." Diana slid onto the long bench seat next to Michael and nudged into him. "Well, I could have told you that."

Everyone continued to stay busy, but impatience was invading the pleasant atmosphere. Michael pushed himself up, mostly motivated by the coffee. Fortified after sucking down half the gigantic mug of his mom's all-day superstrong brew, he recounted what had happened with Andrew in the playground.

"Dude." Stephen, second-youngest at twenty-three, could make "dude" a word to be used in all forms.

"I know, I know." Michael winced. "Now he hates me and never wants to see me again, but we live in the same town of under ten thousand people! And I still really like him," he said pitifully. "I'm doomed."

"Sweetheart." Rita whisked over and refilled his coffee mug, setting a plate of homemade cookies next to him. "You're only doomed if you don't apologize."

That only managed to annoy Michael, probably because she was absolutely right. "But I don't even know—" He was going to say he didn't even know Andrew's last name but caught himself just in time. Instead he distracted by waving his hands and making noises. "Like, anything important! Where he works now, where he lives, nothing."

"Weren't you a detective or something? Aren't you still a cop?" Stephen leaned across the table and grabbed two cookies. He shook his head sadly. "Dude."

Of course, everyone knew Michael had been a detective. Everyone had been proud of his achievement, making it and doing good things in Indianapolis. Everyone also understood why, after his father's heart attack at only fifty-seven, he'd given up that life and returned home.

"Yeah, but I've already been a jerkface. I don't want to be a creepy stalker too."

Michael frowned, because in his despair he'd genuinely forgotten he could work the angles and figure out a lot about Andrew. That said volumes about how upset he truly was, beyond being humiliated and feeling like the world's biggest shitheel.

Sarah loosened a notebook and a pen from her stack of school things. "Here." She grinned. "Start by writing down everything important."

"Be sure to make your heading 'Mikey is a Jerkface,' and don't just doodle hearts and his name." Moriah waggled the potato peeler in his direction. "This is serious business. We can't have that guy you couldn't shut up about for the past year get out of our clutches."

"Even if I have to go ask him out myself," Daniel kicked in. "I know Leslie would be okay with it once she realized it was for the good cause of putting you out of all of our misery."

Leslie and Daniel had been high school sweethearts. They had four kids, and Leslie would probably celebrate having an evening to herself if asking Andrew out for the cause would get Daniel out of her hair. He was a bit of a homebody and they were very much in love, but if it wasn't the farm or his own house on the neighboring property, Daniel had no interest.

Michael almost pointed out it'd been way less than a year but thought better of it. At least they weren't threatening to go find Andrew themselves en masse. Yet. It also made him smile, because before he'd left for Indy, light teasing and tacit acceptance of him wanting to bring a boy home wouldn't have happened as easily. No one had ever renounced him for being gay, but it had been an adjustment. Michael had never lied about who he was, but he'd also gone away to Indy and tirelessly worked to make himself a success there for reasons beyond small-town cabin fever.

It had been good for him. Good for his family too. It let them come to terms in their own ways without having to watch him experiment or hide from them what he was up to. He'd returned home comfortable in his skin and well past the sweaty-palmed high school senior who'd been terrified to tell his father he wanted to go to away to the police academy and that he eventually wanted to get married and settle down—with another man.

"Whose misery?" Pops strolled into the kitchen and took his place at the head of the table. His overalls were stained with oil and fingerprints, meaning he'd been tinkering on the ancient Farmall tractor Michael remembered always being there and never having run.

"Mikey's. And ours." Moriah filled their father's water glass. "We found him. Apparently he lives here, even! You know, *him*," she stressed.

Pops took a long drink. Michael could almost see the cogs turning. He gave a moment's fervent thanks that this topic of conversation was no longer so awkward or brutally embarrassing.

"Ahh, you mean 'that guy.'" Pops looked at Michael quizzically. "If he lives here, I'm sure we know him or at least his family. Have him to dinner."

Michael would have told any of his siblings coming late to this discussion to catch up on their own time, but for Pops it was different. He doodled in the notebook and said, "It's more complicated than that. Actually, it's really complicated. He lives here but he's not from here, and he doesn't have any family except the kids he assumed care for."

Pops absorbed the information. "Okay, so then we know the family of the kids, in all likelihood." He waited, clearly expecting Michael to provide the surname.

The notion wasn't a lark. In a town this size, with as long as and wide as their own roots had spread, they really did know just about everyone in some way or another.

Michael shook his head. "They're his sister's kids, but two different dads. She had been living with number two until recently, after they got pregnant, but apparently she fell in with a bad crowd again. Wound up dying in a car wreck a few years ago."

"Hmmm." Pops started to cut and clean the celery Rita had brought over after she'd not at all subtly plunked a knife at his elbow. "You know, Hank Reed's good-for-nothing boy went and had a kid out of wedlock, along the same time as you're saying. Went off to Evansville after factory work, came home towing a young girl, her daughter, and their newborn son."

Pops had an uncanny knack for connecting specific dates and details with specific people, no matter how many he learned, and no matter the years since having learned them. He'd also lived a long life and seen a lot of things, despite living in a small town, so he made assessments without rigidly unforgiving judgments. Michael liked to think he'd inherited this knack and that it was what made him a good cop.

"That at least tracks. Andrew—that guy—is taking care of a girl around seven and a boy around three." He wrote "Hank Reed" down in the notebook.

"Jayce." Stephen poked at the paper with his own pen. "Went to school with him. Jayce Reed. Pops is right. He did go to be a big man in the big city, came home soon after that with a kid and a pretty, but young, girl who maybe should have been, but wasn't, his wife. We weren't friends, though, so I didn't keep up to find out what happened to them."

Michael nodded and his mind started whirring busily. "I've popped Jayce a few times on speeding tickets. What a d-bag. Mostly harmless seeming, but still a douche-canoe."

Pops tsk'd with satisfaction. "See? There you are. A good place to start."

Michael smiled.

The phone rang and Stephen jumped up to answer. "Dude! Were your spidey senses tingling? Guess what?" He covered the mouthpiece. "It's Ava."

Michael laughed and groaned. He dutifully started writing down everything he could think of about Andrew.

CHAPTER 5

THREE days later Michael had written down almost everything and was hesitating at Gallagher Nursery and Supply, where he'd learned Andrew sourced jobs as a landscape architect.

He'd confirmed the Reed connection, but that wasn't how he wanted to approach Andrew. No reason to build a terrible second impression on what everyone described as a chilly, at best, kin relationship.

An article in the paper and a chat with some other people, then some carefully placed conversation seeds, had led to Michael's discovery that Andrew had been tapped to landscape the newly built middle school. The new middle school was a big deal, so it had gotten a lot of press coverage. Andrew had landed the job in part from doing great work at the principal's house and also for the small, naturalized park near the long-abandoned train depot the city had been working to restore.

This information had Michael placing a phone call to Gallagher's under the pretense of pricing rock to redo the parking pad in front of his barn apartment. Luckily, Clay Gallagher was an old friend—he'd played football with Aaron, and Clay's oldest boy was giving Aaron's daughter a run for her money. Michael had casually mentioned how great a boost it must be for Clay to be able to supply all the goods for that new middle school. That's how he'd learned—even luckier—that Andrew rented a small office from Clay in the back of the store, but didn't work for Clay directly. Michael had been able to sleuth Andrew's whereabouts without having to try and wriggle Andrew loose from Clay or anyone else to get a chance to apologize.

Of course, he still had to get up the courage to go inside.

Michael took stock and set his shoulders and told himself not to be a wuss. He could do this; he owed at least this to Andrew.

Clay had let Andrew add a side door so clients could come and go directly instead of having to meander past an obstacle course of fertilizer pallets and wheelbarrow displays. Michael considered knocking, but he figured that would be weird, so he rebalanced the coffee he'd bought them and the pie he'd asked his mom to make and with a deep breath he pushed open the door.

A castaway wind chime bonged and Michael almost turned and bolted when Andrew called out, "Just a minute!"

He'd been preparing himself for some friendly chitchatting with a receptionist to warm up before getting down to the business of having to face Andrew. But no one else was here. The office was tidy and efficient and very quiet.

Watercolors and technical drawings hung on one wall, interspersed with photographs of scenes and spreads of those drawings brought to life. In the center of that display was Lucas Landscaping's emblem printed on natural paper stock: a minimal white tree with two scripted L's carved into the trunk. The rest of the small room was spare, painted in a relaxing deep sage green, with two comfortable chairs tucked under the window. It was nice—obviously had gotten more neatnik attention than the store did—but it didn't feel personal. Michael was beginning to wonder if anything relating to Andrew did.

Andrew popped out of the connecting office, and his ready smile tightened when he saw Michael.

"Hi." Michael huffed silently, annoyed with himself. "Landscape architect, yeah?" He gestured at the wall of Andrew's work. "Nice. You do work for Clay sometimes but mostly work for yourself, right? That's cool. I also bet that's why you were at the horticulture convention in Indianapolis."

"Are you interrogating me?" Andrew crossed his arms.

"No!" Michael's voice went up a notch and he rolled his eyes. He cleared his throat. "No, sorry. I'm here to eat crow with a side of humble pie." He held up one hand. "I also brought you real pie. My mom made it and it's delicious. I'm sorry to spring myself on you like this, but it was that or avoid you for the rest of my natural life and in a town this size, I'm not sure that would be possible. In all honesty, that's not the only reason, but it's not really fair to get into that, so…."

"You don't have to talk to me, okay? You can never talk to me again, just like you said, but I had to track you down so I could absolutely say I am absolutely so sorry, and that I deserved your anger, and I'm ashamed I jumped to such terrible conclusions. With full disclosure, I'll also tell you I was such a jerkface because I had liked you so much and still thought about you a lot, so it was a shock to think this guy I'd spent months agonizing over and remembering was here, in my town, and with kids! I guess, too, I connected all the wrong dots because anger is safer. It was easier than thinking you just didn't like me back."

"I suppose you found my file, seeing as you found me." Andrew didn't take the pie or the coffee, simply kept careful watch of Michael's rambling.

Michael blushed, then blanched. Those were loaded words if ever he'd heard any.

"Yeah, kinda," he admitted reluctantly. "But I didn't pry beyond what could get me to right here." It was obvious Andrew didn't appreciate meddling, or nosiness, or maybe even getting close to anyone. Michael had probably blown it before he even got here just by cracking things open far enough to find Andrew in the first place.

"I did look up about your kid sister. Saw it happened in Kentucky." He didn't get into what he'd discovered about why they'd been a state away, running wild looking for cheap fixes, leaving her kids behind here in Starling. "I was still in Indy then, but no wonder I hadn't heard, even by the family grapevine—I'm real sorry for that too. Awful."

Andrew still hadn't moved, and Michael's smile and babbling was growing perilously thin.

"I'll just… leave this here. The kids can have it, even if you don't want any." Michael set the pie on the table between the chairs. "The coffee is black but I brought sugar and creamer. You can keep that too. And look, I know, okay? I know I was a total asshole—if nothing else, I hate that I lost my cool like that in front of the kids. So, you get a free pass for whatever. Throw a punch at me, key my car, let your daughter convince the second grade I smell funny. Anything that might start to make this up to you."

He hesitated, then shrugged awkwardly. "Sure, well, okay then." Michael turned and put one hand on the doorknob, a ridiculous tightness in his throat.

"You called her my daughter."

Michael's eyebrows furrowed and he turned back around. "Well, yeah. I mean, she is. Uh. Sorry?"

Something indefinable had changed about Andrew, brought about in the scant moments just past, but Michael felt the shift as palpably as he would have a rumbling earthquake.

"I take it black." Andrew reached for the coffee and sniffed it appreciatively. He took a sip and his eyes widened. "Wow, this is good. I'm used to the gas station sludge." He tapped at the rim of the cup. After a thoughtful pause, he said carefully, "You don't look like a Wiercinski."

"What?" Michael frowned. When the words registered, he flashed a smile. "No, I take after mom. Hernandez, on that side."

"Ah. Definitely more like it." Andrew chewed his lips, which was adorable and distracting.

"You were a star baseball player in high school. A picture of you getting your detective's pin in Indy was front-page news, and under that was a picture of the banner the local VFW hung to congratulate you. You traded being a detective for a small-town cop because your father got sick." He smiled, looking endearingly bashful. "The Starling Sentinel's online archive is a treasure trove."

That told Michael so much, and it loosened the throttle around his neck and the sense of foreboding he'd carried since deciding to do this.

"All true," he said and bit his tongue to keep from saying more. He wanted to ask if that meant Andrew had forgiven him and if so, could they go on a date. Probably not the best time to ask and definitely not good for him to push. "I'll just be going, then. The pie really is delicious."

"I believe it." Andrew actually walked over to open the door for Michael. Heat and sparks flared up between them just from the proximity—the electricity Michael remembered from the first moment their eyes had met at the club.

Michael was fascinated with watching Andrew's jaw work and grind and the blush that had crept up Andrew's nape. He realized his own breath had gone shallow, and Andrew was staring at the telling pulse point on his neck.

"I—" Andrew tilted his head and blinked back into the present, and seemed to reorder his words. "About my sister, that's over and done and I didn't expect you to know. But don't be sorry about calling Chloe my daughter. The rest you can definitely grovel over, but not that."

"Deal. Sorry, and not sorry." Michael grinned because otherwise he'd grab hold of Andrew and do more than was decent or likely welcome. Relief was starting to make him giddy. As he stepped onto the slate-lined path that led from the parking lot to Andrew's office, Andrew stayed in the doorway.

"Thanks."

Andrew sounded almost reluctant but not final, and that gave Michael hope.

"No, seriously, thank you." Before he could think better he added, "See you around?"

Andrew had been on the point of turning away, but he paused. "If only so you can tell me where you get this amazing coffee."

"Yeah, definitely. That I can for sure do." Michael lost all his cool at that and grinned hugely.

He couldn't tell if Andrew regretted saying more or was surprised by having given Michael an opening, because the blush was back and he shook his head. But he smiled in response to Michael's grin and sketched a wave, then disappeared inside.

Michael waited until the door fully closed and the shadow of Andrew's profile was gone from the window before punching the air in victory. It wasn't much, but it was a start, and a start was all he needed.

CHAPTER 6

"SO, Lucas Landscaping—Andrew Lucas—making you one of those guys with two first names?" Michael dropped onto the ground next to Andrew, passed him the water jug, and smiled.

Andrew took a long drink, then surveyed the job site and was more than satisfied. He could say the same about having Michael sitting so close at his elbow but avoided dwelling on the idea.

"Actually, they are my two first names. When I turned eighteen I had it legally changed from my mom's last name to the two that were mine. That I wanted." Andrew licked his lips and shrugged tightly.

He supposed that meant Michael really hadn't pried overly into his business, as it would be easy enough information to glean from whatever files a cop could get on his less-than-stellar history. He felt Michael tense up and sighed inwardly. He was so bad at chitchat, at anything offhand, and clearly, he was just as bad at relaying personal and sensitive information. It didn't even hurt anymore to think about the past—almost ten years ago, and long before then he'd stopped nursing unwarranted affection for a mother who didn't care—but he'd said it almost like a challenge.

Probably because Michael had wormed into his life far too easily and without invitation, but almost by default, because apparently them working on being friends made that a default. It ruffled Andrew and made him wary, instinct and lifelong habits in reaction to anyone taking an interest in him, even while he was trying to be better and offer more.

It had been two weeks and three days since Michael had shown up at Andrew's office to apologize. Since then, they'd run into each other more than Andrew could reasonably think was coincidence, but he found he didn't mind. Quite the opposite. He was flattered and almost pathetically relieved, because, beyond an undeniable attraction to Michael, he flat-out liked the guy, enough to want to be friends.

Friends had been a rarity Andrew's entire life and allowing himself to want any even more so. Michael insinuating into the fabric of his days had made it easier to accept that being friends could happen and would be okay.

Today's just-so-happens dividend of being friends with Michael had seen nearly the entire horde of Michael's siblings descend to help Andrew do the work of planting and installing everything at the middle school. Andrew had estimated it would take him a week, Saturday included, but with the clan of brothers, sisters, and some stray cousins, it had taken Saturday only. Andrew was still in mild shock over someone having that many close relations, never mind that they'd all show up to give this much effort for a complete stranger.

Michael had laughed when he'd gaped at the mass arrival.

"We're a Polish Mexican Catholic household living up to every stereotype those words just conjured up for you. I have seven siblings, with nieces, nephews, and cousins coming out my ears! I might as well put that to good use now and again."

Andrew had still boggled.

He'd been introduced to each in turn, reassured he didn't have to remember them all after one meeting, swapped handshakes and waves. They gave him long, assessing looks before muttering things to Michael. What he'd caught being said was everything to Michael's detriment and Andrew's benefit, merciless sibling ribbing that was foreign to Andrew's experience. Still, he'd managed to fit in with them rather well, trading barbs and banter as they all fell into a steady rhythm of work to help him get the job done.

He'd offered to buy lunch, but the Wiercinski brood had brought a cooler full of goodies. He'd offered to pay for gas, but they'd demurred. He'd been at a loss for what else to offer besides unending gratitude, which they'd all accepted as their due and said was more than enough.

When he'd stood grasping at straws for something else to offer them, Daniel had said outright that they'd been dying of curiosity over Andrew and this let them get a good long look at him to see what he was like, and that would be payment enough.

It'd left Andrew mildly discomfited but not offended. He'd managed to hit the right tone of voice to invite Daniel to look and keep looking, then he'd wiggled his butt and gone to check on the mulch delivery while everyone else catcalled and gave Daniel the business.

Several days before, Michael had managed to get out of Andrew that he'd won the landscaping contract in part because his labor came so cheap. He'd work himself flat-out until it was done, while Chloe and Tanner would be appeased with toddling around digging unnecessary holes, well supplied with PBJs and juice boxes. Michael had also managed to guess his schedule after having discussed the arrival of the huge order of plants and materials with Clay. Over coffee two mornings prior, Michael had mentioned it so nonchalantly Andrew had found himself confirming before he'd quite realized what he was saying.

They'd met for coffee nearly every morning the past weeks, at Michael's insistence that if Andrew was seen with him, he'd get preferential treatment. It was absolutely true—Michael teased and flirted and gossiped with everyone in the shop like a champ—but Andrew had come to discern that the preferential treatment was meant for him, as bestowed by Michael.

He didn't mind that either, which, of course, contrarily bothered him too.

"It looks great," Michael said, breaking the short silence between them. "I like the fieldstone border edging everything."

Andrew smiled. "Me too. Plus they were free, picked out of nearly every field in the county."

One of the major selling points—and points of pride for Andrew—of his landscaping plan had been the use of so many locally sourced materials. The indigenous plants would flourish and grow around the school to make it seem a natural part of the land instead of a huge ugly block that'd been plunked down and left to stick out. Even with everything freshly done, it was already taking on that appearance, the planting beds undulating in organic shapes to soften the building's contours. The sustainable waterway he'd engineered to irrigate everything, using stored rain, trickled delightfully like a hidden creek waiting to be found. Larger boulders had been scattered across the front lawn, softened by ornamental grasses and trees that would bloom in spring and color vividly in fall.

"Even ours?" Michael's brows came down, and he looked almost disappointed.

"Probably, but I'm not for sure. What, did you need those rocks?" Andrew snickered. "I thought farmers picked them out on purpose."

"Oh, it's just that I'd have helped you if I'd known. Which says a lot, because, yes, farmers pick them out on purpose and hate the tedium of doing so besides."

"Hmm." Andrew was noncommittal, because that was safe. He focused on the playground where Chloe and Tanner ran with abandon, absorbed into and delightedly playing with Michael's nieces, nephews, and littler cousins.

"They're fine." Michael dipped his head to catch Andrew's eye. "Yeah?"

"Yeah," Andrew admitted. It was true. They were fine, and having a ball, and that scared him.

Michael nodded and whistled, and Pinto rolled from his nap under a far tree and came bounding over, then pushed between them to pant happily and get petted. Pinto was Michael's enormous dog of uncertain pedigree, silky gray with piercing amber eyes. He had accepted Andrew and the kids like a foregone conclusion. Chloe had warmed to the dog after being unsure at first, but Tanner had taken one look and wrapped Pinto in a little boy bear hug, and they'd been best friends ever since.

Pinto was a stray Michael had found just before leaving Indianapolis. He'd said he knew he was in for trouble because even then Pinto had been a bottomless pit with gigantic paws. He'd also said Pinto was slow to trust, but Michael was tenacious and willing, and now look at them.

Andrew had tried not to read too much into it as some kind of metaphor.

"Go find Tanner—go check on him, buddy, go on!" Michael encouraged, and Pinto's whole body wagged excitedly before he was off to tend the playground, tongue lolling from a wide grin as Tanner greeted him with equal enthusiasm.

"Yup, just fine." Michael nudged Andrew. "'Andrew Lucas' is a good name. Thanks for telling me."

He left it at that, sincere but no fuss or slight taken from Andrew's blunt explanation. Andrew appreciated that, relaxed fully into Michael's company again. They sat in companionable silence, listening to everyone else's chatter and the swarm of kids playing and the passing of cars nearby.

"After all this," Michael lifted a finger and circled it around, "I'm thinking you can buy me dinner or something."

"Oh, so I owe you now, is that it?" Andrew teased. At least, he hoped it sounded teasing. Given their prickly start to, well, everything, he didn't quite trust them to understand each other yet.

Michael took the bait Andrew had intended, and he grunted. "You bet your cute butt you do."

"I owe you and you're calling in my butt as your marker, got it. I suppose you have terms in mind?" Andrew flushed hotly but managed to sound cool and unaffected.

That changed when Michael raked him up and down with an exaggerated leer that turned warm and affectionately interested the more they stared at each other.

Since reuniting after their night together, they'd kept everything friendly, steering clear of innuendo, even if only to tease. Michael always asked about the kids, and Andrew always asked if Michael had rescued any cats from trees, relying on neutral topics like slight acquaintances getting to know one another. The chemistry between them remained, simmering under the surface, but so far they'd been careful not to push.

This exchange pushed—suddenly and with roughly ripe awareness—and Andrew couldn't deny it felt good. He waited for Michael to make a move, wanted it, lips and skin tingling as if to presage a purposeful touch or lingering kiss, but the moment was broken before he could find out.

"Dad! Michael!"

Chloe was tearing across the lawn and Pinto had started barking. It was enough ruckus that the whole assorted family took notice and paused in clearing tools and cleaning debris from the worksite.

As Chloe reached them, Andrew gained his feet, Michael right behind him. He distractedly noted how Chloe included Michael in her call, but his main concern was why she'd come shouting for them at all and what had caused her to look annoyed and pensive at once.

"Right here, Pumpkin." Andrew crouched and kneaded her shoulders. "What's up?"

Chloe frowned, so reminiscent of Andrew's sister that it bent his heart. She poked a thumb behind her toward the playground.

"He's here. He said it's his turn with Tanner until Monday." Chloe's frown deepened. "But he's not supposed to just show up and find us like this. He's supposed to call first." She sounded reproving, more like Tanner's mother than sister.

She put a certain emphasis on "he," one that told Andrew it had to be Jayce, Tanner's father. Andrew sighed and tucked Chloe next to him so they could walk to the playground. Michael fell naturally in step with them. Andrew found he didn't mind that.

As they approached, Andrew felt his mask revert, felt how it shifted into place so he could hide his emotions and observe without giving himself away. He caught Michael's keen glance, indicating he'd noticed the change and Andrew's withdrawal. That wasn't a usual occurrence, but more because he so rarely let his guard down. Andrew quirked a smile and nodded, and before it became a worry, Michael nodded back.

Jayce was there waiting for them, trying to coax Tanner from the jungle gym, but obviously nervous about Pinto.

Andrew plucked Tanner from the monkey bars, trying to ignore how Tanner burrowed to hide against his chest, saying quietly that he wasn't ready to go.

"We're almost done now anyway, bud," Andrew soothed. "You know you'll have a good time with your father and Gran and Gramps. We'll all be here Monday when you're home for dinner."

"Even Pinto?" Tanner pushed away to gaze at Andrew, pale eyes wide and trusting, with a hint of belligerence.

"Ah, well." Andrew never promised what he couldn't deliver, and his hesitation had Tanner's mouth setting mutinously.

"Of course, even Pinto." Michael tickled Tanner's side. He was matter of fact about it and waited for the storm to clear from Tanner's expression.

He turned to Jayce, and his tone of voice changed completely. "Hello again, Mr. Reed. I'd expected to see you in court earlier this week. I guess this means you decided to just pay the fine on that ticket, then."

Michael sounded like a cop, all business, and held Jayce's eyes until Jayce let out a breath and squirmed.

"Something like that," Jayce mumbled and scratched at the back of his neck.

Jayce wasn't a bad guy, but he had no backbone or ambition. It's what Andrew's sister, Kenzie, had liked about him—a marked contrast from Chloe's father—and for a time she'd been happy to have someone to boss around. It hadn't lasted long; just enough for her to get pregnant, Jayce to freak out, and his parents to put their foot down that they wouldn't be marrying nor would their grandson be taken from their lives.

"Good, good. So long as you keep out of further trouble, things should turn out just fine for you," Michael said crisply, and then he dismissed Jayce, leaned in, and said something soft and apparently hilarious to Tanner. "See you soon, Bean."

"Yeah, Bean," Andrew echoed the nickname Michael had given Tanner, something to do with being a matched pair to Pinto. He planted a huge, wet kiss on Tanner's cheek and blew it into a raspberry so Tanner would laugh, then he got Tanner standing and handed over. They didn't have to exchange anything. Tanner had a room at his grandparent's—where Jayce lived—with more than was needed to keep a little boy happy.

Jayce continued to squirm under Michael's watchful eye, but he made nice, waiting for Tanner to say good-bye to Chloe and Pinto, then Michael and Andrew a final time. Andrew stood and watched Tanner trot away, and it gave him a pang, but no apprehension. Jayce wasn't a model adult or anything, but he'd never mistreated Tanner, and his folks went a long way to making sure Tanner was well cared for.

It wasn't like Andrew hadn't known this was coming. Although he'd have preferred Jayce to meet at the time they'd set, in the parking lot, instead of an hour early, interrupting Tanner's day, he had to concede he was grateful Jayce showed up so close to their agreed-on plans. Usually, it was Mrs. Reed who came for Tanner, because she was who remembered, and also who made herself responsible while allowing Jayce to skirt along.

"You okay?"

Michael pulled Andrew from his reverie. He turned to find Chloe hanging off Michael, ready for a piggyback ride, and Pinto dancing between them, ready to run.

"I'm okay." Andrew smiled as they walked toward their cars, and he took in a last sweeping look at the work they'd done today. "It really does look good—thank you, all of you."

"It wasn't a problem."

"Maybe not, but I'd never be able to muster an army of willing hands just from a Facebook status update. Or from sheer curiosity. And it saved me a week's worth of doing this on my own, so pass along my thanks, would you?"

Michael hipped into Andrew. "Come over for dinner at the farm and you can tell them yourself."

"I thought it was me who owed you dinner."

"Oh, you do. But I'm good for both." Michael grinned and tugged on Chloe's ratty braid that hung down over his shoulder. "Whaddya say, Squash? Want to come over for a Fiesta-Q?"

Chloe's face puckered. She loved being called Squash, Michael's take on Andrew always calling her pumpkin. "What's a Fiesta-Q?"

"It's what we called the ginormous celebration dinners my folks put on when we were growing up. It stuck."

"Celebrate what? Are they good?" Chloe wasn't a picky eater, but she was most definitely choosy about who she let close to her.

Andrew had done his best to downplay it, but her taking to Michael as she had, and so readily, said a lot in Michael's favor. He added it to the mental tally he had going of reasons why he hadn't outright pushed Michael from their lives yet.

"Good? They're the best!" Michael enthused, then he swung Chloe around as they approached Andrew's truck. He popped her into the back bench, where she situated herself in the booster seat while he buckled her in. Then Michael kissed her, quick and light and natural as anything. "And oh, July Fourth, or Labor Day, or Wednesday because Wednesday is midweek and that means the weekend will be here soon."

"Then y-e-s," Chloe said emphatically, and kissed Michael back.

Andrew waited for Michael to come back around the truck to his side, waved and called passing good-byes and thanks to the departing familial legion. When Michael was near enough to touch, he reached out, and greatly daring, fiddled the fraying belt loop on Michael's jeans.

"You know, I think you almost made Jayce pee himself there with your little power play."

Michael hummed. "No, no. I mean, not quite. I was simply—"

"I liked it," Andrew cut Michael off and tilted his head so he could see Michael's eyes full-on. He grinned mischievously. Michael's eyes danced in answer.

"Okay then, you got me. Total power play, total show of grr-cop-boyfriend dominance." Michael blanched, then he stammered. "Uh, of a sort. You know, of the sort a grr-cop boyfriend would make in that situation."

Andrew surprised them both by letting it be. He climbed into his truck, and before he pulled the door shut, Michael leaned in and kissed him, just as light and naturally as he had Chloe.

"Oh." Andrew blinked, then Michael closed the door and patted the window frame.

"See you soon." Michael said it differently than he had to Tanner, more like an order mixed with a promise than a question.

Andrew only nodded and let that be too.

CHAPTER 7

AFTER that Saturday, and Michael's daring overposturing with Jayce, then upping the ante with his casual kiss, things had developed from accidental run-ins and shared coffee to actual dates (that weren't called dates) and a lot of making out between playing with the kids.

They were on not-date number several, tucked into the back of a movie theater at a nearly empty matinee screening of an action-adventure movie Michael had actually been excited to see. But as soon as the lights dimmed for the previews, he forgot to pay attention to anything but Andrew. He'd propped his arm on the rest with Andrew's to enjoy the heat of electricity that always sparked whenever they made contact. Before long, their hands were busy, fingers exploring knuckles and tendon lines, light and enticing scrapes of their nails.

Michael shifted enough so they could start to play footsie, too, and chased that with light kisses up Andrew's neck. He grinned when Andrew leaned toward him and tilted to whisper something full of ridiculous innuendo when their eyes met in the flickering pale green of whatever was on the screen. After a moment, Andrew abruptly pulled away and got up, hurrying out of the theater.

Michael crawled to a stand and gave chase, but had to trot to the parking lot to catch up with Andrew's quick retreat.

"Hey! Is everything okay? Did your phone go off or something?" Michael snagged Andrew's arm, suddenly worried that one of the kids was hurt.

"No, I just shouldn't be here. I should go get them and not be doing this." Andrew shifted weight to separate from Michael. "I'm sorry, I wasted your time. But you can still catch the movie, I bet."

Michael rolled his eyes. "Screw the movie." He closed the gap between them again, insistent without being creepy or controlling. "And, you know, I'm sure the kids are great. Besides, you know how it is. Two more mouths to feed among the usual swarm at the farm isn't going to make a difference."

Chloe and Tanner spent a lot of time at the farm. They liked it there, and Michael was thrilled to have them—not simply because having them meant Andrew was around too. The kids were there now, not minding at all it was for babysitting purposes so he and Andrew could have their not-date.

He smiled, but Andrew's eyes shuttered and focused somewhere middistance past Michael's shoulder.

"We don't need charity. They don't, and I don't either."

Michael licked his lips and tried to think through what would be best to say. He always said too much and gave way too much away no matter what, but among the eggshells he walked around Andrew, he'd discovered surprise landmines. He was trying to get better at not tripping one with every conversation. It didn't help that they hadn't said or really learned that much about each other. They'd drifted into being constant company, drawn by the undeniable attraction between them and Michael's stubborn tenacity not to let Andrew slip away.

"Forget that," he said lightly. "You know the score on that count, and none of us consider having people to lunch charity, certainly not you or Squash and Bean. Okay? It's fine that you're here and that they're there."

It was into summer now, with plenty to do on the farm to keep them occupied and content. Chicks were becoming nuisance chickens, there were tomatoes and strawberries and masses of zucchini to pick, old tractors to pretend ride, and the trough they used as a swimming pool to cool down in. Summer was magical, hot and dusty and full of things like praying mantis in the corn cribs to discover that Michael had loved growing up—he couldn't think it was any different for Chloe and Tanner. Summer also meant Andrew's work had slowed from spring plantings to drawing up bids and plans for fall, leaving more time for them to steal together like today.

Andrew nodded slowly and Michael was about to give himself a positive tally mark when Andrew looked back at him, eyes gone cold instead of remote.

"Okay then. How about we really take advantage of it, go to my house, and have sex."

Michael blinked, and for a perilous second the want he had for Andrew and the heat that shot like quicksilver through him almost had him agreeing. Instead, he instinctively took a step back. The flare of heat iced over. It disturbed him the way Andrew had suggested that, hardly an intimate invitation and not even a question, but rather thrust in his face like a thirty-foot-thick barrier.

"Yeah, you know, as much as I'm amazed to be saying this, no." Michael swallowed and imagined the strewn carnage around them in some kind of cartoonish relief drawing from that mine hit squarely on center. "If you need to go get the kids, we'll go get them. Or we can take a hike in Hoosier National Forest. But sex at your place—no."

Saying "sex at your place" warped more ripples of heat through Michael's gut, but he knew it would happen for the wrong reasons. The fleeting satiety that would allow Andrew to push him farther away was the last thing either of them needed.

"Great. So I'm not even good for that." Andrew sucked his teeth, then laughed flatly. "I get it."

Andrew spun away on a heel. Michael made a low exploding noise in his cheeks and imagined another pothole and debris of ruin raining down around them. He let out a long, long sigh, and once again chased after Andrew's abrupt exit.

"You know," he said once he'd caught up and basically had to jog alongside, "I have issues big enough they could bellhop my baggage. We all do. But don't do this. Please. For one thing, the car is the other way and it's a half day's walk to the farm, which is where you left your truck and your kids. For another, not wanting sex from you right now isn't rejection. It's like, completely the opposite of rejection."

Andrew scoffed but slowed his pace.

Michael figured he might as well blunder bravely on.

"Believe me, wow, do I want to do every dirty thing together I've ever seen in porn that I thought was impossible unless you were a yogi master, but that's not what's important to me right now. I don't measure this"—he gestured to himself, then waved at Andrew, and back again—"between us, by sex. I won't let you use it against me. Not my saying no, or if I said yes and you thought that proved something or meant you could freeze me out. I don't measure your worth or whatever's happening with us by that. And, I might as well add since I've got my no-filter babbling going, I didn't even think in terms of what you could do for me in the sack that first night."

Andrew stopped. Michael stopped.

"I know they're okay, at the farm, and that's what bothers me. They're okay for now." Andrew shook his head tersely. "But they're already getting attached, and I don't know if that's wise. To your family, all those cousins and nieces and nephews, your big stupid slobbery—"

"Hey," Michael interrupted with a lopsided grin. "I don't slobber."

Andrew clenched his fists, clearly not ready for teasing. "They're all that really matters to me. They're what's important. I don't want them to get hurt if I'm making a mistake."

That hurt Michael. It cut through him swift and sharp, the idea of not being important and maybe being a mistake, but he didn't show it. He forced his grin to stay in place, and when his tentative reach for Andrew wasn't denied, he tightened his hands around Andrew's upper arms.

"I can absolutely promise you that they'll always be welcome at the farm. By everyone. Nothing can happen that will take that away." He massaged Andrew's arms gently and felt Andrew's tightly controlled, almost imperceptible, tremors.

The mall parking lot was no place for this conversation, but Michael was sure he couldn't let it end there. He was also sure they'd be trapped in this stop-start tension forever if he didn't get them talking. The punishing midday sun glittered off the pavement and cars, so Michael guided them to stand under the trees at the edge of the lot.

"We're generous to a fault. I learned that early following my parents' example and kept it up of my own volition. Letting people in— being generous and sharing—it can be risky and plenty of the wrong people line up to take, same as with the good. It's gotten my heart stomped more than a few times. Never truly broken, but definitely stomped." Michael shrugged equanimously. "Eventually, what I learned wasn't that I shouldn't be generous or so headlong about what I throw myself into, but to be aware of who I'm offering it to. We'll give lunch, dinner, even dessert, to just about anyone. But not everyone is asked to stay."

Andrew absorbed that and was quiet for a while, then leaned against a tree trunk so he could look at Michael.

"I like being a landscape architect, but it's not quite a passion. I chose that because it was practical, and drawing and the neglected neighborhood park at one of my foster homes were my favorite things as a kid. I chose a university in Chicago to get away from everything, including having tried so hard to keep Kenzie from becoming our mother, only to watch her get pregnant at fifteen and be the only one around when Chloe was born. I left them behind—told myself I'd done all I could—started school and just kept plowing ahead into a career." His mouth pulled wryly. "Being on my own and free from constantly worrying about Kenzie was a relief, and I sealed myself off from feeling guilty about that. I had a lot of practice doing that, so it wasn't difficult."

That made Michael ache for Andrew. For the little boy he imagined learning to hide early—in parks and in doodling and in shutting down—from an uncaring mother and unreliable situations. For the man who, by default, hid almost everything now, braced for disappointment and shielded not only from loss, but warmth and spontaneity and even love.

"Most guys I met wanted one thing—well, a few things, but you know. But to me, stability and normalcy were so exotic, all I wanted was a committed relationship and a gourmet coffee maker. I got that in Neil—my first real relationship, older than me by a lot and glad to show me off, glad to let me slot into his life without really disrupting anything for either of us. Honestly, I think I liked Neil's upscale apartment and the certainty he wasn't going anywhere more than I ever did him." Andrew huffed shortly. "I've never done anything headlong or risky."

Michael shook his head. "Maybe we have different definitions, because I'd say dropping everything and giving up something so hard-won as your life in Chicago to take on two kids as your own is both headlong and risky." He trailed a finger up Andrew's arm, encouraged enough when Andrew righted to sway closer to him to add, "And amazing."

"Or making up for responsibilities I never should have abandoned in the first place. I'd wanted to believe after Kenzie and Jayce got pregnant that her being older, and him having reliable parents, meant she'd be okay. She already resented the hell out of me for trying to be a father and a big brother, was glad to have me quit meddling. Said I'd failed at both anyway."

"Whew." Michael let out a long breath, and he couldn't keep from reaching out and dragging Andrew into a tight hug. It helped him understand a lot more about Andrew, made him hurt even more. "You were just a kid yourself. You deserved a chance at your own life."

Andrew made a low noise, one that didn't negate or agree with Michael.

"I suppose this Neil is who freaked out when you decided to take custody of the kids and just like that let you go?"

"Leaving him wasn't a wrench. It didn't even really give me pause." Andrew's tone was brittle, laced with self-derision, and his arms remained stiff at his sides. "I didn't know if I'd do any better than with Kenzie, but I'd be damned if I was going to let them fall through the cracks like we had."

Michael closed his eyes, and for the first time since finding Andrew again, he had a pang of fear that they wouldn't be able to figure this out. He was almost sorry he'd forced the conversation.

But he didn't let on. Instead he kissed Andrew's temple and said, "Yet here you are, as loving and devoted a father as I've seen. In my life and line of work, trust me to know. Definitely amazing."

Andrew pulled from his embrace, and Michael steeled himself but was surprised at his softened expression and searching gaze.

"Since your mom will feed just about anyone, I'm assuming that means us, even if unexpected. I could use some lunch. I'm willing to do dishes."

It took Michael more than a minute to process that, then catch on, then half-nod in reply. Andrew smiled, and Michael pictured the broken cartoon world around them healing over and sprouting into flowers and butterflies and happy bluebirds. He gave himself three positive points, because managing to turn that potentially devastating scene into such a smile deserved at least double that.

"If you offer to do dishes, she'll let you start your lunch with pie."

Andrew's smile did that adorable side-quirk thing that made Michael crazy. He lifted gentle fingers to Michael's neck and pressed them there. Michael's pulse point jumped erratically, then settled again, and Andrew's smile widened. They had started sweating despite the shade, and Michael was parched. He thought nothing sounded better than being at the farm, where it would be several degrees cooler and they could indulge in unending fresh lemonade and being pampered by his mom. They could both use more than a little of each.

"I'm sorry," Andrew whispered, then he nodded. "Thank you."

"Hey man, the pie is worth it, so no problem. Just don't go sharing that tip with anyone though, okay? I don't want word getting out." Michael snagged Andrew's wrist and propelled them back toward his car.

Andrew didn't correct what the thanks had been for, and Michael was glad to give Andrew some breathing space. He was gladder still they both knew what Andrew meant and that Michael was accepting of everything Andrew was willing to give. The encroaching fear that they couldn't find their way lifted, became merely a passing shadow as they moved toward brighter light, and Michael grinned.

He cranked the engine and rolled the windows down, letting the stifling heat be cleared away by sweet, corn-scented wind, and took them home.

CHAPTER 8

ANDREW followed Michael out to stand on the small front porch of Andrew's house, leaving the door open so he could hear if the kids needed anything. Summer was in full swing, and the air was thick and humid, sticky after being in the air conditioning. The street was quiet except for the whirr of cicadas.

"Thanks for the ice cream. I'd complain that you're spoiling them horribly, but since I'm reaping the benefits, that'd be counterproductive." Andrew smiled. "It was a good night."

"It has been. And, my pleasure." Michael leaned in and gave Andrew a quick kiss, looping an arm around Andrew's waist, and stepped in close again for a deeper kiss.

Andrew had, with momentary reluctance and lingering doubt, invited Michael for dinner after his shift ended. Chloe and Tanner had been so excited about the evening, it had done a lot to calm his nerves. He'd let them set the table, and they always helped him cook. The house had been filled with that indefinable quality of anticipation and contentment as they'd made ready. Andrew worked to provide them with stability and happiness, but this was something else altogether and felt different—was different.

He felt it too.

They'd seen a lot of one another in the past few months, and these months had been nice, steadily building to nicer. Nothing had pointed to this overture from Andrew's side, though. He'd started to admit he'd been lonely, for friendship as much as anything, and further admitted Michael was the best cure for that.

Michael had readily accepted without making it seem like a huge milestone had just been hurdled. He'd arrived with flowers and a bottle of wine and promises to take them to the Dairy Dream if they ate all their vegetables without complaint. Once seated, he had complimented the centerpiece of Chloe's pink princess jewelry spilling from Tanner's toy construction vehicles with a perfect enthusiastic sincerity kids need to hear and devoid of adult condescension.

When it had been time to decide if they'd earned ice cream, Michael and the kids had humored Andrew, allowing him to act as if he had the final (or any) say on the matter. Michael had volunteered to drive—as he was blocking Andrew's truck anyway—and had casually explained the booster for Chloe and car seat for Tanner already buckled in as outgrown castoffs rescued from moldering in various family garages.

Michael had said it was no big deal; it just made sense and things easier. Besides, what if one day he had to help get the kids around if Andrew needed something? He'd grinned and turned on the radio, sung loudly and offkey maybe a decibel below Chloe and Tanner's efforts, then piled them out at the ice cream stand to debate the merits of all the treats on offer, Chloe leaning on Michael's leg and Tanner held comfortably in his arms.

Chloe had known before they'd arrived she was getting a cookie ice cream sandwich. Tanner had some sherbet confection in the shape of a cartoon character. Michael had gorged on an extra large gooey chocolate-and-cherry blended monstrosity, while Andrew had opted for his favorite, a plain vanilla cone.

The four of them had squeezed onto one of the poured concrete benches and watched the nearby little league game. Michael had elbowed him and stolen a lick of his soft serve, made a terrible joke about things sort of that shape and him being vanilla which didn't make sense, but despite rolling his eyes Andrew had laughed anyway. Back in the car, Michael had explained to Chloe about moon phases after they'd caught sight of it in the distance, heavy on the horizon and colored like an apricot. Once home, Michael had seamlessly taken part in their nightly rituals. They'd had bath time and story time and goodnight time.

Later, Andrew and Michael had made out on the couch under the guise of watching some baseball.

Such things might be everyday to Michael, but each was a very big deal to Andrew. His entire life experience had proven and reinforced, time and again, that no one went out of his or her way for him. He'd learned painful lessons to be suspicious of anyone's motives if they did, or braced himself to have any offer negated, because nothing good lasts. He marveled over Michael having so fluidly and amiably accepted Andrew as a package deal. Not kids-in-the-way to be shunted aside, and never resented, simply accepted as part of what being with Andrew meant.

Andrew's natural, hard-won defenses were disarmed by it. He was motivated to allow whatever was happening between them to continue. He was further mollified by them maintaining important boundaries, neither of them pushing too far or too hard, but enjoying an affectionate closeness without getting closed in.

He and the kids here in their own home, safe and secure, Michael a welcome visitor. They were welcomed in turn into Michael's orbit. Connections and friends for Chloe and Tanner, the surprisingly gratifying common ground he and Michael's father had quickly established discussing planting and parenting woes. It was a good place to be, Andrew decided, with a pleasant rhythm and more than a few benefits. It was a place he thought he could stay in for a long time, without bringing trouble or heartache to any of them.

Andrew shivered when Michael's hand slipped into his loose-fitting cutoffs and palmed his ass. He shut his eyes, then sucked in a sharp breath and twisted from their kiss. Michael made a short, impatient noise and pursued his retreat.

"Hey, no." Andrew kept evading Michael's mouth.

Michael grunted. "Light's not even on—no one will see me ravishing you."

"Such a gentleman." Andrew laughed. "But I don't know, some of my neighbors might appreciate getting an eyeful of this action."

"And here you said you weren't neighborly with anyone," Michael teased. He started to nibble along Andrew's jaw, but he added thoughtfully, "Just so long as no one would mind."

"I'm not—and I doubt it, but who knows. Who cares. People would probably be more shocked by me having company like a regular person might than by seeing us doing this." Andrew was a neighbor in the same way he was out; he was private and tended to his own business, as with all things in his life.

Until Michael, he'd had no reason to declare being out regardless, as there'd been no one but the kids in his life. But he'd made it clear to the Reeds who he was, because where the kids were concerned, being "discovered" and having that used against him trumped his desire for privacy. He'd always assumed that, from there, word had just gotten around, as happened in small towns. When he'd explained that to

Michael after they'd started not-quite dating, Michael had laughed and said hiding had never been an option for him, considering his family knew and right there was a large portion of Starling's population.

"I feel like an old man saying this but, it's late."

"But it's summer. Not even a school night or anything," Michael wheedled.

Andrew straightened and said steadily, "Yeah, and those brats won't get up any later than their usual o-dark-thirty just because it's summer and I'm dragging."

Michael huffed but nodded, kissed him fast and light, then pulled back. He trailed his fingertips up Andrew's sides then down Andrew's arms, laced their hands together.

"Come over for dinner tomorrow. We can have a sleepover. The kids can stay at the house and you can come stay with me." Michael smiled, but the dim light revealed how widely he'd opened his eyes to gauge Andrew's reaction and the licking of his lips was a nervous tell.

They'd kept each other well satisfied in the intervening months, stealing quickies at his office or Michael's loft between work and the kids. When that wasn't feasible, they had long, almost tortuous necking sessions they couldn't allow to inflame too far. Whenever they were together, Michael was in his space, touching him in some way. Andrew had experienced nearly no physical contact growing up, no one to cuddle or hug or soothe him; his relationship with Neil, in the end, hadn't been much different. He'd learned that was normal, learned to avoid being touched, thought he didn't enjoy it.

With Michael his whole view upended. He'd discovered he more than enjoyed being sought out to touch and be touched. He craved it, thrived on it, wanted more.

Andrew had a passing, fervent desire to drag Michael back inside, not just to the couch but to his bed, to wake up there with him and do this all over again tomorrow. Forget waiting, forget hiding behind the kids having somewhere else to stay. It would be another thing entirely from what they'd done to this point, an escalation on every front, and the idea of doing so scared and thrilled him.

But he viciously compartmentalized and locked that thought away. Because he wanted to keep things working, and too many complications or inroads into their life chanced upsetting the good balance they'd found.

The invitation and Michael's desire tugged sharply, urgently, at the locks and his barriers. He tightened his hands involuntarily but was already shaking his head.

"It's cool," Michael said quietly in immediate retreat. "You can still come for dinner, though?"

"We'll see." Andrew smiled and disentangled a hand, patted Michael's chest. The gesture should have been soft, intimate, but instead effectively set Michael apart from him. "I mean, probably, but I want to see how our day goes before I agree."

The locked-away part of Andrew was screaming and hammering at the boundaries, making him feel hollow, calling him a fool. The cold truth was that he wasn't a fool, and he couldn't get complacent about this.

"I'll call," Andrew said into their silence, and the cicadas' drone seemed to surge in volume.

"Okay." Michael shifted weight and stepped off the porch. His expression darkened, as if he was going to argue or at least needle Andrew about withdrawing, but that cleared and he accepted Andrew's answer. "Thanks for dinner—it was a good night."

Andrew waved as Michael left. He stood and watched the taillights of Michael's car as they turned a corner and disappeared behind a house, until the afterimage of dancing spots dissipated. He realized that suddenly he felt lonely again, then angrily dismissed the notion. He went inside and firmly shut the door.

CHAPTER 9

PINTO'S low warning bark and his nails scrabbling down the stairs followed by a violent thunderclap startled Michael awake. Storms had been predicted for the night, as they always came to herald one season's change to the next. Michael thrilled to a good storm, and he'd fallen asleep watching lightning approach, thinking about Andrew and the stasis they seemed to be lodged within.

He groped to get his phone as he stumbled out of bed. Pinto hadn't shown signs of weather anxiety before, and there was an indefinable energy compelling him to check on things instead of roll over and go back to sleep. He rubbed his eyes and flicked his phone display on. It wasn't quite three o'clock, but there were no messages or texts.

When he'd converted the loft into an apartment, his family had added a staircase at the back so he didn't have to contend with a rickety straight ladder. It exited neatly out a door cut into the barn.

"Pinto? Buddy?" Michael peered through the darkness into the stairwell but couldn't make anything out. The storm and early hour prevented even ambient light from brightening the window.

He had stumbled halfway down the stairs when lightning flashed and a figure emerged from the gloom.

"Holy shit!" Michael fell backward, landing with a sudden bump, then sat on a stair. He shot his breath and patted his chest. "God, Andrew. You scared me."

It didn't begin to occur to him to mind Andrew's sudden arrival, despite the hour and tearing him from sleep. It did, however, alarm him, and he raced to think what might have happened to cause it. The last he'd seen Andrew was a whole day and a half ago, another pleasant evening that ended with him cautiously testing the boundaries before listening to and agreeing with the reasons Andrew gave why he shouldn't stay. It was a familiar pattern, one that held them stuck fast. It frustrated Michael but, otherwise, everything had been okay.

"Pinto's out. I'm sorry, I know it's really late. Or really early. And I woke you up and I'm sorry."

Michael stood, climbed back up the stairs to the sitting area, and turned on a lamp. The glass shade's soft amber glow cast into the dark loft like a harsh floodlight.

They squinted and blinked at each other. Andrew's face was pinched and he looked miserable, high-strung, and was shaking bodily with the minute tremors Michael had learned meant he was truly upset or agitated about something.

"Pinto will be fine. After he snuffles around, he'll go in the house to snooze in front of the wood stove." Michael was direct. "What about you? What's going on?"

"The kids are there too. On the daybed in the kitchen. I dropped them off first because it seemed the best place for them." Andrew's lips flattened. "They went right back to sleep, so I don't think they'll be a nuisance, but—"

"But it's a farm. Pops is probably already up to do the barn work, and Mom gets up with him to load wood, then get going on breakfast." Michael rolled his hands dismissively. "It wouldn't matter anyway. Middle of the day, middle of the night, no one minds you being here."

Andrew nodded distractedly. His pensive expression didn't change, nor did he react to the splitting crack of thunder that rattled the barn. Michael was about to prompt him over what was wrong when Andrew met his worried gaze.

"I tried to wait until later, but I just couldn't anymore, not all the way until lunch. I thought I could hold out, discuss this with you then, tried to sleep but that didn't work either. I would have been able to, before—sleep and wait—but not anymore."

They had planned for Michael to bring a late lunch to Andrew's office during his shift. He nodded encouragingly, glad Andrew would seek him out, but still didn't understand why.

Andrew's shaking became more marked and his shoulders rose. "Jayce is suing for custody of Tanner. The papers arrived in yesterday's mail. Apparently, his father is ready to retire and they're moving to Florida and want to take Tanner with them." He jerked his head tersely as if to negate even the possibility. "Of course I immediately thought, no way, no way will they take him from me. But what if it gets nasty and drawn out?

Am I doing more harm than good digging my heels in? What if they win? Do I pack Chloe up and move to Florida too? I just—I don't know."

"I bet I have family in Florida, if it comes to it." Michael didn't like at all how pale Andrew had gone. He kept his tone light, tried to draw Andrew back out from pitching toward that obsessive loop of thoughts. "It wouldn't be ideal, but I'm almost willing to bet we could drum up a third cousin, have a couch or even a spare room to sleep in while you get settled. I honestly can't believe they'll be granted custody, but we'll figure out and help you deal with whatever does happen."

"That I do know." Andrew smiled tremulously and reached for Michael. Some of his color had returned. He cleared his throat. "I will need help to get through this, and you're who I can count on to ask for it without having to leverage anything. That right there was a big deal to acknowledge, and could have kept until at least breakfast. But I couldn't wait, not another minute. Because I realized, more than needing help, is that I need you. So much. Just, you."

Michael recognized, and greatly appreciated, the enormity of that admission.

"I'm here," he answered, voice tight with emotion and equal need.

A nerve jumped at Andrew's jaw and Michael's heart leapt, then they moved, surged into one another's arms and toward the bed.

Andrew's clothes were rain-wet and cold. Michael grunted an apology for not having attended to that. Andrew shushed and kissed him, then hastily stripped the clinging layers away, shoved at Michael to do the same. He did, loose pajama pants and his worn tee sliding off with ease, then he nudged and shoved Andrew down onto the bed, landing on top of him.

The air rushed from them and Michael lifted, but Andrew protested and wrapped both legs around his, held him tightly in place. Michael relented, nipped and kissed the straining tendon in Andrew's neck. He reveled in the exquisite sensations of them so close like this, heating, then hardening, together. The slick, heavy feel of Andrew's cock trapped alongside his, the warm taut expanse of Andrew's skin, damp with rain and sweat, the good trembling that had overtaken Andrew's earlier tension.

He pushed up enough to brace on his forearms so they could kiss and watch each other. The dim lamp and intermittent lightning revealed Andrew to him in shifting shadows and relief. Michael couldn't think of anything more beautiful. That might have shown in his face, in the way he stared at Andrew, because Andrew smiled and arched into him, tangled long fingers in his hair to urge their pace faster.

"I'm here," he said, harsh with breath and emotion. He rutted without cease, then stuttered roughly and lost rhythm when he felt Andrew's surrendering orgasm.

Michael went wide-eyed, levered up onto his palms, chased the almost-there coiling of his own orgasm with desperate, determined intent. He moaned when Andrew fingered the cleft of his ass then teased further in, anchored into his knees so he could deepen the thrust of his hips. Andrew murmured encouragements, circled a fingertip over his hole, and Michael shuddered forcibly, then came.

He lodged back tucked into Andrew's neck, kissed and sucked and tasted there, listened to the rain and the slowing of Andrew's pulse. Andrew's hands skimmed the knobs of his spine, the twitching muscles in his back, the overheated uselessness of his arms. It wasn't the most they'd done in bed, but Michael thought it by far the best.

Andrew finally shifted from under him and sighed, drew Michael to spoon around him with a soft kiss and a smile. Michael fit them so every curve and angle met, and they watched the thunderstorm's vivid antics from the hayloft doors Michael had turned into an enormous window.

"Why don't you get some sleep? In a couple hours, we can check on the kids, have some breakfast, figure this out."

"At least I'll be able to, now," Andrew said, slurred with lassitude and fatigue. He laced his hand to entwine with Michael's on the bed in front of him, took in a long breath, and held it. "I'm glad I need you," he whispered, so quietly it was almost lost in the pattering rain, then he half-shrugged as if to excuse having said it.

Michael knew the quiet uncertainty wasn't about him, knew what it meant and cost Andrew to allow that sentiment, never mind having said it. From anyone else, that would have been weird. He tamped down the impulse to shout and break from the bed to run around like a fool, telling everyone who would listen that this had happened—that it was real and it was his. He decided it was more than enough that Andrew had to feel the rapid, strong beat of his heart after Andrew's words had brought it to a standstill.

He kissed Andrew's shoulder, leaned in, and smiled. "I'm glad to be here." He wrapped them in blankets and held on, was right there, so Andrew could sleep.

CHAPTER 10

ANDREW stepped from the shower and smiled when Michael wrapped him up in a towel. It wasn't quite five and the autumn dawn was still a few hours away, but he was surprisingly refreshed and altogether calm, the anxiety and scattershot fears from last night turned into readiness to face what had to be done about Tanner.

"I've never minded having a stand-up shower only I fit in before." Michael buffed and scrubbed at Andrew, framed Andrew's face with the towel, and grinned.

On a different morning, Andrew might have pointed out that at least it kept them on task, but they both were filled with an urgency for getting started dealing with the situation. They kissed briefly, then Andrew got dressed, damp skin sticking to the clothes Michael had set out for him to borrow. Michael was dressed already, watched him in a mix of interest and companionable intimacy, then caught his wrist to pull him into a tight embrace.

"You look good in my tee and flannel and inch-too-short jeans." Michael breathed against Andrew's neck. "You ready? I'm ready."

Andrew nodded, and they moved in smooth tandem, Andrew toeing into his shoes as they gained the stairs and headed to the farmhouse. The stars were still bright, the air brisk and the wind sharp, but Andrew welcomed the bracing shift. It helped wake him the rest of the way, shook the last of the warm sleepiness from what he and Michael had shared not too long ago, without negating any of its import.

Light from the kitchen windows spilled onto the shadowed lawn and wood smoke was a heavy scent. Michael pushed the back door open and showed Andrew in, and everything continued to feel right and familiar and reassuring.

Tanner had emptied the toy box of nearly everything and was currently running around the kitchen being chased by Pinto, babbling about this and that at Rita who was busy cooking breakfast. He caught sight of Michael and Andrew and beamed, babbling now delighted and excitedly telling them about the morning since Andrew had left them here: napping on the daybed in the corner of the kitchen near the wood stove, having Pops wake them and trudge to do the barn work, and what a big boy and a big help he'd been.

Andrew swept Tanner into a hug. "That's my good little man," he said. He tried not to act any differently, but already holding and reacting to Tanner felt different. More loaded, more important.

"Morning." Michael kissed Tanner's cheek and waved at his mom.

Pinto pushed between their legs, and they all said their good mornings and made a fuss over the dog. Tanner squirmed to get down and back to playing again. The television was on in the adjoining room, and Chloe was tucked into Pops on the big couch, both of them snoozing through the early morning news.

"Two or four?" Rita stood poised at the toaster oven, bag of bread in one hand.

"Four," Michael said. "For me, at least." He winked at Andrew and added lowly, "Worked up an appetite."

Andrew scoffed and got them each a mug of coffee. "Four for me too, please."

Rita sent a smug look at Michael and tutted pleasingly at Andrew. She liked his innate good manners. He grinned and drowned Michael's coffee in sugar and milk, then dropped onto the bench seat opposite the chair Michael had slid artlessly into. As he settled in, the glint of headlights swept through the yard. The arriving car's engine cut, and a door slammed dully.

"Make that an even dozen, Mom." Aaron popped into the kitchen from the side door and planted a kiss on her head. He slung his briefcase on the table and got a cup of coffee too, looking bleary-eyed but unruffled.

"Hey, bro. Thanks for coming." Michael pushed the plate of already-cooked bacon closer to Aaron but looked at Andrew. "I called while you were in the shower. Figured some legal guidance couldn't hurt—and Aaron gets away with not pitching in around here far too often, so…." He snagged two pieces of bacon and munched them down.

"It's not even six," Andrew said almost as an aside to Michael. He glanced at Aaron, blushed at the myriad implications rife in the simple statement about his shower, but no one had taken offense or particular notice.

Aaron yawned and got a notepad and pen out. "I needed breakfast anyway. Plus, if it makes you feel any better, I'm on the clock and you're being billed soon as it's eaten."

"You know, that actually does." Andrew shook his head and wrapped his coffee cup in both hands.

They left it at that until after a breakfast of messy eggs and potatoes with the last of the garden tomatoes, together managing to drain the huge urn of coffee. Andrew started to stand to tackle the dishes, but Rita pushed him back down and distracted him with a plate of sticky buns.

"All right, let's get some basics." Aaron adjusted his glasses and poised to take notes. "You can afford Tanner's care and all attendant expenses currently, right? And you're willing and able to keep both siblings together, rather than have them split apart?"

"Yeah, absolutely." Andrew tried not to bristle and stifled his defensive instincts.

Michael caught his eye and also his feet under the table and smiled reassuringly. Andrew smiled back and didn't stop his impulse to reach over and squeeze Michael's hand.

"If it makes a difference, I actually own the house in the clear." Andrew shrugged. "I liquidated a lot when I had to drop everything and move here from Chicago, and buying was the most expedient solution as I took over caring for the kids. I wasn't particular, just bought what was decent and available. A share of a downtown Chicago high-rise pretty easily covers a small-town '70s tract house."

"Hunh. Nice." Aaron nodded thoughtfully and kept writing things down. "Where were the children when you learned about your sister's death?"

Aaron was direct with the questions, but not unkind. Andrew appreciated the approach.

"In transit, and that didn't last long. It was ten days from my being informed to having handled my affairs in Chicago and arrived here." Andrew spread his free hand and began to explain. "Kenzie had both of them out of wedlock and always had custody. I don't know how she met Jayce, but during her pregnancy, and for a while after, they lived together in Evansville. When Tanner came and they couldn't afford staying, they moved here to be with his folks. At some point, that fell through, and she went to Kentucky to be with Chloe's father. The kids went with her. After she died, the Reeds accepted Tanner but Chloe was put with child services—they had no interest in being saddled with her," he finished acidly.

Andrew's expression darkened as resentment and anger flared, ghosts of his own abandonment overlapping his protective ferocity for both kids.

"So, you have legal custody?"

"Frankly, I don't know. I just assumed responsibility of them and it stayed that way. Kenzie didn't have a will and neither did Chloe's father. His people have never been in the picture. I'm here because it's where Jayce is from. Since I was willing to be close and never threatened to take him away, they never argued with me keeping him full time." Andrew felt a momentary pang of guilt. He frowned. "I should have tried to adopt them, shouldn't I? I should have pushed already, made sure."

Aaron's pen stilled midword. "Not necessarily. Status quo isn't always a bad thing, and you had no reason to push for it immediately. I can argue it was in everyone's best interest that you made the smooth transition to primary caretaker first, without jumping into adoption before settling in." The coffee maker gurgled, and Aaron grabbed a sticky bun. "It's entirely possible that if you'd pressed for adoptive rights, they'd have denied you, and your lives would have been nothing but a disruptive fight over Tanner. Besides, this way looks good for you."

"How so?" Andrew folded and unfolded a napkin. Custody issues had always been in the back of his mind, but until yesterday, that's where he'd left them. He felt like he'd let everyone down, somehow.

Michael eased the napkin away, tapping each of Andrew's knuckles in turn. He covered Andrew's hand over with his, warm and capable and anchoring. He didn't say anything and didn't have to, understanding Andrew's internal recriminations and communicating that they weren't warranted.

"You said Tanner's father and grandparents are from Starling?"

Andrew nodded.

"Yet, after everything that happened, he didn't have interest in shouldering the burden of Tanner's primary care until the issue was forced." Aaron's mouth crimped. "That useless boy probably still doesn't, but he's doing what Mommy and Daddy want so he doesn't have to nut up and stay here on his own to be with Tanner or give up mooching off of them."

Michael snickered meanly, and Andrew smirked. Rita puttered by to refill their coffee cups, kept a keen ear to their conversation and an equally keen eye on Tanner. Pinto was curled up on the kitchen floor nearby. The TV murmured quietly, Pops and Chloe obviously content in each other's company. Tanner found Michael's leg, tugged and started to climb, and Michael hauled him up the rest of the way.

Tanner landed both hands on Michael's chest and grinned. "Hiya, Pops."

Andrew had been told there was a Pops coined for each generation, but the naming had to happen of its own volition. He arched an eyebrow at Michael and Michael looked goofy and besotted.

"Hiya, Bean."

Tanner chortled and flopped into Michael, trusting and sure that Michael would catch and hold him, and Michael did. Aaron continued to take notes, and framed his questions in ways that wouldn't arouse Tanner's worry, while Rita did the dishes. Upstairs, there were noises of Michael's youngest siblings beginning to stir. The kitchen was bright and warm, and smoke from the fire blended with breakfast and farm aromas in a pleasant combination. The whole house felt like a haven, a fortress.

Andrew swallowed and blinked rapidly, suddenly overcome with the intense realization that this, here, was true safety. A place he and the kids could and should belong, with far more to offer than the walled-off and empty life he'd enforced upon himself so long. Safe wasn't back at the house he couldn't care less about, door locked with the three of them isolated inside, Michael allowed in but kept at arm's length.

It made him ache, almost double over. But the aching was at last sweet, like this morning's cold air, fresh and sharp after the storm.

Michael smiled, swaying to lull Tanner into a nap. Aaron took in clipped facts and dispensed sardonic opinions as they began to discuss the nitty-gritty of the custodial process. Chloe and Pops dozed on.

Some months ago, Andrew had adjusted to how this family looked out for each other, ready to go hammer-and-tongs if need be. He knew that, from today, he needed to outright accept that he and the kids were considered part of the family. Michael had more than earned that, and the kids deserved everything being so generously offered. Andrew smiled at Michael and realized something else. He deserved it too.

CHAPTER 11

THE hearing had been set for the first Monday in November. All they could do in the meantime was prepare for the worst, wait out the six weeks, and hope for the best. Andrew worked like hell to keep up with business demands and stay strong and focused for the kids, and Michael worked like hell to keep them all on an even keel.

He went to Andrew's house for dinner, had the kids to the farm to tramp around and enjoy the wonders and fun to be had when the heat mellowed and operations shifted into harvest. They conspired over Halloween costumes, and he talked idly about Thanksgiving plans for the huge dinner the entire family threw together. All the while, he was there for Andrew and trying not to show any strain, even as he researched any distant cousins to call upon in Florida if the time came.

Despite putting on a brave face, they were both on edge. Chloe and Tanner were aware something was off, even though they didn't fully grasp the enormity of the situation. The clock was ticking and everyone heard it.

Change often meant upheaval—even crisis—and Andrew had reached for him to help see them through and overcome. It might have been the best thing that could have happened to them. While he savored none of the upset and stress it caused Andrew, and selfishly had no wish to move from here and be so far away, Michael couldn't deny that he appreciated the unexpected consequences.

Between conversations to debate the merits of being a fireman or a race car driver, a policewoman or a ballerina, he and Andrew had explained to Chloe and Tanner about the custody hearing. There was no anxiety or tantrums, as the children had grown accustomed to stability with Andrew, and further, the support added by Michael's continued presence. They were curious but not fretful, and Chloe distilled everyone's sentiment in the tidy wish that staying near the farm would be best because next year there promised to be kittens, but Florida with Andrew and Pops would do if they could all go to Disney World together.

Instead of knocking them for a loop and then apart, it had awoken something in Andrew that no amount of Michael's careful handling and yearning patience would have unlocked. They prepared for the hearing, but not as an inevitable end. Michael went to Andrew's house for dinner and stayed the night whenever possible. If the kids wanted to extend their days at the farm, Andrew made sure it wasn't any trouble to Rita and Pops, then tucked the kids into the girls' old room and himself into Michael's bed.

There was no dread, no bitterness. There was no fear—not from Andrew at losing Tanner, and not from Michael at possibly losing Andrew—only resolve. Michael had always wanted a family of his own to protect and cherish. Meeting Andrew again, kids included, had given him lofty dreams of having found it. The custody hearing, and Andrew's reaction, brought those dreams down to earth as something much better. Something that felt real.

Michael shook his head, held the good parts close in his heart, and laid the rest aside for now.

Tonight was for fun, and they were going to have a lot of it. He grinned, then moaned loudly, shouldered dramatically in the front door of Andrew's house, and roared. The kids had stood peeking out the front window, thinking themselves hidden in the curtains, to see him approach, but still squealed with frightened glee when he erupted inside and chased them around.

He'd traded several minor holidays to get the night off work—something he'd never have managed in Indy—and had dressed up like a zombie. Chloe was a unicorn zombie fighter. That is, a unicorn who protected the world from the ravening zombie horde. Tanner had opted to be a fireman who helped unicorns fight zombies. Andrew was dressed as Andrew.

"Rauugh!" He lurched at Andrew with his arms outreached and hands grasping. "Braaaaains!"

"You have none, babe," Andrew said tartly, then gave Michael a chaste kiss. "Okay, where's my zombie army? We have to hustle so we can get Operation Candy in the bag before bedtime."

Michael groaned. "In the bag? You're awful."

Chloe grabbed Michael's hand and Tanner was already out the door and into the yard. Andrew shrugged unapologetically and grabbed Michael's other hand.

CHAPTER 12

FOR the first time in a long while, Andrew was grateful for his ability to suppress everything and present a calm, detached front. He sat next to Aaron in the small courtroom, waiting on the judge's arrival for the start of Tanner's custody hearing, and not one of his surging emotions was betrayed.

It had been the general consensus that landing Judge Gerrity would be ideal. The man was known for efficiency, especially with morning cases, to move things along at pace and not have lunch imposed upon. Instead, their case had drawn Judge Curtis, who was a much tougher nut to crack, according to both Michael and Aaron. Andrew was still trying to decide if that was a bad omen.

Judge Curtis had been prompt and fair and inscrutable. She'd eyed Andrew steadily while asking her questions, and with equal authority had stared down Jayce and his parents as she'd grilled them on their attitudes toward vying for Tanner. Then she'd called a recess and asked to talk with Tanner alone. Now, they awaited her return and, presumably, her verdict.

Andrew glanced over at the table opposite theirs where the Reeds sat, Jayce and his parents in their Sunday best. He wanted to hate them but couldn't find it in him. There was no way he believed they deserved Tanner, and especially not, as Aaron had emphasized to the judge, since they'd only stepped up to challenge Andrew because they were moving several states away. But he couldn't hate them.

Maybe a year ago, he would have been able to. Maybe even several months. But not now, not sitting here with Michael's eldest brother dressed to kill in a suit that screamed "competent professional here to cut you to the quick." Not with Michael's entire family and extended family crammed into the bench rows behind him. Not with Michael front and center directly at his back, Chloe curled in Michael's lap.

The other side of the courtroom was empty, no extra show of support for the Reeds' efforts. If so much wasn't at stake, Andrew might have mustered feeling sorry for them.

Andrew tried to quell the conviction that it was a foregone conclusion, that there was no way Judge Curtis could think that Tanner being dragged off to Florida with an anemic father and well-meaning but aging grandparents would be the right decision. He'd learned all too well, and the hard way, how the seemingly obvious "right" way could go cruelly and inexplicably awry. But he couldn't help feel the bolstering presence of Michael and Michael's family and the lack of stigma his relationship had seemed to elicit from the judge. He hoped against hope that was the omen he should heed.

There was shuffling and anticipation of movement. The bailiff opened the door joining the courtroom to the judges' chambers, and Judge Curtis swept in.

The low hum of scattered conversations ended. Everyone rose. Andrew half-turned to find Michael leaned close for just long enough to kiss his cheek and nod before shifting back again.

Judge Curtis took the bench. "The observers may sit. You," she waved imperiously at Andrew and Aaron, then over to the Reeds, "stay where you are."

Andrew's guts lurched. If she wanted them standing, that meant she was going to render judgment. Aaron patted his back reassuringly, and Andrew squared his shoulders.

"I'll be brief. After talking with young Mr. Reed, and going over all the information in the file, as well as the respective testimony in this matter, I see no reason to disrupt what is obviously a stable and happy life for the child. There is nothing compelling enough in the argument that this be so greatly disrupted, and many compelling reasons for me to believe he will continue to enjoy a stable and happy upbringing right here in Starling."

Someone toward the back—Stephen, it sounded like—gave a low yip. Judge Curtis raised an eyebrow. The courtroom quieted again, but an electric sense of excitement and relief hung in the air.

Judge Curtis nodded at each table in turn and smiled. "It is my ruling that full custodial rights be granted to Mr. Lucas, but I will stipulate that the two parties must come to arrangements for visits to

Florida, on such holidays and durations as agreed upon by said parties. That is all." She rapped her gavel and dismissed the courtroom.

There was a second's pause, then the suspension broke, and the Wiercinski clan erupted into jubilant applause. Andrew was so stoically held in check he could only offer Aaron a grateful handshake, almost couldn't let himself accept that the judge's ruling was real and final. He stepped across to stand in front of the Reeds.

They didn't look surprised. Jayce was barely concealing relief, and while that was disappointing it wasn't of true importance to Andrew. He felt secure and magnanimous. It would be no threat to offer them a few weeks every summer and Christmas holidays. Before he could say anything, Aaron was beside him, cool and efficient and very lawyerly, to address Mr. Wren, the Reeds' representation.

"How about you put in writing your requests for Tanner's visits, and I will review them with my client. We can work out an amicable arrangement from there." Aaron smiled blandly.

Mr. Wren smiled with equal blandness. "Yes, we'll discuss it and have our proposal to you by the end of this week."

Only Mrs. Reed seemed upset, but it was more resignation than anything. Andrew didn't offer to shake their hands. All he could think as they filed out of the courtroom was *That's right, he's mine. A few visits won't change that. It never has and never will. And don't you all forget it.*

Once they were gone, he was surrounded by Michael's siblings and even recognized a few cousins among the mix. They had gone all-out on his behalf, glad the same as with anything to throw in where needed when it came to family. Andrew appreciated it more than he could begin to say. But as they congratulated him and chattered about future plans, his heart started to pound. He felt cotton-mouthed and trapped, overwhelmed by the tension finally cut, and just too many people to deal with now that it was over.

He listened to Michael softly tell him to breathe, leaned in when Michael rubbed his sides.

"Better?"

Andrew blinked away the black dots that had gathered over his vision. They were in the hall, tucked into a deserted corner.

"Yes, I'm fine." Andrew pulled himself together by force of habit and nodded curtly.

Michael quirked a smile and stayed right in his space, massaged his shoulders, sought out and kept contact with him until his tiny shudders and vibrations had subsided. Andrew hadn't even realized he'd been shaking and definitely hadn't been aware Michael had learned that about him, but he didn't panic or question that now. Instead, he let the rest of his reaction show, let Michael soak it in and help him recover. He let out a long restorative breath.

"Okay, yeah." Andrew tipped back and met Michael's gaze. "Now I'm better."

"Good." Michael waited another beat, then his face split into a huge grin. "Andrew!" he whuffed.

Andrew knew the feeling, exactly, encompassed so much. Everything they'd discovered and shared and endured to get to this moment. He grinned too. Tears pricked behind his eyelids, and he ducked down and laughed at himself. When he looked back up, Michael was full-on misty-eyed and grinning without shame.

"Right. Enough of that." Michael shook himself showily like a wet dog. "Let's go find Bean and Squash. Pops is with them in another room until I'm done rescuing you and we're ready to go."

"Well then, I'm ready to go." Andrew didn't bristle or even hesitate. He let Michael guide him to get the kids. With one kid each boosted up into their arms, they left the courthouse and put the entire episode behind them.

CHAPTER 13

MICHAEL jogged across a rutted field littered with shorn cornstalks, a hazardous shortcut from his barn apartment to the far lawn where the family gathered for outdoor events. He'd worn his police uniform to the hearing, but was now in soft cord pants and several layers of ratty shirts with a chunky cable-knit sweater over it all.

Upon leaving the courthouse, they'd made a quick stop at Andrew's house so he and the kids could change. During the drive to the farm, he and Andrew had carefully felt the kids out with gently purposeful conversation. Chloe had asked if what happened meant that nothing would change. Andrew had answered yes, that's what it meant. That had been enough, without even a hint of her tendency to overthink things. Tanner had never been truly anxious in the first place.

He could hear them, carefree as their earlier reactions promised, busy with important kid stuff like getting dirty playing pretend and having fun. Michael picked up his pace when he cleared the field. As usual, his gaze was restless until he found Andrew—an involuntary reflex same as breathing—and his smile in response was almost as instinctive.

Andrew held a bottle of beer and was snugly wrapped up in a dun-colored shearling coat that did things to Michael's nerve endings. He was surrounded by Michael's family, but rather than nervously seeking a bolt-hole or looking like the odd man out, Andrew was a seamless fit. The fire pit had been lit and was crackling merrily. The crisp late-autumn air was redolent with delicious food and ringing laughter.

Michael had known for some time now that Andrew could, and did, belong with him. Which of course, by extension, included his family. It was gratifying to see his unerring conviction in that rewarded. Even better to have it as celebration of the court's decision about Tanner, and in a larger sense, what that meant for Andrew and Michael.

Next, he searched and found Squash and Bean, lost in whatever games the brood had set themselves upon. Pinto and the other dogs ran and barked playfully between them, except Henrietta, Dad's old blue heeler, sixteen years young and with absolutely zero interest in anything other than staying near the fire and potential treats.

Michael swooped past the tables groaning with food and snagged a plate of carnitas pierogies—something his mom had tinkered with and perfected over the years. They were a favorite of the family, and he who hesitated when they were on offer lost out. He barely avoided having Moriah snatch the plate from him and slowed his trot to come alongside Andrew.

Pops, Daniel, and Andrew were well entrenched in a conversation that was somehow relating crop yields to football. Michael conceded a pierogi to Pops, then hooked Andrew's arm and started walking them from the group.

"It'll keep!" he yelled behind him when Daniel squawked about Michael rudely interrupting.

Andrew went along with him and smiled, bemused. "Can I help you?"

"Here." Michael thrust the half-gone plate into Andrew's free hand. "Try those. And yes. I want to talk to you."

"Given the circumstances and everything, I'm going to assume that's not a lead-in to something bad. But I'm still working on that kind of thing, so—it's nothing bad, is it?" Andrew wasn't tentative about the food. He neatly shoveled a whole pierogi into his mouth, chewed thoughtfully for a moment, then said thickly, "Damn. Wow. That's amazing."

Michael beamed. "Mom's secret recipe. A Fiesta-Q mainstay. And no, it's not bad."

Andrew nodded and let Michael guide him to stand on a rise framed by towering oak trees, their leaves dry and brown but held tenaciously and rustling in the wind. Here, they had a view of the farm's waterway, a large creek that cut a diagonal from the high easterly corner of their property and past the main house. It ran fast and swollen in springtime, and fed two ponds on its journey—imaginatively named the High and Low ponds. They could also easily still see the party and the tangle of running kids that at least one adult always had a watchful eye on.

"I decided on the drive here that, given how well the day has gone, I should just push my luck rather than lose the streak." Michael turned the collar up on Andrew's coat, using the gesture to pull them closer together, then rubbed his fingertips in the nubbly material.

"I haven't pushed before. I've tried to be patient and respectful and not spook you, but I can't risk being that way anymore. I want us to have a fancy date night and get you back in the fancy suit you wore to court. Then get you out of it, maybe in a fancy hotel room. I want you to keep coming here, to be with me and the family, and have me to your place without feeling like you have to push me out the door before it gets to be too much. I want to believe we got to a different place in our relationship that can stick and wasn't just from the stress and heightened emotions the custody issue caused.

"I don't want us to backslide or forget or lose each other again, that's all. I mean, hah, hardly anything small to put it in such a way but, that's as simple and plain as I know how to say it."

Michael clamped his mouth shut and shook his head. He hadn't runaway-nervous babbled at Andrew in quite a while.

"Fancy date night sounds great. You know, this was the first I've busted my suits from their dry-cleaning bags since I left Chicago? I don't think I missed them." Andrew let the emptied pierogi plate fall to the ground in a controlled slide. He tucked his hands under Michael's sweater and splayed them to grip around Michael's ribs. He grinned. "I'm further along than I thought."

"Hunh? Embracing casual wear?" Michael was distracted by Andrew's touch, and he wasn't quite sure what Andrew was referring to.

Andrew laughed. "No. I was already that. Learning to dress in suits that cost the same as a small country's GNP was the sharp curve. I meant about talking, and listening, before instinctively retreating."

Michael nodded slowly. "I'm going to ditto on what you said before. Given the circumstances, that seems good—but it is good, right?"

"It is." Andrew sobered and leaned their foreheads together. He breathed in deeply, fingers digging almost painfully into Michael's sides. "I want that too. I can't promise I won't still hide sometimes, or that you and all your wonderful family won't overwhelm me, but I don't want to backslide or lose you, either."

All the air left Michael in a rush. He felt weak. Then he flashed over with heat and dizzying elation and clutched Andrew into a demanding kiss.

Andrew let him demand, and answered in full, until they staggered and had to split apart.

"I don't know how I'll ever be able to thank you." Andrew smiled and searched Michael's face. "Everything you've done, everything your family has done, with Tanner, and both kids, and just, well, all of it. You opened our lives, and to be completely sappy, my heart." He fidgeted. "I can't figure out how I'm going to repay that."

Michael laughed and held Andrew's face in his hands. Before, he would have worried Andrew meant that his attentions and generosity came with a price. It seemed Michael was further along and doing a lot better too.

"Done and done." Michael kissed Andrew because he had to, then he shrugged helplessly. "I've wanted kids since I was a kid, to become a boring old married couple all settled down. That has seemed impossible to me for a long time too."

He swept his thumb up Andrew's cheek. "I wanted you since I scoped you out in that awful club and sat there repeating a fervent mantra that you please-please-please notice me. Then seeing you with the kids and how you can be without your protective reserves, I don't know, it's like it lights me up inside. Now, here you are, letting me in, letting me have you, letting me share Chloe and Tanner. Even with my family and coming back here, I was lonely. I needed someone too."

Andrew looked almost bashful and his nose wrinkled adorably. "You not saying Squash and Bean at this point sounds wrong."

"I was elevating the moment." Michael watched Andrew's eyes twinkle, felt like he was twinkling, imagined them surrounded by pinpoints of golden stars and a shimmering halo. He chuckled and leaned into Andrew again. "What I'm saying is, I'm probably going to have to fix all your parking tickets for the rest of our lives, and angle to get you as much pie as you want, and intimidate anyone who even thinks about trying to date Squash before she's thirty with my grr-cop act, and a lot of other things that are too X-rated to name, before we come close to even."

"You mean your grr-cop-father act? Because I've seen the grr-cop-boyfriend shtick and it's effective, so I approve this line of thinking."

Michael swallowed, hard. "Uh. I—" He blinked, for once completely without words.

Andrew pinched him. "You did say the rest of our lives. Unless?" he added leadingly.

"Nope, no, noooooo unless nothing." Michael dove in for another kiss, forget words.

They stayed there, swaying and grinning at each other, until shouts for their attention finally penetrated their mutual absorption. Michael rolled his eyes but he didn't protest, tucked Andrew into him, and started walking them back. Two steps in, Andrew twisted away, retrieving the dropped pierogi plate, and they tried again.

"I do have a confession to make."

Michael was still buzzing from the adrenaline of the day's events, their revelatory talk, and their kisses. He could tell Andrew was in a similar state and downshifted from that intensity.

"Shoot."

"I feel like I'm dating your whole family. Which is weird. Nice, but definitely weird."

"At least we all like you. It'd be really awkward, otherwise."

Michael gathered Andrew back close to him. Whenever they were close enough, he had to touch, and he had come to the conclusion he'd never get enough.

"Then, pursuant to the first, I feel it's only fair I tell you that I find Aaron to be incredibly attractive when he puts his glasses on and is all Mr. Smart Lawyer."

Michael made a short noise. "Is this going to become a problem?" he deadpanned.

"No. But only because I have a rule not to date straight guys. Or married guys. Otherwise"—Andrew gestured meaningfully—"you'd be up against some tough competition."

"Consider it noted. I am not letting on at all, though."

"Would he mind?"

"No, it'd just make him even more insufferable."

Andrew snickered. "So. How much land does your family own?"

"Several thousand acres, including Daniel's spread, which sounds huge. But when it comes to the kind of crops we raise, it's not really." He slowed his breathing and smiled at his mother, watching their approach. "Why?"

"Just curious. I've never been with a land baron before."

"A-ha, I'm hardly that. I have an apartment in a half-gutted antique barn on land that isn't mine." Michael hipped Andrew. "But I will inherit some acreage, one day."

"Enough to build a greenhouse for nursery plants?" Andrew hipped Michael back. "And have you ever considered renovating the entire antique barn into a whole house?"

For a hot second Michael thought he was going to start blubbering and turn into a soggy mess. Maybe even really lose his mind and propose on the spot. He managed to pull himself together and, instead, waggled an eyebrow.

"Funny you should ask. Because, point of fact, yes, I have. Something about the past several months of my life put the idea in mind, and it's been niggling at me ever since." Michael hummed musingly. "Might even be grant money to help flip it, seeing as it's historic and a restoration. As for the greenhouse—well, maybe. Provided the right incentives and all."

Andrew blushed and smiled crookedly. "Hunh, how about that."

"How about that," Michael repeated tenderly, and he leaned in and kissed the jump of Andrew's pulse under Andrew's ear. He felt Andrew's trust, and contentment, more powerfully than even his own.

They were drawn back into the family crowd, then, pulled different directions without feeling like they'd parted. Michael was assigned to get another load of wood from the bin for the fire, and Andrew was tasked with whittling marshmallow-roasting sticks. After that, they were given positions and strategies for the cutthroat game of touch football about to go down. Chloe was very importantly handing out the colored strips of cloth to the various players.

Tanner trundled after Michael and was hefted into his arms. "C'mon, Bean. Let's get this done so we can hurry back."

"Okay, Pops." Bean grinned and waved at Andrew over Michael's retreating shoulder.

ELLE BROWNLEE has always followed her creative, adventuring spirit.

Growing up she loved westerns and taking long hikes. On these explorations she'd craft miniature worlds with moss and rocks while making up stories about everything that happened there. This often included dashing cowboy heroes. As an adult, not a lot has changed. She still loves westerns, long hikes, and allowing her imagination to roam. She also loves spending time with family and friends, rooting for her baseball team, rainy days in autumn, and the perfect cup of tea (black, steeped extra strong, with milk—please!)

Her romances feature flawed but relatable characters in immersive settings, told with wit, tenderness, and a sly note of sarcasm. Though a cynic in many ways, Elle believes love can conquer all. Every story is a little bit naughty, a whole lot of nice, and will always end with happily ever after.

Elle currently lives in New York City, where she maintains her miniature worlds in terrariums and writing. She's so thankful to be able to share her work with a growing audience, and especially grateful to have you reading along.

Website: http://ellebrownlee.weebly.com/index.html

Twitter: https://twitter.com/ellebrownlee

E-mail: brownlee.elle@gmail.com

JUST A
WEEKEND

ELIZAH J. DAVIS

To Elle and Tere for being so wonderful to work with and fabulous in general.

&

To Sabrina and Andy for all their input, support, and encouragement.

CHAPTER 1

COME on, Brent had said. *It'll be fun! Boys' night out! Isn't that why you came to visit?*

In truth, Devin had come to Seattle because he'd had to move back in with his parents three months ago after he lost his job, and while he loved his family more than anything in the world, they were driving him absolutely insane. Devin had needed to get away, and Brent was always good company for blowing off some steam.

The flip side to that, however, was that Brent tended to get a little carried away with his *blowing.* About an hour into the night, he'd taken off with some wannabe cowboy who was wearing skinny jeans instead of Wranglers, leaving Devin to find his own lodgings for the evening. Technically, he could take a cab back to Brent's house, but his roommate Creepy Dave was there, and Devin didn't like being alone with that guy.

It probably shouldn't have been so annoying. It'd been awhile—he certainly hadn't been bringing guys back to his parents' house—and it wasn't like he didn't have some viable options. He'd been getting interested looks all evening, and several guys had attempted to chat him up, though none had been more original than *I haven't seen you here before.* It was eleven o'clock; he should've been naked and sweaty already. Instead he was talking to one of the many straight girls there, and, if he were being honest with himself, having a really good time.

Kara was adorable, short and curvy, with thick curly brown hair and freckles. She was also wearing a T-shirt that said *Jupiter's,* and while the coat she was holding covered the bottom half of the print, Devin was pretty sure there was a rooster under there, which was why he had started talking to her in the first place. What was his problem?

"So, what's your problem, then?" Kara asked, nodding around the bar. "There are plenty of guys to choose from, and we both know you have your choice."

"I don't know." Devin sighed. "I think I'm having hookup ennui." He nudged her with his shoulder. "What's your story? Friday night at a gay bar?"

"I occasionally have to browbeat my friend into getting out of the house. For his own good."

"Of course."

"Plus, my boyfriend is having a guys' night, so it was kind of a win-win."

"Boyfriend?" Devin waited as she pulled up a picture of him on her phone and whistled once she showed it to him. Boyfriend was six-plus feet of hunky gorgeousness. "Damn, girl. High five." He took the phone from her for a closer look and held out his other hand for her to slap. "If I had that waiting for me at home, I'd never leave the house."

"You would on guys' night. Too much sausage for me to deal with."

Devin arched a brow at her and looked around the bar.

"Yeah, no, I heard it," she said. "It's a whole different vibe, though."

"Fair enough. So he's totally straight, then?" he teased.

"One hundred percent."

"Good for you." He finally handed the phone back to her, giving a halfhearted nod to the guy eyeing him a few feet away. "You know that feeling where you're in the mood for a really good book, but you can't even decide on the genre you want to read?"

Kara laughed and gave him a sympathetic one-armed hug. "Okay, okay. Check him out. In the blue." She gestured with her beer bottle to a guy tucked away at a corner table, smiling blandly at the adorable twinky blond trying his damnedest to chat him up.

"He's all right," Devin admitted. The guy was handsome enough in a bland boy-next-door sort of way. He was tall, with light-brown hair and a square, manly jaw. In any given romantic comedy, he'd be cast as the staid, dependable boyfriend. The bed warmer until the charming roguish hero of the story happened along. "Let me guess; your browbeaten friend?"

"Yeah, that's my social butterfly James. Don't look at me like that. I'm not hitting on you for him. I'm just curious about, y'know. The vibe he puts off."

"Besides the flashing neon 'Not Interested'?" Devin shook his head and tsked at the kid still giving it his all. "Give it up, sugar. Mr. Darcy's not going to ask you to dance."

"I am so tempted to smack him," Kara said. "I mean, he's cute enough, right? But he just sits there people watching. He doesn't even try to talk to anyone, unless...." She threw her hands up in exasperation, splashing beer on both of them as another guy walked over to the table. "Yep. There we go. Right on cue. Unless his vapid, trampy ex shows up. *Him* he'll go home with, and then he calls me the next day to absolve him of his shame hangover."

"Really?" Devin looked at James with a bit more interest, though he felt a little disappointed with himself that the shame fucking made the guy so much more appealing. The twink had been chased away by the vapid trampy ex, who James looked only mildly more excited about talking to. The ex was tall and lanky, with an interesting face, though Devin didn't consider him particularly attractive. "What's the story?"

"No story really." Kara shrugged and took another sip of her beer. "Roger is just that guy, and James is too nice to tell him to fuck off." She wrinkled her nose like she'd just smelled something foul, then looked at Devin in a way that could only be described as diabolical. "How would you feel about playing white knight?"

Devin looked at his watch and back at James. Aside from being "cute enough"—he was at least that—James didn't seem to be falling-down drunk, which would be a bonus if they made it to the sex part. The later it got, the fewer guys there were who could stand of their own volition, and in Devin's experience, those guys were generally a terrible lay. At the very least, James's boredom seemed genuine rather than affected, which was new and refreshing. "What'd you have in mind?"

JAMES could hear a voice in his head saying *You will not go home with him* as Roger spoke. The voice sounded a lot like Kara's. He nodded to himself, resolved, only to have it waver a second later when Roger covered his hand with his own. It was predictably pathetic of him, but the sex was decent, and, if he was being honest, Roger was a lot less work than a stranger would be.

Someone sidled up next to him as James was wavering, and for a moment he thought it was Kara finally returning from the bar to rescue him. Instead he turned to find a surprisingly pretty guy with messy brown hair and green eyes smirking up at him.

"Hey, handsome," the guy said, holding up his coat and scarf. "Kara said to tell you she's hit the wall, and she's taking a cab home, so we can go whenever you're ready."

"Uhhh." *Brilliant, James.* He accepted his coat and scarf, trying to remember when he had given them to Kara. The pretty guy was still smiling at him, which made the whole thought process more difficult.

"Excuse me," Roger said before James could come up with a more coherent response. "Who are you?"

"Devin. And you are?"

Roger frowned and ignored the question, shooting James a suspicious look. "James never mentioned you."

Devin leaned against the table and shrugged. "Probably because most of the stories worth mentioning aren't really any of your business." He turned back to James and said, "I'm ready when you are."

"Yeah." James nodded and, for lack of a better idea of what to do, pulled his coat on. "I think we can call it a night. I'll talk to you later," he said to Roger and didn't protest when Devin took his hand and led him toward the door.

"So Kara sent you to rescue me?" James asked as soon as they were outside, his thoughts finally clicking into place.

"White Knight Devin at your service." Devin gave a little bow without letting go of James's hand.

"And now that I'm rescued?"

"A reward is customary."

It couldn't be that easy. It was never that easy. Pretty boys with impish smiles didn't throw themselves at him as a rule. "Do you... want to come home with me?"

"Oh thank God. For a minute there I thought you really might not ask."

James shook his head, not entirely convinced this wasn't a dream. Only his certainty that Kara didn't have a cruel bone in her body kept him from suspecting it was some sort of joke. "Just like that?"

Devin's smile faltered. "I'm sorry. You honestly don't owe me anything. I can just go back—"

"No!" James wanted to smack himself. Good grief, was he really standing there talking Devin out of coming home with him? "I'm not very good at this. I don't want to pressure you."

"How about this?" Devin's smile hadn't fully returned, but he did look mildly amused, or maybe a little bit indulgent. "I, Devin, being of sound mind and body, would very much like to go home with you if you'd like to have me."

"I'd like to have you. I mean—" he added when Devin laughed.

"No, let's go with that. I'm good with that. Shall we?"

"Sure." James frowned when Devin gave him an expectant look. "Oh! You mean go? Yeah, of course. I walked, if that's okay? It's not too far, but I can call a cab."

"Walking is good. Just lead the way," Devin said, gesturing for James to precede him.

"Do you not have a jacket or anything?"

"Nah, I'm good."

"So, I don't generally have Kara pick up guys for me," James said as they started off. "For the record."

Devin laughed. "I'm sure you can get your own dates."

"Well, no, not really, but I do have some dignity." James smiled when Devin laughed again. "A little bit. I swear it's here somewhere. In my other pants, maybe."

"From where I was sitting, you had plenty of attention. You just didn't seem all that interested." Devin tilted his head and gave James a sly look. "What's the story with the ex? If you don't mind my asking. Sorry, I'm nosy." He said it in such a way that made it clear he was still expecting an answer.

James sighed and wished he had a good one to give. "I don't know. We were never a great couple, but at least with him I know what I'm getting. Hookups can be awkward." He winced when he realized what he was saying, but Devin seemed delighted.

"No offense taken, I promise. I totally get it. The devil you know and all."

"Yeah?"

"Yeah." Devin scrunched his nose and leaned toward James conspiratorially. "I know a devil or two myself. Terrible habits to try and break."

"Why does it sound so fun when you say it?" James asked.

Devin shoved his hands in his pockets, giving an exaggerated shrug. "I'm a fun guy."

"Who's obviously freezing," James said instead of making the mushroom joke that so desperately wanted to come out. He stopped and turned to Devin. "Here, take my coat." He started to take it off, but Devin shook his head.

"Then you'll be freezing. I come from lands east of the Cascades and am of a heartier stock."

James gave him a skeptical look and unwrapped his scarf, hooking it around Devin's neck. "Take this, at least."

The nearby streetlight was bright enough to give James a good look at Devin, and he was surprised all over again by how unreasonably attractive the guy was. What he'd mistaken for eyeliner in the bar was, in fact, a set of thick, dark eyelashes. His lips were pink and curved into what appeared to be a perpetual smirk. It was giving James ideas.

"It's only a few more blocks," James said as Devin wrapped the scarf around his neck.

Devin hooked his arm around James's elbow and pressed up against his side, making James's stomach do a little flip.

"Lead on."

CHAPTER 2

"YOU know, it almost seems like it's going to snow." Devin tilted his head back to look up at the sky as James flipped through his keys to find the one to his building. It had clouded over quite a bit in the short time it had taken them to get there.

"Doubtful," James said as he got the door unlocked. "We here in the lands west of the Cascades don't really do snow. Also, it's March."

"Barely." Devin shrugged to cover his shivering. "I'm just saying, tomorrow could be interesting." He smiled when James held the door open for him like an honest-to-God gentleman, and followed him up the flight of stairs to his apartment, taking the opportunity to appreciate the curve of James's ass. Devin smiled in anticipation, his earlier apathy having disappeared completely.

"So, this is it." James unlocked his apartment door and once again gestured for Devin to go ahead of him, his politeness clearly habitual. He flipped on the entryway light as he shut the door behind them. "The living room is down the hall to the left there."

The apartment was much larger than Devin had been expecting. There was a bedroom and an office to the right and another hallway to the left. A second bedroom? The kitchen was sizable, with the dining room directly across from it, and there was a balcony off the side of the living room. Devin's apartment in Portland had been half that size, and he'd had a roommate.

"Nice place," Devin said as he removed the scarf James had given him and set it on the arm of the couch. He rubbed the tip of his nose, trying to warm it a little, but his hands were equally cold, so it didn't have much of an effect.

"Thanks. I've been here about a year and I'm pretty happy with it," James said from the entryway. Devin could hear him hanging up his coat in the closet, and he wondered if James was the type who asked guests to remove their shoes in the entryway. He toed his boots off and tucked them under the breakfast bar just in case.

In addition to the size of the apartment, it was obvious care had been taken in choosing the decorations and furnishings. It was what Devin would classify as a "grown-up" residence, which was a category usually reserved for friends of his parents. While James was certainly older than Devin, he didn't think it was by much. He was early thirties, tops.

"So...."

Devin raised an eyebrow at James, wondering if he had anything planned after that. He found James's discomfort endearing. It had been awhile since Devin had been with someone who wasn't a get-right-to-it "yeah, you like that, baby?" sort of bad porn reject. James didn't seem the type for dirty talk, but that remained to be seen. Sometimes the quiet ones were the most surprising.

"Um, do you want something to drink?" James finally asked. "I have, you know, some different liquors and stuff. Or coffee or tea or whatever if you want something hot?"

"I'm good, thanks." At James's panicked look, Devin decided to take pity on him. "Actually, some water would be good. Thanks."

"Sure."

As James futzed around in the kitchen, Devin wandered over to the bookshelf that dominated the far wall of the living room, curious as to what sort of reader he was, aside from voracious. He smiled when he spotted the unmistakable lineup of the *Twilight* series on the middle shelf. All of them were in hardback and had obviously been read.

"My sister-in-law made me read them."

Devin turned to find James walking toward him, a sheepish look on his face. "Team Edward or Team Jacob?"

"Jacob, are you kidding me? Bella was out of her flipping mind," James said with the vehemence of someone who'd had that particular argument more than once. A good-natured look of chagrin crossed his face when Devin smiled at him. "What are the chances I can convince you I like it ironically?"

"Irony is overrated. I read the whole series in a weekend." Devin brushed his fingers against James's palm as he accepted the glass of water from him and was gratified to hear the tiny catch in his breath. "I was team Edward *and* Jacob. There's some unresolved sexual tension there." He winked at James and felt another tug of giddy anticipation at the warm, grateful smile James gave him in return. "Is your sister-in-law Team Jacob too?"

James shook his head. "Edward. We aren't allowed to talk about it anymore."

Lord, he was adorable. Devin sipped at his water and turned back to the bookshelf. He could feel the weight of James's attention, and he wanted to bask in it like a cat rolling around in the sun. He swayed close enough to James that he brushed up against him as he made a show of studying the titles. There was a little bit of everything: classics, literary fiction, YA, and a good sampling of genre fiction. Devin felt like he'd found the apartment's diary. The secret, fantastical yearnings trying to blend in with their tidy, mature surroundings.

"Have you read it?" James asked as Devin trailed his fingers over *Pride and Prejudice and Zombies.*

"The original, many times, but I can't do zombies. They freak me out." Devin could feel the heat from James's body at his back, but James had yet to actually touch him. It was distracting. "Zombies and spiders."

James made a thoughtful noise. "So you wouldn't be interested in reading my screenplay, *Zombie Spiders from Outer Space?*"

That was enough to make Devin turn, and he grinned at the mischievous sparkle in James's eyes. Mischievous looked good on him. "Do they take over Earth?"

"They try, but Earth is saved by a space pirate that I'm hoping will be played by Orlando Bloom."

"A space pirate, huh?"

"He started out as a space cowboy, actually, but that felt a little cliché."

A warm, affectionate little thrill bloomed in Devin's chest. He'd always been a sucker for guys who could banter, and James's particular sort of bashfulness made it all the more charming. Devin knew it was all superficial, James was a complete stranger, and yet he found that he already genuinely liked him to an alarming degree.

Under different circumstances, they might've been friends, which was not quite what Devin wanted to be thinking about at the moment.

He walked over to the coffee table and set his water down on one of the empty coasters, then straightened to find James watching him. "So, here we are," Devin said, hoping to coax another smile out of James.

"Here we are." James rubbed the back of his neck, managing to look embarrassed, rueful, and pleased all at the same time. When he made no move to close the distance between them, Devin crooked his finger at him, beckoning him forward, which James didn't hesitate to obey.

Once James was close enough, Devin pulled him down into a kiss, because he was curious and saw no reason to deny himself the pleasure. James clutched at his hips, his surprise evident, but only for a moment. Then he was pulling Devin closer, kissing him back with a skill that belied his previous hesitancy. The trampy ex had at least been good for practice, it would seem.

"Yeah, this will definitely work," Devin said when he broke the kiss.

"Glad to know I'm not a lost cause."

Devin shook his head. "That wasn't really a concern."

James grinned and let Devin lead him to the couch, stretched out easily at Devin's urging so Devin could settle on top of him, which took care of the height difference. There was a moment of less-than-graceful maneuvering with the couch only just wide enough to accommodate them. Devin couldn't quite contain his laughter as he finally managed an acceptable position straddling James's thigh.

"Good?" James asked, grabbing Devin's waist to help balance him.

"Yep, I've totally got this." Devin ran his fingers through James's hair, pleased to find it was as soft as it looked and not tacky with product. His own hair had enough wave to it that he didn't need to use any himself, and he couldn't stand the feel of it. "How about you? Can I get you anything?"

"I think I'm set for the moment." James tilted his head back and let Devin kiss him again as he slid his hands under Devin's sweater. Wonderfully big hands that curved hotly over Devin's sides.

Devin had definitely chosen well. He leaned back enough to peel off his sweater and started working at the buttons of James's shirt before kissing him again. James's kissing had a subtle dirtiness to it that, when taken in with everything else, was working for Devin in a profound way. He managed to get the last of James's buttons undone and pushed the material aside so he could get to bare skin.

James's body was thick and solid and it made Devin a little gluttonous as he felt James up. He'd always had a thing for guys with more to them than the typical gym bunny. Devin ran his hands over James's sides, then up over his chest, the hair there tickling his palms enough to make him smile against James's mouth.

"I would like to state for the record," Devin said between kisses, "that you are really, incredibly sexy."

"You're sweet."

Devin snorted. "See if you still think that once I've had my way with you."

In lieu of an answer, James grabbed the back of his neck and kissed him hard, cupping Devin's ass with his other hand. Devin rocked his hips against the hard muscle of James's thigh, his mind shuffling through all the things they could do given enough time together. James definitely had potential.

"Just so we're on the same page, I don't usually bottom on a first date," Devin said, as much of a reminder to himself as anything else, because he was surprisingly tempted for all that they were still in the heavy petting stage.

James nodded. "Yeah, that's cool. It takes some of the pressure off, honestly," he said, earnest where so many guys would've been smarmy or jaded. It caught Devin off guard to the extent that he lost track of his usual script. He had a feeling it would be useless with James anyway.

"No pressure." Devin kissed him lightly. "We're just having a good time." That's all it was, no matter how very likable James might be.

"I am. Having a good time, that is."

"Well, I'm excellent company." Devin rocked against James's thigh again, restless and wound up. He'd intended to take it slow, fool around on the couch for awhile to give James time to relax, but he was pretty sure it wouldn't take much more of that to tip him over the edge.

One-night stand or not, it wasn't the sort of impression he wanted to make.

"Will you think less of me if I try to talk you into the bedroom now?" Devin sat up and moved so he was straddling James's lap. "Because, I'll be honest, I could happily dry hump you until I come in my pants, but they're the only pair I have on me at the moment." He gave James his winningest smile and another slow roll of his hips.

"If I wake up before I get to see you naked, I'm going to be so pissed." James smiled crookedly as he grabbed Devin's thighs, barely giving him enough time to wrap his arm around James's neck before he stood.

"Impressive," Devin said, his arousal kicking up a notch at the unexpected manhandling.

James stopped after a few steps. "Yeah, I can't carry you the whole way there. Well, I probably could, but—"

"Save your strength." Devin laughed as James set him down and gave him a kiss for the effort before following him into the bedroom.

The blinds were still open and the streetlamp outside was bright enough to light the entire room. It was as nice as the rest of the apartment, simple, but tastefully decorated, and Devin felt another unexpected rush of affection for the guy he'd lucked into going home with.

James disappeared into the attached bathroom and came out with a bottle of lube and a hand towel. "For, afterward. Y'know," he said when he caught Devin looking at the towel.

"Yeah, I know." Devin bit his lip to keep from laughing and focused his attention on getting his jeans undone. He shucked them and toed his socks off before turning his attention back to James, who was neatly turning down the covers of the bed, still mostly clothed. Devin doubted it was because James wanted to give him the pleasure of unwrapping him, but that's how he was going to take it anyway.

"So here's what I was thinking," Devin said before they could get too far removed from the rapport they'd established on the couch. He closed the distance between them and pushed the shirt off James's shoulders, letting James pull it the rest of the way off. "I'd like to undress you and suck you off. Then I was thinking you could give me a hand job, because you've got really great hands. What do you think?"

"Yeah, I can— That's good."

James sucked in a breath as Devin undid the fly of his jeans and reached in to rub him through his boxers. He was deliciously hard and Devin's mouth watered at the thought of tasting him. He was torn between dropping to his knees right there and wanting to see James spread out on the bed. In the end, the allure of soft blankets won out, and Devin pushed James's jeans down, motioning for him to kick them off before getting on the bed.

The boxers James wore were simple black cotton, a little faded from repeated washings and far sexier than they had any right to be.

Devin waited until James had settled into a comfortable position before joining him on the bed, crawling between James's thighs. He leaned up to give James another quick kiss, then kissed and nipped his way down James's body, glancing up every few seconds to make sure James was into it. Devin honestly tried to be considerate in bed, but had occasionally been known to get a little too absorbed in what he was doing, and so far he was finding his pleasure in James to be distracting.

Devin traced the shape of James's erection through his boxers before pulling them down until they stretched over his thighs. He smiled at James as he wrapped his fingers around the base of his cock, then bent to take the tip into his mouth.

The noise James made was downright pornographic, and Devin had to stop himself from reaching down to stroke his own cock in response. James was big enough that Devin kept his hand on him, stroking him as he bobbed his head, slow and deliberate. He ran his other hand over the smooth skin of James's hip and clenched his fingers there when James's hand settled tentatively at the back of his head. Devin pulled up far enough to give James an encouraging look, swirling his tongue around the tip of James's cock before sinking back down, his chin already wet and messy.

After another moment, James threaded his fingers through Devin's hair, holding but not directing him. He brought his other hand up to trace over Devin's cheek, and Devin sincerely hoped James didn't notice him humping the bed. He closed his eyes and gave himself over to it, the perfect stretch and ache of his jaw and the weight of James against his tongue. At the rate this was going, he wasn't going to last long enough to get his hand job, which would be a shame, but not enough that it made him want to stop. Everything about James, every gasp and moan, was hitting his buttons, and Devin wondered if it was the man himself, or if it had just been that long since he'd had anything other than mediocre sex with blasé fuck buddies.

James was also a talker, but it seemed more inadvertent than anything, like he couldn't quite keep it to himself, but he didn't intend for Devin to hear him either. All Devin caught was a litany of *fuck, yes, mouth, so perfect, God, please*, James's hips twitching in an obvious effort to keep from thrusting into Devin's mouth. It made Devin wish he had more time to spend, time to get past the polite self-control, to explore and learn what would make James forget himself completely. Would familiarity make James's dirty talk more intentional?

James's fingers twisted and tugged at Devin's hair, gentle at first and then with more insistence until Devin reluctantly pulled off with one last obscene, wet slide of his mouth. He pressed a few kisses against James's stomach, then pushed up onto his knees as he stroked James over the edge, drinking in the sight of him as he came undone.

Sated was an incredibly sexy look on James, and Devin wondered how he'd initially thought him to be average. Devin's cock throbbed, desire curling up his spine at the thought of James's hands on him. He grabbed the towel James had left on the nightstand to clean himself up a little as he waited for James to recover. Once he was done, he folded the towel over and set it on the bed; then he stretched out along James's side, taking the opportunity to paw at him a bit more as he went. There really were so many things he wanted to do. He wondered how many rounds James would be up for in a night.

"Just one more second," James said, turning on his side.

"Sure." Devin scooted closer and tugged James's arm to the other side of his waist, hoping James would get what he was after without him having to ask. He wanted James on top of him, wanted his weight pressing him into the bed.

It took a moment, but James did catch on, rolling them both until Devin was on his back, James pressed between his thighs. James smiled at him, still looking a little dazed as he slid his hand down over Devin's stomach, a light, teasing caress. The muscles in Devin's belly tightened in response, and he grabbed James's shoulders to keep from pushing his hand to where he wanted it. It sometimes took a conscious effort for him to go at someone else's pace. He nearly lost it when James stopped to get the bottle of lube and squirt some in his palm.

Devin's patience was rewarded when James finally wrapped his hand around his cock, too tight for a moment as he swiped his thumb over the head, and Devin tried to twitch away from the overstimulation. Then, with a twist of James's wrist it was perfect, the perfect pressure and pace and hot, slick slide. Devin shut his eyes and clutched at James's shoulders as he arched up, biting his lip to keep from begging. He wanted James in control, wanted to just give himself over to it.

"You're so gorgeous." James's whisper sound like more of an actual statement than meaningless pillow talk, and Devin opened his eyes again, confused.

James was watching him, so intent that Devin's whole body flushed. He didn't have an answer, couldn't think beyond the way James was touching him, so he pulled him into a kiss, relieved that James kissed him back. He kissed Devin senseless, sweet and filthy as he stroked him until Devin wasn't aware of anything beyond James's mouth and touch. He moved against James, restless and desperate, digging his fingers into his back as he finally toppled over the edge. James kissed him through it, soft fleeting kisses against his lips, then down the side of his neck as Devin's heartbeat continued to thunder in his ears.

"Holy shit," Devin said once he'd caught his breath. "Go team." He grinned when James laughed, feeling rather proud of himself. "Don't let me fall asleep. I want to go again. I mean, y'know, if you're game."

"I could be persuaded." James's voice was low and rumbly and pleasing.

Devin drew him into a kiss, and then another. It was way too soon to start fooling around again, but the way James kissed was stupidly addicting. "You kiss good. You should teach a class," Devin mumbled against his lips.

"No way that would be awkward."

The delivery was so deadpan it took Devin a moment to actually process the words, and once he started laughing, he couldn't make himself stop, silly, tired giggles that he was too satisfied to be embarrassed over. He felt James smile against his neck and wrapped his arm around his shoulders to keep him from moving away. "Just give me like five minutes."

"I'm gonna need more than five minutes," James said.

"That's okay." Devin dropped his arm, feeling a stab of disappointment as James rolled off him and onto his back. "I can start without you. It will give me a chance to thoroughly appreciate your person."

"I can't tell if you're joking or not."

"That depends entirely on whether or not you'd be into it."

"Thank you," James said instead of answering.

Devin turned his head to look at him. "For what?"

"For rescuing me."

"My pleasure." Devin slapped his hand over his mouth to cover a yawn, then said, "Three more minutes and I'm good." He rolled onto his side and propped his head up, reaching out to trace the curve of James's shoulder. "Tell me about yourself. What do you do when you're not being rescued by dashing young men?"

"There's not much to tell. I work in HR, I have one brother. I like to read." James shrugged. "I'm afraid I'm not terribly exciting."

"You say that like it's a bad thing."

James gave him a skeptical look. "Are you trying to convince me it's a good thing?"

"There are a lot of things that are better than exciting," Devin said. He'd had his share of exciting guys, and none of them had been worth spending more than a night with. "A car chase is exciting, but it gets old pretty fast."

"But it's fun while it lasts," James said.

Devin pinched him lightly, just enough to convey his annoyance. "If you think you're not fun, you haven't been paying very close attention."

"I guess you have your work cut out for you."

CHAPTER 3

JAMES knew without opening his eyes that it was still early, though the room seemed unreasonably bright. He grunted in displeasure and tucked his head down, his nose brushing against warm, smooth skin. To his complete mortification, it startled him so much that he jerked back before he remembered who it was. Luckily, Devin seemed to be a heavy sleeper because he only hunkered deeper into the covers, and when he resumed his deep, even breathing, James relaxed.

Despite his momentary panic, James was still half wrapped around Devin, his arm slung over his waist and their legs tangled together. They'd managed to create a cozy cocoon of blankets while they slept, and James tried to settle back into his previous lethargy but was too awake to manage it. He moved his head closer, feeling a little bit like a creep, but not enough to stop. He could smell Devin's shampoo, or maybe his soap. Something fresh and clean mixed with the scent of sweat and deodorant, maybe some cologne or aftershave as well. James couldn't really pick out any one thing, but the overall effect was sexy as hell. It was all he could do to keep from pressing his nose against the curve of Devin's neck and inhaling.

Devin was far and away the most appealing guy James had ever slept with, and while his list was admittedly shorter than a lot of guys he knew, it was still saying something. He'd had an amazing time, and it made James think that maybe he really had been selling himself short. Not that he thought a guy like Devin would be willing to stick around beyond breakfast. Devin was a fluke, a happy accident of circumstances that James had stumbled into. He was a fun, gorgeous guy who could have whoever he wanted, and for whatever reason, he'd decided James would be an entertaining choice for the evening. James had no illusions about that and it didn't really bother him.

Okay, maybe it bothered him a little. His night with Devin served as a stark contrast for how stuck James had become, how much he'd compromised on just about everything. Devin was a world of possibilities James had never thought to consider. He couldn't remember the last time sex had been so fun, even with the inherent awkwardness of being with someone new. It was a good reminder that it could be something more than the release and regret of hooking up with his ex. That it *should* be more than that. James needed to stop falling back into bad habits and start making an actual effort. There were other guys out there. Guys he could date and have fun with who might actually stick around.

Of course, it was a little difficult to think of the possibility of other guys when Devin was still very warm and naked and perfect right there in his bed. James wondered if he might be able to convince Devin to stick around for a while yet, or if he would want to leave as soon as he woke up. That was, if James could even work up the nerve to ask him.

Any further thoughts he had on the matter were interrupted by the shrill ring of his phone. Despite all the cute and clever ringtones Kara had loaded on there for him, he was old enough that the actual sound of a phone ringing was the only thing that was sure to get his attention. He turned to smack his hand on the nightstand where his phone usually was, only to remember that he'd never taken it out of his pocket the night before.

Devin shifted away from him as James scrambled out of bed in an effort to locate his jeans. The ringing had stopped by the time he found them, and James sighed when he saw his sister-in-law's name on the screen and decided to skip the voice mail for the time being.

"What time is it?"

"A little after eight," James said as he grabbed a clean pair of sweats from his dresser. It was one thing to strip down in front of a guy like Devin in the dark after they'd both been drinking. It was a different situation entirely to walk around naked in the cold apartment with the harsh morning light there to highlight every flaw.

"Good God, who calls you at eight on a Saturday?" Devin rolled onto his stomach and pillowed his head in his arms, the blankets slipping down to the middle of his back. With his hair falling in soft, messy curls around his face, he looked like some sort of debauched, twinky angel.

"Uh." James blinked and shook his head, looking around the room until he spotted his phone on the dresser. "My sister-in-law. I'm usually up by now, so." He tried not to wince at how much that said about him. *I'm the type of guy who so rarely has something going on in his personal life that his sister-in-law thinks nothing of calling him on a Saturday morning.*

"So, do you have to call her back?"

"Not right now." He probably should've at least listened to the voice mail, but he wasn't feeling particularly motivated. Likely Chris had done something to piss her off and she was calling to vent.

"Well then—" Whatever Devin was about to say was cut off by a loud metallic crunching sound outside. He gave James a startled look and James walked over to the window to see what had happened.

"Holy shit." James pulled the blinds up to get a better look. A truck had slid into one of the cars parked on the street because, sometime during the night, it had actually snowed several inches, which made the small hill that James lived on as good as impassable. "Did you have anywhere you needed to be today?"

Devin slid out of bed and wrapped himself in the down throw James kept folded on his cedar chest before joining James at the window. "Told you it would snow," he said mildly as they watched the driver try to get his truck off the road. "No, to answer your question. I don't have anywhere I need to be and no way to get there even if I did."

"So, then, you can hang out here," James said. "Or, y'know, go sit on a street corner. In the snow. Without a coat."

"Can I think about it for a minute?" Devin glanced at him out of the corner of his eye and grinned. "What about you? Will I be interrupting any plans?"

"I have some work I brought home that I need to get done, but other than that, not really." James wiped his hand over his face and wondered if he could make himself sound like more of a loser. "I'm like a real-life James Bond, I know. Try not to be too intimidated."

"James Bond never did it for me." Devin hooked his fingers in the waistband of James's sweats and started backing toward the bed. "What do you say, Darcy? You want to give it another go?"

"Sex or paperwork, let me think." James let Devin tumble them onto the bed and unwrapped him from the blanket he'd bundled himself in. "I'm sure you hear this all the time, but you are incredibly gorgeous."

"Weirdly, it never gets old."

James laughed at the easy agreement. There was something really refreshing about Devin's lack of coyness, and James wondered if he was like that all the time, or if his forthright manner was something he reserved for people he would never see again. Either way, it helped James relax and let go of whatever reservations he had left. Why not just go with it and enjoy himself?

"Can I?" James trailed his fingers down Devin's side, hoping the open-ended question might grant him a certain amount of blanket permission.

"Someone's feeling adventurous this morning," Devin teased.

"The universe has granted me a snow day with a beautiful guy in my bed. It would be a crime not to take advantage."

"Against nature?"

"Against sex." James felt himself flush at his own brazenness, but Devin seemed pleased by the answer.

"I'm willing to negotiate once you lose the sweats." Devin slipped his hands under the waistband to squeeze James's ass. "Those are definitely a crime against sex."

"Really?" James frowned. "Damn. These are my sexiest sweatpants too. Did you see the back? I think the way they sag around the butt is a particular selling point."

The smile Devin gave him was breathtaking. "Your butt is far too lovely to wear anything that sags."

James shimmied out of his sweats before he could think about it too much and had barely kicked them to the floor when Devin grabbed his hips to pull him back down.

"Yeah, like that." Devin hooked his legs around James's, their dicks pressed together between their stomachs.

It wasn't quite what James had in mind, but they had time. There was no need to rush. They could get off, and then he could kiss every inch of Devin's gorgeous, perfect body. Then they could get off again. James bent down to kiss him and ended up knocking their heads together when his phone started ringing again.

"Popular guy."

James groaned. "I'm sorry. Just—" He gave Devin a quick kiss. "Let me tell her to buzz off and then I'll turn it off, I swear." He kissed Devin again, the roll of his hips more automatic than intentional, but the result was the same. "Or we could...."

Somewhere from the floor, a muffled song started playing. It wasn't something James recognized, but considering his knowledge of pop music didn't extend much beyond the late '90s, that wasn't too surprising.

Devin laughed. "That'd be my phone. Probably my friend checking in to see if I'm still alive."

"So, I guess we should answer those then." James wasn't particularly thrilled with the idea. His call had already gone to voice mail.

"It will only take a minute," Devin said. "Then we can carry on uninterrupted."

"You make a compelling argument." James rolled to the side to let Devin up. He took a deep breath to gather some patience before he got up to get his own phone. There was no way Erin would know he had a guy there. She wasn't intentionally trying to ruin his entire life. He pushed himself into a sitting position and resisted the urge to put his pants back on before walking over to the dresser.

"Yeah, that was Brent," Devin said as he listened to his voice mail. "He's stuck where he is and hopes I found somewhere to crash last night." For the first time since they'd met, he sounded mildly annoyed, and James couldn't tell whether it was the interrupted sex or if it was toward his friend specifically.

James pulled up his voice mail and listened to the first message.

Hi, it's me. Um, maybe you're in the shower or something. Anyway, Chris woke up last night around three with a fever, and we've been up all night and I was wondering if you could maybe take the kids for a little bit. Nobody else can make it here with the snow and I can't watch them and take care of him at the same time. You know what a baby he is when he's sick.

"Shit," James said, skipping to the next message. "Shit, shit, shit."

Hi, it's me again. You're probably working and I know this is a huge imposition, but I need you to take care of the girls for awhile. I'm getting them dressed now, and we'll just walk over to your place. I know, I'm sorry. I have to figure out a way to get Chris to Urgent Care. Please be home. I'll be there in half an hour or so.

"No, no, no. Don't do this to me." James hit number to call her back, but it went to voice mail. He hung up without leaving a message. What was he going to say? *Screw your kids and sick husband, I'm getting laid?*

"Is everything okay?" Devin asked.

"Uh, not so much." James rubbed his hands over his face and sighed. "My brother is sick and my sister-in-law is on her way over with the kids so I can babysit. I need to grab a shower."

"Oh." Devin frowned and looked down at his phone. "Yeah, okay. I'll call Brent and see if maybe—"

"No!" James said a little too forcefully, startling Devin into looking up at him. "I mean, God, sorry. Yeah, of course you can call your friend, but I'm not kicking you out. Not that this is what you were expecting, but…." He really wished he had pants on for this.

The corner of Devin's mouth quirked up. "You still want me to stay?"

"I really do. I have to go take a cold shower right now, but then you could take a shower, and I have some clean clothes you could wear that will be way too big for you." James felt encouraged by the smile Devin gave him. "I don't know how long they'll be here, but I'm hoping it'll only be a few hours, and you can hang out in here if you want and watch a movie or something. Or, y'know, come out and play *My Little Pony* if you're into that sort of thing. Then maybe we could pick up where we left off?"

Devin nodded. "Sounds like a plan."

"Yeah?" James was more relieved than he was willing to admit. He knew Devin wouldn't be staying forever, but he wasn't ready for him to leave quite yet.

"Sure." Devin crawled back under the covers, and James wanted desperately to join him. "By the way, how many kids are we talking?"

"Two nieces, five and one." James pulled out some fresh clothes for himself, then wondered what in the world he had that would fit Devin. He grabbed a ribbed tank top and a sweatshirt that would work, but pants were going to be a problem. "Madison, the oldest, will either talk your ear off or ignore you completely. Zoe's pretty chill. A little slobbery still, but, y'know, she's one. They're great, but I completely understand if you're not a kid person."

"Naw, I like kids," Devin said around a yawn.

"Yeah?" James grinned when Devin nodded. "Cool." He had yet to date a guy who actively liked kids. Not that he and Devin were dating, but it was nice to know such guys did exist.

After another minute of searching, James came up with an old pair of running pants he should've gotten rid of years ago. They would probably still be too long, but at least they had a drawstring waist.

"If you want something clean to wear," James said, setting the clothes on his cedar chest. Devin did, of course, have his clothes from the night before, but they seemed like they might be a little formfitting for all-day wear. "I'm just gonna—"

"Yeah, go take your shower." Devin waved him away, yawning and disappearing further into the blankets. It was adorable. "I'm gonna hang out here."

The phone call from Erin had pretty much taken care of his erection, but James set the water to the cooler side just to be safe. It also ensured the shower was as quick as possible. It was Saturday, so he didn't need to shave. Once he was finished and dressed, he pulled the guest basket out from underneath his sink and grabbed a few things he thought Devin might want and set them, along with a fresh towel and washcloth, on the counter.

Devin was barely visible under the covers when James opened the door, so he tried to be as quiet as possible in creeping back into the room.

"I'm awake," Devin said, making him jump.

"Sorry."

"It's okay, I couldn't actually get back to sleep, but it's warm in here." He stuck his head out from under the covers and gave James a goofy smile.

"I'll turn up the heat," James promised. He usually did when the kids were over anyway.

Devin waggled his eyebrows. "Yeah, you will."

"Stop that. I'm trying to make the switch to uncle mode." It usually wasn't too difficult. James loved his nieces more than anything, but he was still having some trouble shifting his expectations for the day from Adult Things to playing dress-up and at least a few hours of *My Little Pony,* every single episode of which he had already seen at least three times over. Madison, bless her, had come by her obsessive tendencies honestly.

"I'm sorry. I'll be good. I promise I don't make dirty or inappropriate comments around children." Devin sat up and ran his hand through his hair, somehow managing to make it look even more unruly.

"Are you sure your sister won't mind me being here? Is she like—" He made an angry face and curved his fingers into claws.

"Nosferatu?"

"Exactly."

"Nah. She's cool. I'll talk to her when they get here." It was something James had actually wondered about, but seeing as how Erin had sprung this on him, she didn't have much in the way of grounds to object. Besides, it wasn't like Devin had somewhere else to go at the moment.

"I've taken those First Aid CPR classes if that helps."

James grinned, charmed all over again that Devin would care one way or the other what Erin thought. "I'll let her know you have extensive babysitting credentials. Speak of the devil," he said as his phone rang. "There's stuff in the bathroom if you want to take a shower. I have to go let them into the building."

For a moment he was tempted to let the call go to voice mail, just to see what she'd do, but from her previous messages, he guessed she wasn't in the mood for jokes, so he answered it. "I'm on my way down."

"Oh thank God," she said and immediately hung up on him.

When he reached the front door, he was glad he hadn't screwed around with her. Erin looked like she wanted to strangle the world in general, and Madison looked decidedly put out. Only Zoe, strapped to Erin's chest in her puffy pink jacket, seemed okay with the morning's events.

"What would you have done if I hadn't been here?" James asked.

"I would've cried and hunted you down. Not necessarily in that order." Erin handed the bag full of babysitting essentials over to him on her way in, and James took hold of Madison with his free hand as she tried to stomp the slush off her otherwise pristine boots.

"I dislike the snow very much," she told him, adorably ferocious in her ire. They'd clearly had another conversation on using the word "hate" on the walk over.

"Shocking, right?" Erin asked tiredly, already halfway up the stairs. Madison had always been particular about anything she deemed messy. Their one and only attempt to take her camping before Zoe was born had resulted in a meltdown of epic proportions. That she would not be fond of snow was not a complete revelation.

"Hey, hold up." James looked down at Madison, who was still disgustedly wiping her feet, and bent down to scoop her up. "Come on, Cookie. We'll clean your boots up inside, okay?" She crossed her arms but allowed it, and James caught up to Erin just as she was entering the apartment. "I need to talk to you for a sec."

"I know. I'm sorry I'm so crabby. I really appreciate this."

"Thanks, but there's actually something else." James kneeled down to help Madison get her shoes off, then handed her the bag which was half as big as she was. "Take this to your room, okay?" He watched her stagger down the hall, dragging the bag behind her, for a moment before turning back to Erin.

"What's up?" Erin was only half paying attention to him; most of her focus was on getting Zoe unbundled.

"I, uh...." James scratched the back of his neck. "Made a new friend last night?"

"Good for you. And?"

"And he's still here."

Erin did look at him then, her eyes comically wide. "Oh snap. I was not expecting that."

"Yeah, me neither, to be honest. But it happened, and then we got snowed in today, and...." He trailed off and waited for the implication to sink in.

"And babysitting is not what you wanted to be doing right now." Erin rubbed at her eyes as Zoe babbled at her happily. "Shoot, Jay. I'm so sorry. I didn't even think—"

"It's fine. I'm still going to watch them," James said, because she really did seem to be at her breaking point. "I just wanted to let you know that there was someone else here. I mean, he's nice and it'll be fine and everything, but also, how long do you think you'll be?"

Erin laughed, then groaned. "No idea. Chris thinks he's dying. I think he has a sinus infection, which is what I told him days ago when he started feeling crummy, but of course he didn't go to the doctor then like I suggested because that would've been the reasonable thing to do. So now I have to find a way to get him to a walk-in clinic. Without killing him."

"I wish you luck and as much speed as you can manage. I mean, y'know. Seriously. If you could make it back before dinner."

"I'll see what I can do."

"Don't give me that look," James said when she frowned, very much like Madison had over the snow. "I'm the victim here. I mean, really, how often do I get—a new friend?" he finished as Madison joined them again carrying her *My Little Pony* DVDs.

"It's rare enough that you're actually more pathetic than Chris right now. You're giving me details later." She pulled Zoe from the sling and handed her over. "I'll try and be as fast as I can, but I'm making no promises. You're going to be good for your Uncle Jay, right?" she asked Madison, smoothing her hair back from her forehead.

Madison nodded dutifully as she pushed the DVDs into James's hand.

"We've got this," James said. "Don't worry. Just—"

"Hurry back, yeah, I got it." She winked at him to soften the reply, then leaned in to kiss his cheek. "Thank you, dear, really. I owe you one."

CHAPTER 4

DEVIN knew he needed to get up once he heard James arrive back at the apartment with his family in tow, but he wasn't quite ready to leave behind the blanket cocoon he'd created, and he regretted it was necessary at all. By all rights, he should've been halfway to his second orgasm by now. Of course, contrary as he was by nature, the fact that James had agreed to watch his nieces made him that much more attractive. His sister-in-law hadn't even worried that he wouldn't come through for her. That sort of dependability was a huge turn-on.

"Mr. Darcy," Devin whispered as he pressed the back of his hand to his forehead, rolling his eyes at himself. Luckily, there was no one around to witness his stupidity. He rolled over with the intention of getting up but was distracted again by the faint scent of cologne that clung to the sheets. It was something dark and woodsy and expensive-smelling. Devin stayed there for a moment, his cheek pressed against the pillow, then forced himself to push back the blankets and stand.

The clothes James had pulled out for him were sitting on the chest at the foot of the bed, but Devin had to search for his underwear, which was the only item James had forgotten. Devin wondered if that was intentional. Probably not, considering the circumstances. His jeans had been kicked to the side when he'd retrieved his phone, and his briefs had made their way under the bed. The urge to peek at what James kept under there was too tempting for Devin to pass up, but it looked to be mostly storage.

Devin grabbed the rest of the clothes and went into the bathroom, which was as tidy and organized as the rest of the apartment. In addition to the clean towel Devin expected to find, there was a pile of travel-sized goodies waiting for him: deodorant, a razor, toothpaste, and a toothbrush with the name of a dentist stamped into the handle. There was clearly no end to James's charm, and Devin felt an aching sort of fondness for him as he set the items on the counter to get at the towel and washcloth underneath. He wondered what it would be like to actually date a guy like James if this was the level of consideration he showed a virtual stranger.

It was a melancholy sort of thought, and Devin shook off the funk that threatened to settle over him as he got in the shower. As a general rule, he didn't like to dwell on useless what-ifs.

By the time Devin was showered, shaved, and minty fresh, his carefree mood had been more or less restored. He had to roll the waist of the pants James had given him a few times in order to make them work, and the sweatshirt was too big, but it was warm and weirdly comforting. He'd never borrowed someone's clothes in an intimate context. It was nice.

One last mirror check confirmed that he looked a little silly but not entirely ridiculous. Devin could work with that. He was going to be hanging out with kids. It was fine. He took a deep breath, then another, realizing with some amusement that he was nervous about meeting James's nieces. *Madison and Zoe, five and one.* He repeated the information a few more times to commit it to memory.

What if they didn't like him? That was absurd, though. Devin was great with kids. He'd even considered becoming a preschool teacher once upon a time. They would like him. The bigger question was, why did it matter to him so much that they did? They could end up loving him best in all the world and James would still be a nice guy that Devin spent a pleasant weekend with one time.

"No pressure." Devin made a face at himself and left the bathroom.

The bedroom door was still closed, but Devin could hear cartoon voices coming from the living room. James hadn't been kidding about the ponies, apparently. Sure enough, Devin found everyone in the living room on the couch, watching the goings-on in Pony Land. Well, the girls were watching. James was staring off into the middle distance, his expression somewhere between pained and resigned.

Madison was dressed all in pink, with brown eyes and a riot of black curls making a mockery of someone's valiant attempt at taming them into a ponytail. Zoe, dressed in green and seated on James's lap, looked like a chubby baby version of her sister. They were adorable, and must've taken after their mother, as Devin could see no immediate resemblance to James.

Devin cleared his throat, his nervousness returning full force, and patted down his sides, wishing his pants had pockets. He smiled reflexively when James turned to him, calming down a bit at the bemused look on his face. The situation was too ridiculous to get so wound up about. *No pressure.*

"Hey," James said quietly as he stood, adjusting his hold on Zoe to settle her on his hip. "Do you want something to eat? Or coffee? Choose wisely—you can't have both." He walked the long way around the couch to avoid crossing between Madison and the TV.

"Coffee would be fantastic," Devin said, even as his stomach betrayed him with an unseemly rumble.

"I was joking. You can have both. Hey, Cookie, this is my friend, Devin. Can you say hi?" When she didn't respond, James leaned over the back of the couch and grabbed the remote to pause the TV. "What do we say when we meet new people?"

Madison kneeled up on the couch and turned to them, taking a moment to glare at James before delivering a very flat "Nice to meet you," to Devin.

"It's nice to meet you too." Devin pressed his lips together to keep from laughing as she flopped back on the couch, her arms crossed. "You can let her watch her show," he said when James looked like he wanted to chide her for being rude.

James sighed. "Sorry, she's a little bit contentious this morning."

"Am not!"

"Are too," James said as he pressed play. He winked at Devin, who was still struggling to muffle his laughter. "Honestly, I don't know where she gets it from."

"Must just be one of those things."

Zoe, who had previously been occupied smacking James's chin, spotted Devin then and lunged for him with enough force that James struggled to keep his grip on her. "Jeeze. This is Zoe. She's super shy."

"I can take her," Devin said as Zoe continued to make grabby hands at him.

"Are you sure?" James asked, even as he shifted to hand her over. "She's an armful."

"I believe I was promised coffee." Devin accepted Zoe, settling her on his hip. "Hi there. How are you?"

Zoe waved her arms in delight and made a happy cooing noise.

"Lady of few words."

"Yeah, when she's not otherwise occupied, her sister does most of the talking for her." James motioned for Devin to follow him into the kitchen. "How do you take your coffee? I'd offer to make it Irish, considering the amount of cartoon watching your immediate future holds, but…."

Devin laughed. "Just a little bit of sugar is fine. I can handle a few cartoons."

James poured the coffee and passed it over with a spoon and an adorably grandma-like ceramic sugar bowl. "Famous last words," he said as he took Zoe back, much to her dismay.

"Is that a challenge?"

"I suppose that depends on the terms."

Devin sipped at his coffee and considered it. "Winner gets to call the shots, within reason, for the next round of grown-up play time. First one to break loses."

The smile James gave him was a little too confident. "You're on."

THREE solid pony hours later, Devin was ready to admit defeat. While Madison had warmed to him once she realized she could narrate the show to him as he watched, it had come at a terrible price. Namely, Devin wanted to watch the rest of the series to see what happened, which was worrying enough for him to try and talk Madison into a break.

"Did you get to play in the snow on your way over?" he asked when James got up to change the disc.

"I hate the snow."

"Madison."

"I dislike the snow very much," Madison amended.

"Well, then." Devin fished around for something else. He could see James's shoulders shaking and he suspected he was being laughed at. James was enjoying this way too much. Aside from the cartoons, Zoe had fussed until James had handed her over to Devin, which meant that, really, Devin was doing all the heavy lifting babysitting-wise. "What about lunch?"

James turned as the disc loaded, still looking incredibly pleased with himself. "I could eat. Are you hungry, Cookie? I can make mac and cheese."

"From the box?" Devin asked a little too excitedly, realizing once the words were out of his mouth that James probably had big people food in mind for them. "I'm asking for a friend."

"It's the hippie kind, but yeah. Same basic idea." James was at least polite enough not to laugh at Devin outright as he confirmed the macaroni selection. He kneeled down in front of Madison to get her attention. "Hey, look at me. Does that sound good?"

When Madison nodded her agreement, James straightened and patted the top of Devin's head like he was one of the children. "Do you want a sandwich or something to go with your mac and cheese? I have some deli ham and roast beef."

Devin batted his hand away. "A ham sandwich would be lovely, thank you. And some juice. And a cookie."

At the word "cookie" Madison perked up, and James gave Devin an accusatory look. "I'll see what I can come up with."

Once James disappeared into the kitchen, Devin turned to Madison, determined to convince her that they should do something else while James was otherwise occupied. "Do you want to play a game? I think I saw some board games over there." It spoke to Devin's level of desperation that he was willing to embark on an afternoon of Monopoly with a five-year-old. "We could play pretend," he suggested when Madison shot down the board game idea. "We could have an adventure to rescue princess Zoe, who was captured by an evil dragon!"

Madison tilted her head and considered Devin out of the corner of her eye, clearly convinced this was some sort of trick or dastardly plot.

"Help me," Devin said in a high-pitched voice. He waved one of Zoe's hands, making her giggle. "Help me, Madison! You're my only hope." It was fair game. She was too young to get the reference.

"I want to be a princess," Madison said, which was encouraging. If she was willing to bargain, he at least had her interest.

"You can be! You can be an adventuring princess, out to rescue your sister."

"Ugh, don't you know anything?" Madison rolled her eyes in a display of truly impressive disdain. "Only a prince can rescue a princess."

"Nuh-uh. Only if you want it to take forever." Devin leaned forward and whispered, "Princes take forever to get there." He nodded to emphasize the point. "Besides, I didn't see any ponies waiting around to get rescued by some silly prince. Did you?" He had her there, and they both knew it.

"Maybe," Madison finally conceded. Then she looked around the room as if to imply it was not the most adventurous setting ever. It wasn't really, but Devin wasn't about to let that stop him.

"We could make a fort!" Devin said, the combination of desperation and excitement making him restless. "We could make caves and a castle and… things." Devin eyed the couch cushions, which were definitely usable. He had made do with less.

"What kinds of things?" James asked from the doorway, making Devin jump. He'd been so momentarily consumed with the idea that he'd forgotten he really ought to check with James first. Devin was saved from an immediate answer by Madison, who had been won over by the prospect.

"Can we make a fort, Uncle Jay, and go on an adventure?" She hopped off the couch and ran over to him, wrapping her arms around his leg and tilting her head back so she could look up at him in the most blatantly-manipulative-yet-effective way possible. "Please?"

"May we," James corrected absently. "What does this fort building involve?" He looked at Devin expectantly, but it seemed like he was willing to humor them.

"Oh, you know, a few couch cushions. Maybe some chairs. A few blankets and sheets. Old sheets," Devin amended, thinking of the very nice, very soft, bajillion-thread-count sheets that were currently on James's bed. "Clothes pins or safety pins, and your *imagination*." Devin threw in some jazz hands with that to coax a full-blown smile from James and felt a happy little flutter in his stomach when it worked.

"Can we? May we?" Madison bounced as she asked.

"Why don't you go wash your hands for lunch and let me think about it."

"Sorry," Devin said as Madison tore down the hall toward the bathroom. "I should've run the idea by you first."

James hummed noncommittally. "Is this you admitting defeat?"

"Mr. Darcy!" Devin gasped in mock outrage. "Are you using your niece's very happiness as a tool to win our wager?" He grinned. "How opportunistic. I didn't know you had it in you."

"You'd be surprised." James made a show of studying his nails, his expression intentionally bland. "Well?"

It hadn't escaped Devin's notice that James had grown more confident with his nieces there. Maybe because they served as a buffer, or perhaps it was the by-product of him being an authority figure to them. Either way, the result was unarguably appealing, even in their current G-rated context. James was relaxed and indulgent with Madison without allowing her to run roughshod over him. Circumstances were proving him to be attractive as a person on every level, and Devin found he was no longer as bothered as he'd originally been by the change in their plans for the day.

"My hands are clean," Madison announced as she raced back into the living room. "Can we?"

Devin knew that, despite James's expectant look, he was going to say yes whether Devin admitted defeat or not. Still, he was curious as to the terms of surrender James had in mind. What would he do with Devin at his mercy? The possibilities were tantalizing and endless, and James was watching him with enough interest to make Devin squirm.

There was no downside that Devin could see, so he nodded and was rewarded with a brief, shockingly dirty smile before James turned his attention back to Madison.

"Yes, we can build a fort. *After* you eat your lunch."

"Yay!" Madison hopped up and down, clapping her hands.

Devin was sorely tempted to do the same.

CHAPTER 5

JAMES had known skipping nap time would be a bad idea when he made that call, but Madison had been so excited about the fort, there'd been a near meltdown when he suggested they get a nap in first, and after it was built, he knew tearing her away from it would be impossible. In his defense, he'd still been laboring under the illusion that it would be Erin and Chris dealing with the bedtime fallout. By the time Erin had called to apologize profusely and ask if he could keep the girls for the night, it was too late to do anything but brace himself for the battle of trying to put two very exhausted girls to bed after a day of fun.

It *had* been a fun day, at least, and Devin had been a huge part of that. He'd shown an amazing amount of patience in letting Madison help him with the fort—the blanket and pillow monstrosity that now covered most of James's living room. Madison, in return, had been on her very best behavior in helping. They'd spent the rest of the afternoon playing, though James had been relegated to playing the part of Lady Princess Knight Madison's trusty steed, leaving Devin to play the wicked sorcerer, the grumpy dragon, and the handsome prince who was always late to everything.

"Where have you been?" Madison had asked when he arrived. "I already slayed the bad guys and rescued the princess. Why are princes always late?"

"If only I knew, dear Lady Princess Knight." Devin had bowed low and kissed her hand at that, making her giggle. "I know now who I shall call if ever I am in need of a rescuing."

Following that there'd been a very brief, embarrassing moment where James had been jealous of his niece. Madison was not the only one who would've benefitted from a nap, it seemed.

In light of Devin's unwavering good humor throughout the day, James let him off the hook for getting the girls ready for bed. He knew that having Devin there at that point would only make them fight harder when they were already so desperately sleepy. Madison had nearly done a face-plant into her dinner.

"It took a while, but exhaustion finally worked in my favor," James said as he walked back out into the living room. "I didn't even get through the first page of our bedtime story. Where are you?" He looked around, expecting to find Devin at the table, as that was the only seating that hadn't been consumed by blankets.

"In here," Devin said from somewhere in the middle of his creation. "Come on in. The water's fine."

Since he'd spent his day as a horse, James hadn't really had a chance to explore the fort, so he knelt down, hoping Devin missed the sound of his knees cracking, and crawled inside. It was really quite an impressive structure, considering the fact that it was using couch cushions as support beams in places. James could definitely see how this would be magical to a kid Madison's age.

Devin was stretched out on his back, under the dark-red sheet that was tented between the coffee table and two barstools. The light filtering through gave that whole section of the fort a decidedly brothel-like glow, and James wondered if Devin had noticed. He looked very much like exhaustion was about to do him in as well. The sheet was high enough at the barstool end for James to sit upright, so he sat and crossed his legs, careful not to knock anything out of place.

"I picked up most of Madison's things and put them in her bag, but I wasn't sure what's supposed to go home with her, and what stays here. So—" Whatever he was about to say was cut off by a huge yawn. "I thought I'd hang out in here for a few minutes before we took it down. I was the weird little kid who used to hide in cabinets and stuff."

"You've done this before," James said.

"The fort?" Devin tilted his head back to look at him and nodded. "Yeah, I make them with my nephews whenever they come to visit, but they live in California, so it isn't super often. Weirdly, my mom frowns upon me just building them for myself. Says it's 'childish'." He brought his hands up to do the air quotes, then laced his fingers together over his stomach.

"Your mom?"

"Oh, hey. There's an embarrassing fact I wasn't going to share. I lost my job a few months ago and had to move back home. Temporarily."

"That's not all that uncommon right now," James said. He'd realized more than once over the past few years how lucky he was to not only still have his job, but to enjoy what he did and the company he was working for. True, it wasn't exciting or glamorous, but it suited him. Things could definitely be worse. "You shouldn't be embarrassed."

"Yeah, nothing ramps up a guy's sex appeal like sleeping in his childhood bedroom." Devin reached up and patted his knee. "Thank you, though. You're a nice man."

"You keep saying that."

"It keeps being true."

"Well." James rubbed the back of his neck. "About tonight...."

"I'm completely okay with a 'no sex with kids in the house' rule, really. I don't know how straight couples manage it." He looked back at James again. "God, I hope that's what you were going to say."

"That was the gist of it, yeah." Devin's laughter triggered James's own, and he figured they were probably both tired enough to be a little punchy. Sitting under the cover of sheets and blankets only made him feel sillier. "What about the next best thing?"

"I'm curious to see what you consider the next best thing to be." Devin waved his hand. "I'll allow it."

James leaned over and kissed his nose. "Stay here. I'll be right back."

The camping gear was stashed in the front hall closet, including the very expensive backpacking sleeping bag James had bought a week before he and hiker Rob had both admitted that sometimes opposites were just opposites. He pulled that out along with the flashlight. Most of his spare blankets had been used in the structure of the fort, so he detoured to the bedroom to grab the pillows and blankets off his bed. It occurred to him as he waddled into the living room with his oversized armload that it might have been better to make two trips. He dropped everything at the entrance to the fort and pushed the sleeping bag in front of him, dragging his duvet along beside him like a demented hamster.

"What is this?" Devin sat up as James rolled the sleeping bag toward him.

"You wanna camp out tonight? No s'mores, but I have a flashlight, so we can do shadow puppets and stuff." James wasn't sure what he was expecting as a response, except maybe more laughter at the absurdity of it. Instead, Devin smiled, looking genuinely touched.

"Really?"

The offer seemed more fragile and important than it had been a moment ago. James had hit on something, and he nodded, wanting to walk the right line between light and sincere so as not to ruin it. "I have the blankets, more blankets and pillows out there too. And none of my scary stories include zombies."

"Except for the spider zombies."

"That one's actually more of a love story."

"Interspecies?"

"Not until the sequel." James shrugged. "You went to all the effort of putting this up. I don't know that I'm ready to tear it down quite yet."

"Yeah," Devin said quietly. "Same here."

"Right, so, um." James nodded at the sleeping bag. "If you want to get that unzipped and spread out, I'll get the rest of the bedding and hit the lights and stuff."

James got all the pillows and blankets into the brothel area of the fort for Devin to arrange as he wanted, then went back out to make sure the rest of the apartment was in order. Luckily, the girls, once out, generally slept like rocks. He flipped on the nightlight in the bathroom and turned on the light over the sink in the kitchen in case Devin needed something in the middle of the night. He turned off the living room lights and smiled when the flashlight flickered on in the middle of the tent a moment later.

By the time he crawled back into the fort, Devin had arranged a cozy little nest for them and was practicing his shadow puppets against the ceiling.

"I can only really do a duck. Or...." He frowned at his hand. "Whatever that is. A raptor, maybe."

"Where's its teeth?"

"A baby raptor."

"A raptor zombie."

"Don't even joke about something like that." Devin flipped back the blankets so James could join him. "*Jurassic Park* gave me nightmares. I know what you're thinking, and the answer is yes, I am a giant chicken."

James bit his tongue against the joke he wanted to make, knowing it would only date him. He'd made that mistake too many times with

Kara, and the vacant stare of someone too young to understand his pop culture references was not something he typically enjoyed. Instead he crawled between the covers and settled on his back next to Devin so he could watch his shadow duck raptors attack each other.

"To be fair, I think most people would be afraid if confronted with an actual dinosaur."

Devin nodded but didn't really seem to mark the comment. "There's this closet at my parents' house under the stairs. It's not like a creepy spider closet. It's nice. There's carpet and a slanted ceiling so it's not like the back of stairs. I used to hang out in there so much as a kid that my mom stopped trying to use it for storage."

"What'd you do in there?"

"Read, mostly. Sometimes I played with my G.I. Joes or whatever. I made them make out in there when I got a little older and, y'know." He grinned then. "Made out in there a few times myself in high school. With other people," he said, glancing at James. "I wasn't in there alone."

"Yeah, I got that."

"Good. I mean, not that you even asked. I just have always kind of liked closed spaces like that. They feel…."

"Cozy?" James asked.

"I was gonna say secure." Devin sighed. "At the risk of sounding dumb, it seems like, as you get older, you grow out of everything that once made you feel that way."

"Yeah." James wasn't sure what else to say to that. He couldn't exactly argue the point, but it seemed like an odd sentiment coming from someone who had seemed so fearless the night before.

"So, sometimes you've just gotta make a pillow fort. That's my philosophy."

"This is more like a pillow castle, really," James said. "You have a talent."

"You don't know the half of it. The list of delightful yet ultimately useless things I have mastered is staggering. The lollipop ghosts I make at Halloween would knock your socks off."

"Yeah? Those don't give you nightmares?" James teased.

"Sometimes. I never said I wasn't willing to suffer for my art."

"Speaking of suffering, thank you for being such a good sport today. I know this wasn't exactly ideal."

"Nah." Devin waved the comment away. "Don't worry about it. It was fun. Okay," he conceded at James's dubious expression. "I'm not saying I wasn't completely on board with our original agenda, but it really wasn't too bad. And, hey, your sister-in-law owes you now, right?"

"I will definitely be reminding her of this the next time I need a favor," James said. "But the truth is, we've known each other for so long it's impossible to know who owes who at this point."

"Yeah? How long have you known each other?"

"Since high school. We were best friends all four years, and we went to college together. Then she went and ruined it by seducing my baby brother like a giant creepy brother-seducer." James gave an exaggerated shudder. He really had been appalled when Chris had told him they were dating, and while he'd eventually accepted them as a couple, and even admitted they were good together, he still liked to occasionally give them grief about it.

"So much explained." Devin laughed. "How much younger is your brother?"

"Three whole years."

"Aw, come on. That's not so bad."

"It's gross," James said decisively. "I try not to think about it too much. They got the girls from a cabbage patch."

"Isn't that a little sexist? I mean, guys date younger women all the time. Or younger guys, for that matter." He raised an accusatory eyebrow at James.

"It has nothing to do with her being a woman and everything to do with him being my baby brother. To put it another way, if she were a dude and my brother was a girl, I would be equally creeped out. So really," he said, crossing his arms behind his head. "You're the one who's sexist for assuming it has to do with her being a woman."

"Touché. That's really great, though, joking aside."

"What?"

"That you guys are such good friends. That you can count on each other and you don't keep track. When you start keeping track.... Well. That's not good, obviously."

"Voice of experience?"

"I'm a little low in friends I can depend on at the moment." He laughed. "Sorry. Lack of sleep makes me a little too true confessions."

"It's fine," James said, hoping he sounded more casual than insanely curious. "What happened? If you don't mind my asking."

"Just one of those things. I was living in Portland with my college roommate. He was straight, but we were really good friends. Or, I thought we were really good friends. We had our little hipster coffeehouse group, and everyone was really great. Then I lost my job, and Josh more or less said if I wasn't going to be able to pay my share of the bills, he had a buddy who was moving there who could use the room." He shrugged. "There was some other stuff too, before that. The little stuff that builds on itself."

James tried not to be outraged and failed spectacularly. "Still, that's so shitty!"

"It wasn't unfair. Rent isn't cheap," Devin said evenly. "But once I moved back home, that was pretty much it with everyone else too. I got a few e-mails and phone calls for the first couple weeks, then nothing. The people I'd started to think of as family were just gone. Out of sight, out of mind, I guess."

"I'm sorry." James wished there was more he could say. *That sucks* seemed a little inadequate. "For what it's worth, I don't believe you're even a little bit forgettable. Also, they're idiots."

"Thanks," Devin said, his voice warm and amused.

"What about the guy you're staying with?"

"Brent? Brent is… who he is."

"Meaning?"

"We've known each other forever. Brent was my high school friend with benefits. Neither of us were really out, so we fooled around with each other." He paused for a moment, and James wondered what he was thinking about. "That's a pretty apt description of our friendship, really. Brent is the guy to call when you need a break, but he's not all that reliable. I'm not bad-mouthing him, by the way. He'd be the first one to tell you he's a gigantic flake."

"That doesn't mean he's not a good friend." James felt the need to point it out, despite feeling weirdly jealous of Brent. He wanted to think there was at least one friend out there who Devin could depend on.

"That's true, as long as you don't have any expectations. That's a good rule in general, actually."

James frowned. "Aren't you a little young to be that cynical about people?"

"Do I seem cynical?" Devin sounded honestly surprised. "I'm really not. I don't think I am, at least. I mean, a cynic would expect people to be disappointing, right?" He nodded at that, not waiting for James to answer. "Somehow that's the part that always catches me off guard. Now, quick, tell me something appalling so I don't feel embarrassed."

"The *Twilight* thing wasn't enough?"

"Nope. Too endearing."

"Erin and I took a weekend trip to Forks when she was pregnant with Zoe. It was my idea."

Devin laughed low and easy as he turned over, propping himself up enough to kiss James once, chaste and fleeting. James held his gaze until the moment stretched thin and Devin looked away, reaching to switch off the flashlight. He settled with his head curved toward James's shoulder, close enough that James could feel the puff of his breath, but not quite touching. "You're surprising in all the good ways, Darcy. I hope you know that."

"I'm glad you think so." Devin hummed in response, and James tried to think of something else to ask him, something that would keep them awake just a few minutes longer. "You said you had nephews?"

"Three nephews," Devin said on a sigh. "Ten, seven, and two."

"How many siblings do you have?"

"Just the one older sister."

"So you're the baby of the family?"

"Kinda obvious if you think about it, huh?" Devin's words were slurring together, and James decided the polite thing to do would be to let him sleep, much as he hated to let go of the intimacy the darkness of the fort provided.

"M'awake. I'm awake," Devin said without prompting, and he shifted again until he was curled up against James's side, his head actually resting on his shoulder. "Tell me something 'bout you."

"Like what?"

"Doesn't matter. I like your voice."

"Well, I just have the one brother. We are nothing alike, but we get along pretty well." Devin made a sound of acknowledgement, so James continued. "I wanted to be a fireman when I was a kid. A few years down the road, I realized I didn't want to necessarily *be* a fireman. There was a station just down the street from us."

When James received no response to that, he sighed. "I think I really like you," he said and wondered if he'd be brave enough to say it again in the morning.

CHAPTER 6

"HEY, Devin."

Devin groaned and pushed blindly at the hand that was prodding him awake. He rolled onto his side in order to escape it, but the hand kept after him.

"Come on, babe, wake up. You don't have to stay awake, we just need to relocate you."

"D'you call me babe?" Devin asked, because that was sort of nice, really. He could be babe for James.

There was a definite awkward beat of silence that followed the question before James said, "The girls will be getting up pretty soon, so I thought I'd give you a heads-up. If you want to sleep a little longer, you can hide out in my bedroom."

"Hmm." Devin took a deep breath and forced his brain to start working. When he opened his eyes, he realized they were, in fact, still in the fort. James was sitting cross-legged at his side, his hands wrapped around a cup of coffee. He looked unfairly handsome sitting there, his stubble dark enough to make him look ever-so-slightly roguish. "How much time do we have?"

"A few minutes. They'll sleep until I get them up, but the roads have cleared, so Erin will be here in a little while to get them, and I need to have them upright by then. Coffee?" he asked when he caught Devin eyeing his cup.

"Can I just steal a sip of yours?" Devin was still weighing his options of more sleep versus being awake. He accepted the cup with a smile and took a much larger sip than he should have. James drank his coffee very black and very strong. "Refreshing," Devin said once he'd managed to swallow the mouthful.

James was doing a terrible job of not laughing at him as he took the cup back. "Sorry, I should've warned you. You should see your face."

"Well, I'm awake now." Devin did actually feel well rested, considering they'd spent the night on the floor. He sat up and leaned forward to kiss James's cheek. "Thank you for the campout."

"Sure. Any time."

James said it like he meant it, and Devin found himself indulging in the momentary fantasy that *any time* was an offer. That Devin could have more mornings with James calling him babe and terrible coffee.

"You still with me?" James asked.

"Yeah. Sorry." He blinked and rubbed the sleep from his eyes. "It usually takes me a few minutes."

Devin helped James haul his blankets back to the bedroom and make the bed up. He wondered if they'd get a chance to mess it up again before he had to leave.

"I'm gonna go get the girls up," James said. "Feel free to do whatever. If you want to shower or get coffee or go back to sleep."

"Thanks." Devin rubbed his eyes with both hands and willed himself to shake off the morning lethargy and come up with a plan of action. He didn't even know what time it was. A quick scan of the room revealed no obvious clocks, so Devin grabbed his phone from the nightstand where he'd left it the previous morning.

The wake-up screen showed that it was nine thirty and that he had five missed calls and three new texts, all from Brent. Devin dialed his voice mail and listened to the messages.

Hey, it's me. Call me back when you come up for air.

Hey, it's me again. Just checking in. I'm still stuck here, but it looks like the roads should be good in the morning. Call me back.

Dude. I'm sure you're having, like, tons of crazy awesome Olympic marathon sex, and that's great, but if you could text me or whatever to let me know you haven't been axe murdered, that would be nice.

You're such a dick.

Okay, I have to go into work at noon, so if you want me to come pick you up, it'll have to be before that. So fucking call me back.

Devin dialed Brent's number, not bothering with the texts. He assumed they were more of the same.

"You're such a little bitch," Brent said by way of a greeting.

"If I didn't know any better, I'd swear you were worried about me."

"Hardly. I'm merely disconcerted by this unexpected role reversal. You are the responsible one, I am the inconsiderate flake who goes home with a guy and then doesn't check in for a whole fucking day. It works for us, Devin. Why mess with a good thing?"

"Sorry," Devin said, because Brent had a point. It was a dick move and he usually knew better. "It's been a weird weekend."

"Was there a sex swing involved?"

"What? No, nothing like that. Why would you even ask that?"

Brent hummed and said, "A story for another time. Am I coming to get you or is the sex dungeon your new home?" If Brent had to be at work by noon, he would need to come get Devin almost immediately.

"Can I get back to you on that? The pick-up part, not the sex dungeon." It was best not to let Brent run with some things. "I just need to figure out a couple of things."

"Where are you?"

"Within walking distance of the bar."

Brent sighed. "I need to know within the next half hour. Otherwise I'll assume you found your own ride, so to speak. I think Kathy is home tonight, so she can let you in. Creepy Dave is out with his friend Creepy Mark, so he'll be gone most of the day."

"Have I met Creepy Mark?"

"If you have to ask, you definitely have not. Anyway, I have to go grab a shower. Shoot me a text once you know what your plans are."

"Yeah. Thanks, man. I'll let you know."

Devin ended the call and debated whether or not he wanted to take a shower himself, but decided he should probably talk to James first. As soon as he figured out what to say. The etiquette books didn't really cover a polite way to say *I would like you to fuck me if you're interested, but I'll also need a ride home.* Even if twenty-four hours ago, that's exactly what Devin would've said without a second thought.

Now there were second thoughts, and third thoughts, and the stupid little part of Devin that wanted James to ask him to stay. Playing over their earlier conversations didn't offer Devin any clues on that front. James had mentioned the kids being picked up, but hadn't given an indication of what his plans for the day were beyond that. The only way to find that out was to ask him directly.

Devin could do direct. It was sort of his thing.

James was at the dining room table with the girls having a family breakfast of oatmeal and fruit, Madison in her booster seat with five different coloring books spread out in front of her, and Zoe strapped in to her high chair tapping her spoon against the tray. It was sweet and wholesome enough to make Devin's confidence falter. He didn't fit into the picture anywhere. This was a family, and Devin was the guy James had brought home to fuck. No, even that wasn't the full truth. Devin was the guy who had talked James into bringing him home and charmed his way into his bed. Was he really considering trying to talk James into letting him stay longer?

"Breakfast?" James asked, pointing to his bowl with his spoon. "There's other stuff too if you're not an oatmeal guy."

"Uh, no. Thank you, though. I was actually— My friend called. Brent, who I'm staying with, and he has to work tonight. He works at a restaurant, so he has to go in at noon, so if he is going to pick me up, he has to come before that."

"Oh." James seemed surprised for a moment but recovered quickly. "Right. Of course. Well, like I said, you're welcome to the shower or anything here. I think all your stuff is in the bedroom on the chest. Um." He looked around the room like he was searching for anything else that might help send Devin on his way. "Is there anything else you need from me?"

"Just the address." Devin waved his phone and smiled, wondering if it looked as forced as it felt. "I have to text him and let him know where I am."

"Right."

Devin typed the street address James rattled off into his phone, hoping for a foolish moment that James might add his phone number in there, but he didn't. So, that was that. He sent the address to Brent and sent a follow-up text reading *I'll be ready whenever. Text me when you get here.*

"Okay, so. I think I will maybe take a shower, then. And, um. Yeah."

"Sure. Okay." James nodded and Devin nodded in response.

"Okay."

The shower was a good idea, as it gave Devin time to reflect on his rambling idiocy and then regroup. It wasn't fair for him to expect James to ask him to stay. James had a life to get back to, and he'd mentioned that he had work to catch up on over the weekend. Nor was it fair for him to expect James to give him his number when Devin had presented himself as a no-strings good time sort of guy, and James had proven himself to be somewhat shy at the very least.

If only Devin could quiet the nagging voice in his head that kept asking *But does he like me?* Sex and attraction Devin could handle, and he and James were good on both those counts. The liking part of it is where things got fuzzy. Devin liked James. He had liked James almost from the word go, but he had no real handle on what James thought of him. That was the ultimate problem with genuinely nice people; they were genuinely nice, and therefore impossible to read.

Devin hadn't arrived at a satisfactory sort of answer by the time he was dressed in his own clothes again and ready to go. Without a clear message from James, he was operating blindly. That in and of itself didn't usually bother him, but between the liking-James thing and his recent streak of crap luck, Devin was feeling uncharacteristically vulnerable to the possibility of rejection.

James was still at the dining room table when Devin came out, and while Madison was nowhere to be seen, there was a woman sitting there in her place, her hands wrapped around a coffee mug. She was very obviously Madison and Zoe's mom—the girls were mini versions of her—and Devin very much wished he was still in his borrowed sweats rather than his blatantly "gagging for it" bar outfit.

"Sorry. I didn't mean to interrupt."

"You're fine. It's just Erin," James said. "Have a seat. I'll grab you some coffee."

"I believe the big fat interrupter award goes to me this weekend. Hi, I'm Erin," she said, standing to shake Devin's hand. "It's nice to meet you, and I apologize again for dumping my spawn on you guys yesterday."

"No worries." Devin hesitated for a moment, then took the seat across from her. "We had fun. We watched some cartoons, built a fort."

"I see that. Madison wanted to spend just a few more minutes in there before we left."

"Yeah, sorry about that. Thank you," Devin said when James set down a cup of coffee and the sugar in front of him. "I wasn't really thinking about the long-term consequences when I suggested it. How is your husband?"

"Well, no one has ever suffered the way he suffers when he's sick, but aside from being a giant baby, he'll be fine."

"Motherhood has really brought out her nurturing side," James said dryly.

"Nurturing side, my foot." Erin leaned forward conspiratorially. "Their mom still comes to take care of them when they're not feeling well. It sets up a terrible precedent."

"Hey, that's just Chris. I never get sick."

Erin gave him a considering look, like she wanted to argue the point. Instead she nodded. "Fair enough. If there is an actual caretaker in the family, it's James."

The corners of Devin's mouth twitched into a smile before he could stop himself. "Yeah, I can see that." He shifted under the interested look that earned him and cleared his throat. "So."

"So, Devin. Are you from around here?"

"Ellensburg, actually. I'm just visiting a friend." Devin was saved from any further questions by the ding of a new text. "Speak of the devil. He's here to pick me up, so I guess I should get going." He set his phone back on the table and stood. "I'm just gonna go grab my shoes."

His boots were sitting next to the chest where he'd moved them, and Devin checked the room after pulling them on to make sure he hadn't left anything else behind. His wallet was in his pocket, and he didn't have keys or a coat, so he was good.

Both James and Erin were standing when Devin walked back into the room, and Devin wondered just how much more awkward this could get. James was holding Zoe, so it looked like they would not be getting another moment alone together, which maybe was for the best.

"It was nice to meet you, Devin."

"Yeah, nice to meet you too." Devin shook Erin's hand again. "Good-bye, Madison. Thanks for hanging out with me."

"Bye!" Madison called from the far corner of the room.

"You know, I think Zoe and I are going to check out the fort. Thanks again for babysitting." Erin grabbed Zoe from James's arms and crouched down, crawling into the fort with more grace than Devin could've managed with a kid on his hip.

"So...."

"I'll walk you out," James said, like the idea had just occurred to him. "Just let me grab my shoes."

"Sure."

Devin walked back to the table to grab his phone, his gaze catching on the spread of coloring books Madison had left there. A notepad would've been better, but he didn't see one. There was probably something in James's office, but Devin didn't feel comfortable going in there uninvited. He bit his lip and glanced toward the bedroom. Before he could lose his nerve, he grabbed a red crayon and flipped the nearest coloring book to the back page, jotting his number down. After another moment of hesitation, he added *Call me.*

"Ready?" James asked, coming out of the bedroom as Devin dropped the crayon back on the table.

"Yep. Just getting my phone." Devin held it up as evidence, then slipped it into his pocket.

The morning was cold and wet, and the snow that had been so pretty and white the day before had melted into gross, dirty slush. Brent's car was idling at the corner, and he hit the horn as soon as they stepped outside.

"That's my ride." Devin stopped and turned back to James, tugging on the open edges of the jacket he was wearing. "Thank you for the unforgettable weekend, Darcy."

"Thank you for rescuing me."

"Yeah. Any time." Devin smoothed the jacket down and reached up to cup the back of James's neck and pull him into a kiss or three. Despite keeping it relatively chaste, by the time he stepped back, Devin felt a little dizzy. "You really are amazingly good at that. Don't ever let anyone tell you otherwise."

"Thanks. I'll keep that in mind."

Devin nodded. "Take care of yourself."

"Yeah, you too."

"Will do." Devin sighed when Brent honked again, taking a few steps backward and waving before he turned to walk toward the car.

"So that's the guy, huh?" Brent asked as Devin pulled the door shut. He didn't hide the fact that he was checking James out before he pulled into the street and did a U-turn. "A solid seven."

Devin gave one last halfhearted wave as they drove away but didn't check to see if James waved back. "Fuck you, he's a nine at the very least."

"Yeah, okay." Brent glanced at him out of the corner of his eye. "What's up with you? You don't seem like someone who spent the weekend having sex."

"We didn't. It's a long story," Devin said in hopes of heading off any more questions.

"Was he an asshole?"

Brent sounded genuinely concerned, which was rare, so Devin shook his head. "No, he was a really nice guy."

"Oh." It was a particular talent Brent had that he could make such a small word so incredibly loaded.

"Oh what?"

"Nothing. I just see what this is now."

"Yeah? Care to enlighten me?"

Brent laughed. "Come on, Devin. This is you with your whole unhealthy Prince Charming nice guy fetish."

"What are you even talking about?" Devin was honestly baffled by the comment. "I don't have a fetish."

"Dude. It's me. I know you."

"You're full of shit."

"Adam Hill," Brent said, like that was the end of the argument.

"From high school? What in the world does Adam Hill have to do with anything?"

"When you guys were lab partners? You talked about him every single day. 'Oh, Adam did this! Oh, Adam said that! Isn't Adam the nicest guy you've ever met?'" Brent fluttered his eyelashes and sighed dreamily. "And then when he started dating Ashley, you were heartbroken."

"I wasn't heartbroken over Adam and Ashley," Devin said, even if he could still feel the echo of that horrible gut-clenching sickness at seeing them walking down the hall holding hands that first time. That was just stupid high school bullshit.

"You listened to Sarah McLachlan for a month."

"Yeah, well, sometimes I like some easy listening folk ballads. What's your point?"

"Just that you have a thing."

"Well, I don't actually think there's anything unhealthy about liking guys who are nice to you," Devin said defensively. "Some might even consider that a positive thing to look for."

"The nice part is fine, but you always make them so unattainable. Like they could never actually like you, so you hang out with assholes like me." Brent sounded exasperated, and Devin wondered where all this was even coming from.

"I don't *always* anything." He paused for a moment, then added, "And, current conversation aside, I don't think you're an asshole."

"Fine. Whatever. Are you going to see him again?"

"Dunno. I left my number."

"It's a start, at least. No," Brent said, shaking his head when Devin would've protested. "We're not getting into it right now. I'm done with your issues. I have other news. You remember me telling you about Drama Gary at work?"

"Vaguely. He's the one with the on-again-off-again sugar daddy?"

"Right, well, Sugar Daddy got some hotshot promotion and is transferring to the California office, and he wants to take Drama Gary with him, which, bitchy side note, Gary must have some extreme hidden talents in bed, because he does not have the face of a kept boy. Or Sugar Daddy is a real troll and Gary's as good as he can get with his millions. Maybe both."

"Is there a point to this?" Devin usually enjoyed Brent's work gossip, but it wasn't really working for him at the moment.

"My *point*, Miss Priss, is that Gary turned in his two weeks, so John is looking for another waiter, and I talked him into meeting with you."

"What?" Devin looked at him, surprised. "Why would he meet with me? I haven't waited tables since freshman year."

"A, because I vouched for you and I'm amazing, and B, because you are pretty and you like people. The rest you can learn, and if you take a bartending class, you can work the bar as well." Brent tilted his head. "The tips are awesome and it will get you out of your parents' house. You may thank me now."

"Thank you," Devin said. "I mean, really. Thank you. But where would I stay? I can't afford my own place here, even with awesome tips."

"I was saving the best for last! Creepy Dave is moving at the end of May, so you can be my new roommate, and I will beg if I have to because Kathy loves you and will allow it, but otherwise she wants her friend Beth to move in and I cannot stand that bitch." He waved his hand. "She's sweet and all but has the most bizarre never-ending man drama. I cannot deal with that in my life right now."

"Where would I stay until the end of May, though?"

"There's room in the basement."

"Ah." Devin nodded. There was the catch to Brent's otherwise perfect plan. There always was one, though as far as catches went, a couple of months in the basement wasn't too terrible.

"Basement in Seattle, childhood twin bed in Ellensburg." Brent held his hands up as scales and Devin grabbed the steering wheel.

"Yeah, I get it."

"Good. Now say, 'Thank you, Fairy Godmother Brent.'"

"Thank you, Fairy Godmother Brent," Devin said dutifully. "I did notice that this plan of yours benefits you in a variety of ways."

"Well, that is because I'm an excellent planner. Just be grateful that I'm using my powers for good."

CHAPTER 7

"WELL, I think my rooster-blocking duties are fulfilled," Erin said as soon a James got back inside. She had Zoe's coat in her hand and was halfheartedly trying to get her into it. "Madison, get your coloring books picked up. Your uncle had everything packed for you." She turned back to James once Madison started clearing her stuff off the table. "I really am sorry about the family disaster."

"It's fine," James said. It wasn't, but he wasn't sure the weekend would've ended any differently had it gone the other way. Devin was gone and James wanted to curl up on the couch and mope.

"He was really cute. Like, way cuter than I was expecting." Erin sounded impressed. "How did you manage that?"

"He actually picked me up, if you can believe it."

Erin's expression suggested that she did not believe it.

"Kara may have pointed him in my direction."

"There it is." Erin nodded, satisfied with that explanation. "You owe Kara a very nice birthday present."

"Her birthday isn't for another six months."

"Start planning."

"You know, he was actually attracted to me," James felt the need to point out. There was healthy skepticism, then there was offensive disbelief. "Kara may have pointed me out, but I, y'know... let him pick me up."

"Whew!" Erin made a show of fanning herself. "You stud, you."

"Yeah, yeah. Real nice, considering the level of your rooster-blocking offense."

She laughed. "Okay, sorry. I'll be good. So when are you seeing Devin Cutie McTightpants again?"

"I'm not."

"You're kidding, right?" She started laughing again and then stopped. "James, tell me you're kidding. Why wouldn't you see him again? That's insane."

"It wasn't like that. It wasn't a date, it was just a weekend fling." James shrugged defensively. "And, as you so clearly intimated, Devin is way out of my league. It was a fluke."

"It was a heck of a fluke. Out of your league or not, that kid had the biggest puppy dog eyes for you I've ever seen. Tell me you completely missed that." She rolled her eyes at him. "My god, you're an idiot."

"Momma, you shouldn't call people names," Madison said, pausing in her packing to admonish her mother. "It's not nice and it hurts their feelings."

Erin gave James another irritated look before turning to Madison. "You're right, honey. That wasn't very nice of me. You shouldn't call people names and hurt their feelings."

"You should say you're sorry."

"I'm sorry, James."

"I accept your apology," James said for Madison's benefit. He waited for her to resume shoving things into her overfull backpack before asking, "You really think he liked me?"

"You are so lucky the kids are here right now," she said quietly. "I can't believe you didn't get his number. Maybe you can find him online, though. What's his last name?"

"Um."

"Okay, you know what? You deserve what you get."

"He's from Ellensburg and he's in his twenties. I should be able to find something with that, right? Ellensburg is not that big." He nodded, because that seemed reasonable. "How hard can it be?"

AS IT turned out, finding someone based on a ballpark age and a first name was a lot more difficult than it seemed, even in a town the size of Ellensburg. James had quickly exhausted the usual, reasonable, Internet methods, and had even tiptoed over a bit into a few tracking methods that would've been difficult to explain had he managed to find Devin that way, but he hadn't so it was a moot point.

So, James had done what any reasonable person would do when faced with the choice of giving up or full-out stalking; he'd gone back to the bar where they met in hopes that Devin might magically be there again.

"Hey, if this were a movie, *All By Myself* would totally be playing in the background right now." Kara set a new bottle of beer in front of him.

"That's helpful, thanks."

"I'm sorry, you just look so pathetic." Kara's sympathy was laced with a healthy dose of amusement at his expense. "It was a one-night stand, and it's been a month. Don't you think it's time to maybe move on? Other fish in the sea, yada yada platitudes."

"Why did I invite you again?"

"Because you desperately need a wingman." Kara set her chin in her hand and frowned at him. "Seriously, James. All joking aside, I'm a little worried about you being so hung up on this guy. It isn't like you to be this fixated. I mean, I get it, he was hot, but—"

"He wasn't. Well, okay, yeah he was," James said. "But that's not why. I really liked him, I guess, and I wish I'd gotten the chance to tell him that. Or used the chance I had. Whatever."

"Okay," Kara said slowly. "And while that is completely valid, I'm wondering how much longer you're going to be beating yourself up over it."

"How about when I stop actively missing him?" James knew he sounded petulant. He knew Kara was wondering how he could miss someone he'd only spent a couple of days with, and James couldn't explain it. He just did. They'd connected, Lord help him if he ever used that word in front of her, and James missed him in a stupid, aching, miserable way.

"I know you're really bummed right now, but maybe it was never supposed to be a thing. Some people are in your lives forever, and some people happen along to be there when you need them." It was a testament to how upset he must seem that Kara had done away with the sarcasm entirely. "Maybe Devin was just what you needed to get you out of your funk."

"If that's the case, the universe did a terrible job of planning that one," James said.

"You know what I mean."

"I know what you mean," James agreed. "He didn't feel temporary, though, Kara."

"Well, then, the universe will make it right."

"You think?"

She nodded, then rolled her eyes, and James looked up to see Roger approaching them.

"I haven't seen you around lately." Roger took the third seat at the table without being invited. "Kara," he said to acknowledge her presence. "Did your new pet twink finally lose his sparkle?"

"He wasn't—" James cut himself off, unwilling to discuss Devin even a little bit with Roger. "Was there something you needed? Otherwise, we were sort of in the middle of a private conversation."

"Beg your pardon, then. I would hate to interrupt whatever important heart-to-hearts you decided to have in the middle of the bar." He stood again, brushing his hand against James's. "I'll catch you some other time."

"Sure." James watched Roger walk away and wondered why he had stuck with him of all people for as long as he had. He shook his head at Kara's impressed look. "I feel like the universe is sending me mixed signals," he finally said.

"Yeah," Kara agreed. "The universe can be a dick."

CHAPTER 8

"YOU said he'd be out of here by the end of May, and we are now halfway through June," Devin said in a furious whisper as he mixed a Lemon Drop for the lady at the end of the bar. Brent kept making up excuses to duck into the back so he could avoid their argument, but Devin was determined to have it out while they were both stuck bartending.

The first full week of spring had finally arrived in Seattle, with five straight days of sunshine and warm weather, and the whole city was determined to make the best of it. It was barely five and the restaurant was already packed, and if the past few days were anything to go by, they wouldn't slow down any time before closing.

"That's what he told me. Look, it'll be another week. Two, tops," Brent said.

Devin poured the drink into the glass Brent had sugared for him and delivered it to his waiting customer. He chatted with her for a moment, then took three more drink orders before he managed to get back over to where Brent was stacking the freshly washed glasses. "He came down there while I was sleeping."

"He was going to do some laundry. Okay, fine. I know," he said when Devin gave him an incredulous look. "I maintain that he's harmless, but he is justifiably creepy. That's how he got the nickname. Do you want to sleep with me until he moves out?"

"Um."

"Oh please. If I wanted to get in your pants again, you'd know it. Mopey bitches are not exactly a turn-on for me."

"I'm not mopey."

Brent snorted and reached up to pinch Devin's bottom lip. "Right. Don't think I missed the Sarah McLachlan CD in your car."

"Shut up, that's been in there forever." Devin batted his hand away. "I'm just annoyed that I'm working on my night off."

"Mike is sick."

"Mike is having a barbecue."

"How do you know?"

"He sent me a text half an hour ago inviting me over."

Brent laughed. "Now *that* dude wants in your pants."

The number of drink orders they had to fill kept Devin from needing to comment on that, which was good. It was a whole can of worms he didn't want to open with Brent. Mike hadn't been subtle in hitting on Devin, and he was an attractive enough guy. Devin just wasn't interested in having a fling at the moment. Especially not with a coworker.

"He's not bad, you know," Brent said half an hour later when there was a lull in the action.

"Who isn't?"

"Mike. He's a decent lay. There were a few things he did I wasn't crazy about, but you might be into it."

"Are there any of our coworkers you haven't slept with?"

"Most of the girls."

"Most?" Devin asked.

"Tequila is a fickle mistress. Surprisingly enough, that wasn't terrible either, though she might have a different opinion on it."

Devin shook his head, torn between feeling exasperated and fond. "You're so ridiculous."

"It's why you love me. Hey, okay, don't look now, but the dude that just walked in the door." He slapped Devin's arm when Devin started to turn. "I said don't look! The guy at the hostess stand, isn't that your Prince Charming hookup that you've been morose over for like a thousand years now?"

"What?" Devin froze, the mere possibility of it making his heart pound in his throat.

"Wait, maybe you actually shouldn't look. A cute-in-a-goofy-sort-of-way twink just joined him. Now they're headed to the bar. Shit." Brent's fingers were locked around Devin's wrist, and he was tugging at his arm and generally making Devin a thousand times more anxious. "Go take your break."

"I'm not going to take my break. It probably isn't even him." Devin shook Brent off and took a breath to calm himself, then turned to find that it was, in fact, James sitting a few feet away with a cute-in-a-goofy-way kid who couldn't have been too far removed from his twenty-first birthday, jeez. He turned back to Brent. "Shit. It is him. Do you think he saw me?"

Brent looked back and then nodded at Devin. "He definitely saw you."

"And we're being super conspicuous right now, aren't we?"

"So, so conspicuous," Brent confirmed. "Do you want me to take him?"

"In a fight?"

"As a customer, jackass."

"Here I thought you were going to defend my honor," Devin said, trying to joke his way through the horrible jittery, nervous feeling in his stomach. "No, thanks. I've got this."

Devin squared himself and took another deep breath before turning back to the bar, the closest approximation of a smile he could conjure plastered on his face. "Hey, James. Long time no see."

"Devin? I thought that was you." In contrast to his own expression, James's smile was completely genuine. It made Devin feel a thousand times worse, because James probably was genuinely happy to run into him again. They had parted on good terms. There was no reason for him not to be.

"In the flesh. What can I get started for you?"

"Are you living here now? How long have you been in town?" He looked like he was about to say more, then he froze, his expression going weirdly flat. "Never mind. I, um. I'll just have a vodka tonic."

Devin glanced at his date, who was still looking over the drink menu, completely oblivious. "I've only been here a couple of months. I moved to town at the end of March."

"Yeah?" James smiled again. "That's great! Wow. That's really... so awesome."

"Awesome?" Devin glanced at the date again, completely confused. The kid did not seem at all bothered by James beaming at him.

"I'll have a whiskey sour, please."

"Sure." Devin nodded and turned to start the drinks. Shit, what had James ordered?

"Wait," James said. "I didn't introduce you. I should introduce you. This is Kara's brother, Ben, and he is Kara's brother, and straight. And visiting from California. And straight. Kara is joining us, but she got caught up with a project or something so she's not here yet."

"She's also straight," Ben said dryly. "I think I am going to hit the head and, yeah. That feels right." He stood and slapped the bar before walking away.

"So, that's Kara's brother. Ben," James concluded.

"I heard he's straight," Devin said, still feeling a little dazed. What was actually happening?

James laughed and covered his eyes with his hand. "When I pictured this in my head, I was way, way smoother."

"When you pictured what?"

"Seeing you again. It's really great to see you again."

"Aw. Point to Charming."

Devin turned to find Brent standing right behind him, his back to them, which was the only nod he made to pretending he wasn't eavesdropping. "Dude."

"I'm just mixing my drinks, don't mind me."

"You, uh." Devin cleared his throat and waited for Brent to move away. "You imagined seeing me again?"

"Yeah. I was the world's biggest idiot for not asking you for your number and I've been kicking myself ever since." James scratched the side of his neck, adorably sheepish. "Is it too much to hope that it's not too late?"

Devin shook his head and James's face fell. "No, I mean, yeah, I'm still single and everything. It's just, I left you my number."

"What? Please tell me you're joking." James looked too genuinely appalled at the possibility to be faking it.

"Yeah. I wrote it on the back page of one of Madison's coloring books and... I should've torn the page out of the coloring book." He smiled, too pleased at the fact that James hadn't purposefully not called him to be upset at how completely stupid it was. "You didn't find my number?"

James shook his head. "I didn't find your number. Trust me, I would've called. I definitely would've called."

"Soooo," Ben said as he arrived back at the bar. "If I hang out in the men's room any longer, I think someone's going to call the cops."

"Right. I'll get your drinks."

"I'll get your drinks," Brent said, hip checking Devin out of the way. "It's time for your break."

Devin nodded. "It's time for my break."

"Which you'll be taking outside. There's a nice little alley around the side of the building." Brent snapped at James. "Around the side of the building, Charming. Ten minutes, Devin, I'm serious. Any longer and I will hunt you down."

"You're a prince," Devin told him as he undid his apron and tossed it under the bar.

"God forbid," Brent muttered.

"SO I wasn't misremembering that," Devin said as James moved back to kiss down the side of his neck. "God-given talent, I'm not even kidding."

James laughed and kissed him again, sweet little kisses that made Devin greedy for more. "This wasn't exactly how I was picturing this part, either," he said against Devin's lips.

"How were you picturing this part?"

"Fewer dumpsters, anyway." He kissed Devin one more time and took a step back. "Have I mentioned yet how sorry I am for not asking for your number?"

"Why didn't you?" Devin asked. It wasn't really a point he wanted to dwell on, but it seemed weird how easily James had let him walk away before.

"I don't know what the rules are for that sort of thing, or if you were interested. I was fine at first with it just being what it was, and then, y'know, you kind of wowed me, and I didn't know what to do with that."

"I wowed you?" Devin felt his cheeks heating, James's earnestness making him shy. "That's such a fantastic answer," he said when James nodded. "Okay, give me your phone."

James pulled his phone out and unlocked it, and when he handed it over the contacts screen was already pulled up. "I tried to find you online, but 'Devin from Ellensburg' didn't yield the results I'd hoped for."

"Yeah, I never got into the whole Facebook thing," Devin said as he typed in his number. "And Devin isn't my real name."

"What?" James sounded so outraged Devin couldn't keep from laughing.

"It's my middle name. My first name is Christopher, but there were like six Christophers in my kindergarten class, so I've always gone by Devin. I'm not on the lam or anything, I swear."

"Okay, then," James said dubiously. "That makes me feel better about my Internet stalking prowess, I guess."

"I'm sure you're very capable."

James shook his head. "Don't patronize me."

"I wouldn't dream of it."

"So, your ten minutes are almost up, and your friend scares me a little, so how late do you have to work tonight?"

"I get off at eleven."

"And then again afterward? Wow." James cringed and rubbed his hand over his mouth. "I was nowhere close to pulling off that line, was I?"

"Not even in the same hemisphere."

"Let me try that again." James cleared his throat and rolled his shoulders back. "Would you like to join me for a nightcap after your shift is over?"

Devin nodded, his cheeks starting to ache from smiling so much. "That's more your speed. As to your question, Darcy, I would be honored." He hooked his arm around James's elbow as they made their way back to the front of the restaurant. "I do believe there is the small matter of a wager between us, with you the victor with winnings yet unclaimed."

"I think you're right, now that you mention it."

"You have hours to think about it. You'd better come up with something good."

James stopped and wrapped his arm around Devin's waist, pulling him close. "Correction," he said, leaning down enough that his lips brushed against the edge of Devin's ear as he spoke. "I've had months to think about it. I promise you, it's very good."

"Well then." *That* line he had definitely pulled off, holy shit. Devin took a step back, then another, bumping into a guy leaving the restaurant as he did so. "It's a date."

"Yeah." James nodded, back to looking adorably pleased with himself. "It's a date."

ELIZAH J. DAVIS has lived in various parts of the United States, but currently resides in the Pacific Northwest, enjoying the abundance of coffee readily available there. Once upon a time she had journalistic ambitions, but switched to creative writing after she realized journalism involved too many facts and not enough unicorns. She loves stories of all kinds, but has a particular fondness for romance and fantastical adventures. When she isn't busy making things up, Elizah enjoys reading, laughing at cats on the internet, buying girly shoes, and trying to come up with world domination plans that don't require the donning of pants (her endeavors toward which have thus far been unsuccessful).

Website: http://elizahdavis.com

Twitter: https://twitter.com/ElizahDavis

Tumblr: http://elizahdavis.tumblr.com

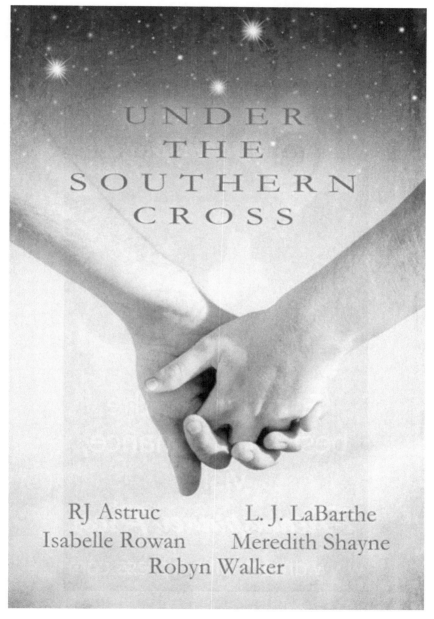